Aristotle and the Gun and Other Stories

Aristotle and the Gun and Other Stories

L. Sprague de Camp

with an introduction by Harry Turtledove

Five Star • Waterville, Maine

Five Star First Edition Science Fiction and Fantasy Series.

Published in 2002 in conjunction with
Tekno-Books and Ed Gorman.

Set in 11 pt. Plantin by Myrna S. Raven.

Cover illustration by Ken Barr.

Printed in the United States on permanent paper.

Library of Congress Cataloging-in-Publication Data

De Camp, L. Sprague (Lyon Sprague), 1907–
    Aristotle and the gun and other stories / L. Sprague
de Camp ; with an introduction by Harry Turtledove.
       p. cm.—(Five Star first edition science fiction and
fantasy series)
    Contents: Aristotle and the gun—The gnarly man—A
gun for dinosaur—The honeymoon dragon—The mislaid
mastodon—Nothing in the rules—Two yards of dragon.
    ISBN 0-7862-4311-2 (hc : alk. paper)
    1. Science fiction, American.   I. Title.   II. Series.
    PS3507.E2344 A85 2002
    813'.52—dc21   02067512

Aristotle and the Gun and Other Stories

Table of Contents

Introduction

If you are picking up this collection, there's a chance you've never before run into any stories by L. Sprague de Camp. And if you haven't, you're in for a treat. For more than fifty years, Sprague wrote witty, elegant, impeccably researched, and wryly humorous tales of ordinary people with their share of human flaws and foibles—and of what might happen to them when they find themselves in circumstances altogether out of the ordinary. Robert A. Heinlein, who commonly knew what he was talking about, characterized de Camp's fiction as "a *very* dry Martini," which neatly sums up the flavor and the kick.

De Camp was trained as an engineer (he graduated from the California Institute of Technology), but reached the job market at a time when the Depression made it next to nonexistent. After a series of odd jobs, he began selling as a writer in the late 1930s, and, except for serving as a naval officer during World War II, earned his living that way for the rest of his life.

In such seminal works as *Lest Darkness Fall*, "The Wheels of If," and (in collaboration with Fletcher Pratt) *The Incomplete Enchanter* and *Land of Unreason*, he made the study of history and literature a legitimate part of science fiction and fantasy. Along with the speculative fiction for which he was best known, he wrote entertaining, erudite nonfiction on subjects as diverse as engineering in the ancient world, the elephant, anthropology, paleontology, Atlantis, and the history of occultism. He contributed important biographies of fantasy authors H.P. Lovecraft and

Robert E. Howard. And he also wrote a series of five historical novels—too little known today—set in the days of ancient Greece that are the only works I've ever found that can stand alongside those of Mary Renault. The stories in this collection nicely illustrate his strengths. The title piece, "Aristotle and the Gun," is simultaneously a time-travel story, a splendid piece of historical fiction illustrating the times of the young Alexander and the strengths and weaknesses of Greek philosophy, and a study of how history might be changed by some seemingly small thing. A lot of writers have done much less in much more space.

Similarly, many writers have dealt with the theme of a Neanderthal brought up into modern times. "The Gnarly Man" is a classic of its kind. Its long-lived main character is delightfully well drawn, while the men—and women—who plague him are also recognizably human, all of them acting at least in part on motives they find good. As he usually does, de Camp here finds the conflict between two differing visions of good more dramatically interesting than that between self-perceived good and self-perceived evil.

"Nothing in the Rules" first ran in the lamented *Unknown* in July 1939. When it appeared, it was, no doubt, seen as a pleasant bit of fluff, nothing to take too seriously. In these days of athletes improved by stimulants, steroids, blood doping, and other products of the pharmacist's art, it is perhaps less funny and more relevant than it used to be—not bad for a yarn more than sixty years old.

"Two Yards of Dragon" became the first two chapters of de Camp's fantasy novel, *The Incorporated Knight*. As the title of the novel suggests, Sprague does what few other authors would either think or dare to do: he brings some of the virtues and economic practices of our world into one where magic works—here, specifically, one based on the fantastic tales spun by that master prevaricator of the fourteenth century, John Mandeville.

"A Gun for Dinosaur" is another classic, taking Australian hunting guide Reginald Rivers back through time to hunt the biggest and most dangerous land game that ever lived. It first saw print in 1956, and has stayed in print, in one collection or another, almost continuously ever since. Again, it shows the de Campian virtues of intelligence, scrupulous research, and deep insight into the nature of the characters involved. Proving that de Camp kept right on turning out excellent tales to the very end of his career, the other two Reginald Rivers stories appearing in this book, "The Honeymoon Dragon" and "The Mislaid Mastodon," both came out in the early 1990s. The former takes Rivers to the Pleistocene in his native Australia, while the latter is also set in the Pleistocene, but in North America.

Not least because he was a shy, self-effacing man, Sprague de Camp never quite got the recognition his work earned for him. This collection goes some way toward giving him his due; if it also introduces his work to some who haven't been lucky enough to find it before, so much the better. Have fun!

Aristotle and the Gun

From:
Sherman Weaver, Librarian
The Palace
Paumanok, Sewanhaki
Sachimate of Lenape
Flower Moon 3, 3097

To:
Messire Markos Koukidas
Consulate of the Balkan Commonwealth
Kataapa, Muskhogian Federation

My dear Consul:

You have no doubt heard of our glorious victory at Ptaksit, when our noble Sachim destroyed the armored chivalry of the Mengwe by the brilliant use of pikemen and archery. (I suggested it to him years ago, but never mind.) Sagoye-watha and most of his Senecas fell, and the Oneidas broke before our countercharge. The envoys from the Grand Council of the Long House arrive tomorrow for a peace-pauwau. The roads to the South are open again, and I send you my long-promised account of the events that brought me from my own world into this one.

If you could have stayed longer on your last visit, I think I could have made the matter clear, despite the language difficulty and my hardness of hearing. But perhaps, if I give you a simple narrative, in the order in which things happened to me, truth will transpire.

Know, then, that I was born into a world that looks like this one on the map, but is very different as regards human affairs. I tried to tell you of some of the triumphs of our natural philosophers, of our machines and discoveries. No doubt you thought me a first-class liar, though you were too polite to say so.

Nonetheless, my tale is true, though for reasons that will appear I cannot prove it. I was one of those natural philosophers. I commanded a group of younger philosophers, engaged in a task called *a project*, at a center of learning named Brookhaven, on the south shore of Sewanhaki twenty parasangs east of Paumanok. Paumanok itself was known as Brooklyn, and formed part of an even larger city called New York.

My project had to do with the study of space-time. (Never mind what that means but read on.) At this center we had learned to get vast amounts of power from seawater by what we called a fusion process. By this process we could concentrate so much power in a small space that we could warp the entity called space-time and cause things to travel in time as our other machines traveled in space.

When our calculations showed that we could theoretically hurl an object back in time, we began to build a machine for testing this hypothesis. First we built a small pilot model. In this we sent small objects back in time for short periods.

We began with inanimate objects. Then we found that a rabbit or rat could also be projected without harm. The time-translation would not be permanent; rather, it acted like one of these rubber balls the Hesperians play games with. The object would stay in the desired time for a period determined by the power used to project it and its own mass, and would then return spontaneously to the time and

13

place from which it started.

We had reported our progress regularly, but my chief had other matters on his mind and did not read our reports for many months. When he got a report saying that we were completing a machine to hurl human beings back in time, however, he awoke to what was going on, read our previous reports, and called me in.

"Sherm," he said, "I've been discussing this project with Washington, and I'm afraid they take a dim view of it."

"Why?" said I, astonished.

"Two reasons. For one thing, they think you've gone off the reservation. They're much more interested in the Antarctic Reclamation Project and want to concentrate all our appropriations and brain power on it.

"For another, they're frankly scared of this time machine of yours. Suppose you went back, say, to the time of Alexander the Great and shot Alexander before he got started? That would change all later history, and we'd go out like candles."

"Ridiculous," I said.

"What, what would happen?"

"Our equations are not conclusive, but there are several possibilities. As you will see if you read Report No. 9, it depends on whether space-time has a positive or negative curvature. If positive, any disturbance in the past tends to be ironed out in subsequent history, so that things become more and more nearly identical with what they would have been anyway. If negative, then events will diverge more and more from their original pattern with time.

"Now, as I showed in this report, the chances are overwhelmingly in favor of a positive curvature. However, we intend to take every precaution and make our first tests for short periods, with a minimum—"

"That's enough," said my superior, holding up a hand. "It's very interesting, but the decision has already been made."

"What do you mean?"

"I mean Project A-257 is to be closed down and a final report written at once. The machines are to be dismantled, and the group will be put to work on another project."

"What?" I shouted. "But you can't stop us just when we're on the verge—"

"I'm sorry, Sherm, but I can. That's what the AEC decided at yesterday's meeting. It hasn't been officially announced, but they gave me positive orders to kill the project as soon as I got back here."

"Of all the lousy, arbitrary, benighted—"

"I know how you feel, but I have no choice."

I lost my temper and defied him, threatening to go ahead with the project anyway. It was ridiculous, because he could easily dismiss me for insubordination. However, I knew he valued my ability and counted on his wanting to keep me for that reason. But he was clever enough to have his cake and eat it.

"If that's how you feel," he said, "the section is abolished here and now. Your group will be broken up and assigned to other projects. You'll be kept on at your present rating with the title of consultant. Then when you're willing to talk sense, perhaps we can find you a suitable job."

I stamped out of his office and went home to brood. I ought now to tell you something of myself. I am old enough to be objective, I hope. And, as I have but a few years left, there is no point in pretence.

I have always been a solitary, misanthropic man. I had little interest in or liking of my fellow man, who naturally paid me back in the same coin. I was awkward and ill at ease in company. I had a genius for saying the wrong thing and making a fool of myself.

I never understood people. Even when I watched and planned my own actions with the greatest care, I never could tell how others would react to them. To me men were and are an unpredictable, irrational, and dangerous species of hairless ape. While I could avoid some of my worst gaffes by keeping my own counsel and watching my every word, they did not like that either. They considered me a cold, stiff, unfriendly sort of person when I was only trying to be polite and avoid offending them.

I never married. At the time of which I speak, I was verging on middle age without a single close friend and no more acquaintances than my professional work required.

My only interest, outside my work, was a hobby of the history of science. Unlike most of my fellow philosophers, I was historically minded, with a good smattering of a classical education. I belonged to the History of Science Society and wrote papers on the history of science for its periodical *Isis*.

I went back to my little rented house, feeling like Galileo. He was a scientist persecuted for his astronomical theories by the religious authorities of my world several centuries before my time, as Georg Schwartzhorn was a few years ago in this world's Europe.

I felt I had been born too soon. If only the world were scientifically more advanced, my genius would be appreciated and my personal difficulties solved.

Well, I thought, why is the world not scientifically more advanced? I reviewed the early growth of science. Why had not your fellow countrymen, when they made a start towards a scientific age two thousand to twenty-five hundred years ago, kept at it until they made science the self-supporting, self-accelerating thing it at last became—in my world, that is?

I knew the answers that historians of science had worked out. One was the effect of slavery, which made work disgraceful to a free man and therefore made experiment and invention unattractive because they looked like work. Another was the primitive state of the mechanical arts: things like making clear glass and accurate measuring devices. Another was the Hellenes' fondness for spinning cosmic theories without enough facts to go on, the result of which was that most of their theories were wildly wrong.

Well, thought I, could a man go back to this period and, by applying a stimulus at the right time and place, give the necessary push to set the whole trend rolling off in the right direction?

People had written fantastic stories about a man's going back in time and overawing the natives by a display of the discoveries of his own later era. More often than not, such a time-traveling hero came to a bad end. The people of the earlier time killed him as a witch, or he met with an accident, or something happened to keep him from changing history. But, knowing these dangers, I could forestall them by careful planning.

It would do little or no good to take back some major invention, like a printing press or an automobile, and turn it over to the ancients in the hope of grafting it on their culture. I could not teach them to work it in a reasonable time; and, if it broke down or ran out of supplies, there would be no way to get it running again.

What I had to do was to find a key mind and implant in it an appreciation of sound scientific method. He would have to be somebody who would have been important in any event, or I could not count on his influence's spreading far and wide.

After study of Sarton and to other historians of science, I picked Aristotle. You have heard of him, have you not? He existed in your world just as he did in mine. In fact, up to Aristotle's time our worlds were one and the same.

Aristotle was one of the greatest minds of all time. In my world, he was the first encyclopedist; the first man who tried to know everything, write down everything, and explain everything. He did much good original scientific work, too, mostly in biology.

However, Aristotle tried to cover so much ground, and accepted so many fables as facts, that he did much harm to science as well as good. For, when a man of such colossal intellect goes wrong, he carries with him whole generations of weaker minds who cite him as an infallible authority. Like his colleagues, Aristotle never appreciated the need for constant verification. Thus, though he was married twice, he said that men have more teeth than women. He never thought to ask either of his wives to open her mouth for a count. He never grasped the need for invention and experiment.

Now, if I could catch Aristotle at the right period of his career, perhaps I could give him a push in the right direction.

When would that be? Normally, one would take him as a young man. But Aristotle's entire youth, from seventeen to thirty-seven, was spent in Athens listening to Plato's lectures. I did not wish to compete with Plato, an overpowering personality who could argue rings around anybody. His viewpoint was mystical and anti-scientific, the very thing I wanted to steer Aristotle away from. Many of Aristotle's intellectual vices can be traced back to Plato's influence.

I did not think it wise to present myself in Athens either during Aristotle's early period, when he was a student under Plato, or later, when he headed his own school. I could not pass myself off as a Hellene, and the Hellenes of that time had a contempt for all non-Hellenes, who they called "barbarians." Aristotle was one of the worst offenders in this respect. Of course this is a universal human failing, but it was particularly virulent among Athenian intellectuals. In his later Athenian period, too, Aristotle's ideas would probably be too set with age to change.

I concluded that my best chance would be to catch Aristotle while he was tutoring young Alexander the Great at the court of Philip the Second of Macedon. He would have regarded Macedon as a backward country, even though the court spoke Attic Greek. Perhaps he would be bored with bluff Macedonian stag-hunting squires and lonesome for intellectual company. As he would regard the Macedonians as the next thing to *barbaroi,* another barbarian would not appear at such a disadvantage there as at Athens.

Of course, whatever I accomplished with Aristotle, the results would depend on the curvature of space-time. I had not been wholly frank with my superior. While the equations tended to favor the hypothesis of a positive curvature, the probability was not overwhelming as I claimed. Perhaps my efforts would have little effect on history, or perhaps the effect would grow and widen like ripples in a pool. In the latter case the existing world would, as my superior said, be snuffed out.

Well, at that moment I hated the existing world and would not give a snap of my fingers for its destruction. I was going to create a much better one and come back from ancient times to enjoy it.

Our previous experiments showed that I could project

myself back to ancient Macedon with an accuracy of about two months temporally and a half-parasang spatially. The machine included controls for positioning the time traveler anywhere on the globe, and safety devices for locating him above the surface of the earth, not in a place already occupied by a solid object. The equations showed that I should stay in Macedon about nine weeks before being snapped back to the present.

Once I had made up my mind, I worked as fast as I could. I telephoned my superior (you remember what a telephone is?) and made my peace. I said:

"I know I was a damned fool, Fred, but this thing was my baby; my one chance to be a great and famous scientist. I might have got a Nobel prize out of it."

"Sure, I know, Sherm," he said. "When are you coming back to the lab?"

"Well—uh—what about my group?"

"I held up the papers on that, in case you might change your mind. So if you come back, all will go on organizationwise as before."

"You want that final report on A-257, don't you?" I said, trying to keep my voice level.

"Sure."

"Then don't let the mechanics start to dismantle the machines until I've written the report."

"No; I've had the place locked up since yesterday."

"Okay. I want to shut myself in with the apparatus and the data sheets for a while and bat out the report without being bothered."

"That'll be fine," he said.

My first step in getting ready for my journey was to buy a suit of classical traveler's clothing from a theatrical costume company. This comprised a knee-length pullover tunic or chiton, a short horseman's cloak or chlamys, knitted buskins, sandals, a broad-brimmed black felt hat, and a staff. I stopped shaving, though I did not have time to raise a respectable beard.

My auxiliary equipment included a purse of coinage of the time, mostly golden Macedonian staters. Some of these coins were genuine, bought from a numismatic supply house, but most were copies I cast myself in the laboratory at night. I made sure of being rich enough to live decently for longer than my nine weeks' stay. This was not hard, as the purchasing power of precious metals was more than fifty times greater in the classical world than in mine.

I wore the purse attached to a heavy belt next to my skin. From this belt also hung a missile-weapon called a *gun,* which I have told you about. This was a small gun, called a pistol or revolver. I did not mean to shoot anybody, or expose the gun at all if I could help it. It was there as a last resort.

I also took several small devices of our science to impress Aristotle: a pocket microscope and a magnifying glass, a small telescope, a compass, my timepiece, a flashlight, a small camera, and some medicines. I intended to show these things to people of ancient times only with the greatest caution. By the time I had slung all these objects in their pouches and cases from my belt, I had a heavy load. Another belt over the tunic supported a small purse for day-to-day buying and an all-purpose knife.

I already had a good reading knowledge of classical Greek, which I tried to polish by practice with the spoken language and listening to it on my talking machine. I knew I should arrive speaking with an accent, for we had no way of knowing exactly what Attic Greek sounded like.

I decided, therefore, to pass myself off as a traveler from

India. Nobody would believe I was a Hellene. If I said I came from the north or west, no Hellene would listen to me, as they regarded Europeans as warlike but half-witted savages. If I said I was from some well-known civilized country like Carthage, Egypt, Babylonia, or Persia, I should be in danger of meeting someone who knew those countries and of being exposed as a fraud.

To tell the truth of my origin, save under extraordinary circumstances, would be most imprudent. It would lead to my being considered a lunatic or a liar, as I can guess that your good self has more than once suspected me of being.

An Indian, however, should be acceptable. At this time, the Hellenes knew about that land only a few wild rumors and the account of Ktesias of Knidos, who made a book of the tales he picked up about India at the Persian court. The Hellenes had heard that India harbored philosophers. Therefore, thinking Greeks might be willing to consider Indians as almost as civilized as themselves.

What should I call myself? I took a common Indian name, Chandra, and Hellenized it to Zandras. That, I knew, was what the Hellenes would do anyway, as they had no "tch" sound and insisted on putting Greek inflectional endings on foreign names. I would not try to use my own name, which is not even remotely Greek or Indian sounding. (Some day I must explain the blunders in my world that led to Hesperians' being called "Indians.")

The newness and cleanliness of my costume bothered me. It did not look worn, and I could hardly break it in around Brookhaven without attracting attention. I decided that if the question came up, I should say: yes, I bought it when I entered Greece, so as not to be conspicuous in my native garb.

During the day, when not scouring New York for equipment, I was locked in the room with the machine. While my colleagues thought I was either writing my report or dismantling the apparatus, I was getting ready for my trip.

Two weeks went by thus. One day a memorandum came down from my superior, saying: "How is that final report coming?"

I knew then I had better put my plan into execution at once. I sent back a memorandum: "Almost ready for the writing machine."

That night I came back to the laboratory. As I had been doing this often, the guards took no notice. I went to the time-machine room, locked the door from the inside, and got out my equipment and costume.

I adjusted the machine to set me down near Pella, the capital of Macedon, in the spring of the year 340 before Christ in our system of reckoning (976 Algonkian). I set the auto-actuator, climbed inside, and closed the door.

The feeling of being projected through time cannot really be described. There is a sharp pain, agonizing but too short to let the victim even cry out. At the same time there is the feeling of terrific acceleration, as if one were being shot from a catapult, but in no particular direction.

Then the seat in the passenger compartment dropped away from under me. There was a crunch, and a lot of sharp things jabbed me. I had fallen into the top of a tree.

I grabbed a couple of branches to save myself. The mechanism that positioned me in Macedon, detecting solid matter at the point where I was going to materialize, had raised me up above the treetops and then let go. It was an old oak, just putting out its spring leaves.

In clutching for branches I dropped my staff, which slithered down through the foliage and thumped the ground below. At least it thumped something. There was a startled yell.

Classical costume is impractical for tree climbing. Branches kept knocking off my hat, or snagging my cloak, or poking me in tender places not protected by trousers. I ended my climb with a slide and a fall of several feet, tumbling into the dirt.

As I looked up, the first thing I saw was a burly, black-bearded man in a dirty tunic, standing with a knife in his hand. Near him stood a pair of oxen yoked to a wooden plow. At his feet rested a water jug.

The plowman had evidently finished a furrow and lain down to rest himself and his beasts when the fall of my staff on him and then my arrival in person aroused him.

Around me stretched the broad Emathian Plain, ringed by ranges of stony hills and craggy mountains. As the sky was overcast, and I did not dare consult my compass, I had no sure way of orienting myself, or even telling what time of day it was. I assumed that the biggest mountain in sight was Mount Bermion, which ought to be to the west. To the north I could see a trace of water. This would be Lake Loudias. Beyond the lake rose a range of low hills. A discoloration on the nearest spur of these hills might be a city, though my sight was not keen enough to make out details, and I had to do without my eyeglasses. The gently rolling plain was cut up into fields and pastures with occasional trees and patches of marsh. Dry brown grasses left over from winter nodded in the wind.

My realization of all this took but a flash. Then my attention was brought back to the plowman, who spoke.

I could not understand a word. But then, he would speak Macedonian. Though this can be deemed a Greek dialect, it differed so from Attic Greek as to be unintelligible.

No doubt the man wanted to know what I was doing in his tree. I put on my best smile and said in my slow tumbling Attic: "Rejoice! I am lost, and climbed your tree to find my way."

He spoke again. When I did not respond, he repeated his words more loudly, waving his knife.

We exchanged more words and gestures, but it was evident that neither had the faintest notion of what the other was trying to say. The plowman began shouting, as ignorant people will when faced by the linguistic barrier.

At last I pointed to the distant headland overlooking the lake, on which there appeared a discoloration that might be the city. Slowly and carefully I said:

"Is that Pella?"

"*Nai, Pella!*" The man's mien became less threatening.

"I am going to Pella. Where can I find the philosopher Aristoteles?" I repeated the name.

He was off again with more gibberish, but I gathered from his expression that he had never heard of any Aristoteles. So, I picked up my hat and stick, felt through my tunic to make sure my gear was all in place, tossed the rustic a final "*Chaire!*" and set off.

By the time I had crossed the muddy field and come out on a cart track, the problem of looking like a seasoned traveler had solved itself. There were green and brown stains on my clothes from the scramble down the tree; the cloak was torn; the branches had scratched my limbs and face; my feet and lower legs were covered with mud. I also became aware that, to one who has lived all his life with his loins decently swathed in trousers and underdrawers, classical costume is excessively drafty.

I glanced back to see the plowman still standing with one hand on his plow, looking at me in puzzled fashion. The poor fellow had never been able to decide what, if anything, to do about me.

When I found a road, it was hardly more than a heavily used cart track, with a pair of deep ruts and the space between them alternating stones, mud, and long grass. I walked towards the lake and passed a few people on the road. To one used to the teeming traffic of my world, Macedon seemed dead and deserted. I spoke to some of the people, but ran into the same barrier of language as with the plowman.

Finally a two-horse chariot came along, driven by a stout man wearing a headband, a kind of kilt, and high-laced boots. He pulled up at my hail.

"What is it?" he said, in Attic not much better than mine.

"I seek the philosopher, Aristoteles of Stageira. Where can I find him?"

"He lives in Mieza."

"Where is that?"

The man waved. "You are going the wrong way. Follow this road back the way you came. At the ford across the Bottiais, take the right-hand fork, which will bring you to Mieza and Kition. Do you understand?"

"I think so," I said. "How far is it?"

"About two hundred stadia."

My heart sank to my sandals. This meant five parasangs, or a good two-days' walk. I thought of trying to buy a horse or a chariot, but I had never ridden or driven a horse and saw no prospect of learning how soon enough to do any good. I had read about Mieza as Aristotle's home in Macedon but, as none of my maps had shown it, I had assumed it to be a suburb of Pella.

I thanked the man, who trotted off, and set out after him. The details of my journey need not detain you. I was benighted far from shelter through not knowing where the villages were, attacked by watchdogs, eaten alive by mosquitoes and invaded by vermin when I did find a place to sleep the second night. The road skirted the huge marshes that spread over the Emathian Plain west of Lake Loudias. Several small streams came down from Mount Bermion and lost themselves in this marsh.

At last I neared Mieza, which stands on one of the spurs of Mount Bermion. I was trudging wearily up the long rise to the village when six youths on little Greek horses clattered down the road. I stepped to one side, but instead of cantering past they pulled up and faced me in a semicircle.

"Who are you?" asked one, a smallish youth of about fifteen, in fluent Attic. He was blond and would have been noticeably handsome without his pimples.

"I am Zandras of Pataliputra," I said, giving the ancient name for Patna on the Ganges. "I seek the philosopher Aristoteles."

"Oh, a barbarian!" cried Pimples. "We know what the Aristoteles thinks of these, eh, boys?"

The others joined in, shouting noncompliments and bragging about all the barbarians they would some day kill or enslave.

I made the mistake of letting them see I was getting angry. I knew it was unwise, but I could not help myself. "If you do not wish to help me, then let me pass," I said.

"Not only a barbarian, but an insolent one!" cried one of the group, making his horse dance uncomfortably close to me.

"Stand aside, children!" I demanded.

"We must teach you a lesson," said Pimples. The others giggled.

"You had better let me alone," I said, gripping my staff in both hands.

27

A tall handsome adolescent reached over and knocked my hat off. "That for you, cowardly Asiatic!" he yelled. Without stopping to think, I shouted an English epithet and swung my staff. Either the young man leaned out of my way or his horse shied, for my blow missed him. The momentum carried the staff past my target and the end struck the nose of one of the other horses.

The pony squealed and reared. Having no stirrups, the rider slid off the animal's rump into the dirt. The horse galloped off.

All six youths began screaming. The blond one, who had a particularly piercing voice, mouthed some threat. The next thing I knew, his horse bounded directly at me. Before I could dodge, the animal's shoulder knocked me head over heels and the beast leaped over me as I rolled. Luckily, horses' dislike of stepping on anything squashy saved me from being trampled.

I scrambled up as another horse bore down upon me. By a frantic leap, I got out of its way, but I saw that the other boys were jockeying their mounts to do likewise.

A few paces away rose a big pine. I dodged in among its lower branches as the other horses ran at me. The youths could not force their mounts in among these branches, so they galloped round and round and yelled. Most of their talk I could not understand, but I caught a sentence from Pimples:

"Ptolemaios! Ride back to the house and fetch bows or javelins!"

Hooves receded. While I could not see clearly through the pine needles, I inferred what was happening. The youths would not try to rush me on foot, first because they liked being on horseback, and if they dismounted they might lose their horses or have trouble remounting; second, because, as long as I kept my back to the tree, they would have a hard time getting at me through the tangle of branches, and I could hit and poke them with my stick as I came. Though not an unusually tall man in my own world, I was much bigger than any of these boys.

This, however, was a minor consideration. I recognized the name "Ptolemaios" as that of one of Alexander's companions, who in my world became King Ptolemy of Egypt and founded a famous dynasty. Young Pimples, then, must be Alexander himself.

I was in a real predicament. If I stayed where I was, Ptolemaios would bring back missiles for target practice with me as the target. I could of course shoot some of the boys with my gun, which would save me for the time being. But, in a monarchy, killing the crown prince's friends, let alone the crown prince himself, is no way to achieve a peaceful old age, regardless of the provocation.

While I was thinking of these matters and listening to my attackers, a stone swished through the branches and bounced off the trunk. The small dark youth who had fallen off his horse had thrown the rock and was urging his friends to do likewise. I caught glimpses of Pimples and the rest dismounting and scurrying around for stones, a commodity with which Greece and Macedon are notoriously well supplied.

More stones came through the needles, caroming from the branches. One the size of my fist struck me lightly in the shin.

The boys came closer so that their aim got better. I wormed my way around the trunk to put it between me and them, but they saw the movement and spread out around the tree. A stone grazed my scalp, dizzying me and drawing blood. I thought of climbing, but, as the tree became more slender with height, I should be more exposed the higher I got. I should also be less able to dodge while perched in the branches.

That is how things stood when I heard hoofbeats again. This is the moment of decision, I thought. Ptolemaios is coming back with missile weapons. If I used my gun, I might doom myself in the long run, but it would be ridiculous to stand there and let them riddle me while I had an unused weapon.

I fumbled under my tunic and unsnapped the safety strap that kept the pistol in its holster. I pulled the weapon out and checked its projectiles.

As a deep voice broke into the bickering I caught phrases: ". . . insulting an unoffending traveler . . . how know you he is not a prince in his own country? . . . the king shall hear of this . . . like newly-freed slaves, not like princes and gentlemen . . ."

I pushed towards the outer limits of the screen of pine needles. A heavy-set, brown-bearded man on a horse was haranguing the youths, who had dropped their stones. Pimples said:

"We were only having a little sport."

I stepped out from the branches, walked over to where my battered hat lay, and put it on. Then I said to the new-comer: "Rejoice! I am glad you came before your boys' play got too rough." I grinned, determined to act cheerful if it killed me. Only iron self-control would get me through this difficulty.

The man grunted. "Who are you?"

"Zandras of Pataliputra, a city in India. I seek Aristoteles the philosopher."

"He insulted us—" began one of the youths, but Brown-beard ignored him. He said, "I am sorry you have had so

30

rude an introduction to our royal house. This mass of youthful insolence" (he indicated Pimples) "is the Alexandros Philippou, heir to the throne of Makedonia." He introduced the others: Hephaistion, who had knocked my hat off and was now holding the others' horses; Nearchos, who had lost his horse; Ptolemaios, who had gone for weapons; and Harpalos and Philotas. He continued:

"When the Ptolemaios dashed into the house, I inquired the reason for his haste, learned of their quarrel with you, and came out forthwith. They have misapplied their master's teachings. They should not behave thus even to a barbarian like yourself, for in so doing they lower themselves to the barbarian's level. I am returning to the house of Aristoteles. You may follow."

The man turned his horse and started walking it back towards Mieza. The six boys busied themselves with catching Nearchos' horse.

I walked after him, though I had to dog-trot now and then to keep up. As it was uphill, I was soon breathing hard. I panted:

"Who—my lord—are you?"

The man's beard came round and he raised an eyebrow. "I thought you would know. I am Antipatros, regent of Makedonia."

Before we reached the village proper, Antipatros turned off through a kind of park, with statues and benches. This, I supposed, was the Precinct of the Nymphs, which Aristotle used as a school ground. We went through the park and stopped at a mansion on the other side. Antipatros tossed the reins to a groom and slid off his horse. "Aristoteles!" roared Antipatros. "A man wishes to see you."

A man of about near my own age—the early forties—

came out. He was of medium height and slender build, with a thin-lipped, severe-looking face and a pepper-and-salt beard cut short. He was wrapped in a billowing himation or large cloak, with a colorful scroll-patterned border. He wore golden rings on several fingers.

Antipatros made a fumbling introduction: "Old fellow, this is—ah—what's-his-name from—ah—some place in India." He told of rescuing me from Alexander and his fellow delinquents, adding: "If you do not beat some manners into your pack of cubs soon, it will be too late."

Aristotle looked at me sharply and lisped: "It ith always a pleasure to meet men from afar. What brings you here, my friend?"

I gave my name and said: "Being accounted something of a philosopher in my own land, I thought my visit to the West would be incomplete without speaking to the greatest Western philosopher. And when I asked who he was, everyone told me to seek out Aristoteles Nikomachou."

Aristotle purred. "It is good of them to thay tho. Ahem. Come in and join me in a drop of wine. Can you tell me of the wonders of India?"

"Yes indeed, but you must tell me in turn of your discoveries, which to me are much more wonderful."

"Come, come, then. Perhaps you could stay over a few days. I shall have many, many things to athk you."

That is how I met Aristotle. He and I hit it off, as we said in my world, from the start. We had much in common. Some people would not like Aristotle's lisp, or his fussy, pedantic ways, or his fondness for worrying any topic of conversation to death. But he and I got along fine.

That afternoon, in the house that King Philip had built for Aristotle to use as the royal school, he handed me a cup of wine flavored with turpentine and asked:

"Tell me about the elephant, that great beast we have heard of with a tail at both ends. Does it truly exist?"

"Indeed it does," I said, and went on to tell what I knew of elephants, while Aristotle scribbled notes on a piece of papyrus.

"What do they call the elephant in India?" he asked.

The question caught me by surprise, for it had never occurred to me to learn ancient Hindustani along with all the other things I had to know for this expedition. I sipped the wine to give me time to think. I have never cared for alcoholic liquors, and this stuff tasted awful to me. But, for the sake of my objective, I had to pretend to like it. No doubt I should have to make up some kind of gibberish—but then a mental broad-jump carried me back to the stories of Kipling I had read as a boy.

"We call it a *hathi*," I said. "Though of course there are many languages in India."

"How about that Indian wild ath of which Ktesias thpeakth, with a horn in the middle of its forehead?"

"You had better call it a nose-horn *(rhinokeros)* for that is where its horn really is, and it is more like a gigantic pig than an ass . . ."

As dinnertime neared, I made some artful remarks about going out to find accommodations in Mieza, but Aristotle (to my joy) would have none of it. I should stay right there at the school; my polite protestations of unworthiness he waved aside.

"You mutht plan to stop here for months," he said. "I shall never, never have such a chance to collect data on India again. Do not worry about expense; the king pays all. You are—ahem—the first barbarian I have known with a decent intellect, and I get lonethome for good tholid talk.

Theophrastos has gone to Athens, and my other friends come to these back-lands but seldom."

"How about the Macedonians?"

"*Aiboi!* Thome like my friend Antipatros are good fellows, but most are as lackwitted as a Persian grandee. And now tell me of Patal—what is your city's name?"

Presently Alexander and his friends came in. They seemed taken aback at seeing me closeted with their master. I put on a brisk smile and said: "Rejoice, my friends!" as if nothing untoward had happened. The boys glowered and whispered among themselves, but did not attempt any more disturbance at that time.

When they gathered for their lecture next morning, Aristotle told them: "I am too busy with the gentleman from India to waste time pounding unwanted wisdom into your miserable little thouls. Go shoot some rabbits or catch some fish for dinner, but in any case begone!"

The boys grinned. Alexander said: "It seems the barbarian has his uses after all. I hope you stay with us forever, good barbarian!"

After they had gone, Antipatros came in to say good-bye to Aristotle. He asked me with gruff good will how I was doing and went out to ride back to Pella.

The weeks passed unnoticed and the flowers of spring came out while I visited Aristotle. Day after day we strolled about the Precinct of the Nymphs, talking, or sat indoors when it rained. Sometimes the boys followed us, listening; at other times we talked alone. They played a couple of practical jokes on me, but, by pretending to be amused when I was really furious, I avoided serious trouble with them.

I learned that Aristotle had a wife and a little daughter in another part of the big house, but he never let me meet the lady. I only caught glimpses of them from a distance.

I carefully shifted the subject of our daily discourse from the marvels of India to the more basic questions of science. We argued over the nature of matter and the shape of the solar system. I gave out that the Indians were well on the road to the modern concepts—modern in my world, that is—of astronomy, physics, and so forth. I told of the discoveries of those eminent Pataliputran philosophers: Kopernikos in astronomy, Neuton in physics, Darben in evolution, and Mendeles in genetics. (I forgot; these names mean nothing to you, though an educated man of my world would recognize them at once through their Greek disguise.)

Always I stressed *method:* the need for experiment and invention and for checking each theory back against the facts. Though an opinionated and argumentative man, Aristotle had a mind like a sponge, eagerly absorbing any new fact, surmise, or opinion, whether he agreed with it or not.

I tried to find a workable compromise between what I knew science could do on one hand and the limits of Aristotle's credulity on the other. Therefore I said nothing about flying machines, guns, buildings a thousand feet high, and other technical wonders of my world. Nevertheless, I caught Aristotle looking at me sharply out of those small black eyes one day.

"Do you doubt me, Aristoteles?" I said.

"N-no, no," he said thoughtfully. "But it does theem to me that, were your Indian inventors as wonderful as you make out, they would have fabricated you wings like those of Daidalos in the legend. Then you could have flown to Makedonia directly, without the trials of crossing Persia by camel."

"That has been tried, but men's muscles do not have

enough strength in proportion to their weight."

"Ahem. Did you bring anything from India to show the skills of your people?"

I grinned, for I had been hoping for such a question. "I did fetch a few small devices," said I, reaching into my tunic and bringing out the magnifying glass. I demonstrated its use.

Aristotle shook his head. "Why did you not show me this before? It would have quieted my doubts."

"People have met with misfortune by trying too suddenly to change the ideas of those around them. Like your teacher's teacher, Sokrates."

"That is true, true. What other devices did you bring?"

I had intended to show my devices at intervals, gradually, but Aristotle was so insistent on seeing them all that I gave in to him before he got angry. The little telescope was not powerful enough to show the moons of Jupiter or the rings of Saturn, but it showed enough to convince Aristotle of its power. If he could not see these astronomical phenomena himself, he was almost willing to take my word that they could be seen with the larger telescopes we had in India.

One day a light-armed soldier galloped up to us in the midst of our discussions in the Precinct of Nymphs. Ignoring the rest of us, the fellow said to Alexander: "Hail, O Prince! The king, your father, will be here before sunset."

Everybody rushed around cleaning up the place. We were all lined up in front of the big house when King Philip and his entourage arrived on horseback with a jingle and a clatter, in crested helmets and flowing mantles. I knew Philip by his one eye. He was a big powerful man, much scarred, with a thick curly black beard going gray. He dismounted, embraced his son, gave Aristotle a brief greeting, and said to Alexander:

"How would you like to attend a siege?"

Alexander whooped.

"Thrace is subdued," said the king, "but Byzantion and Perinthos have declared against me, thanks to Athenian intrigue. I shall give the Perintheans something to think about besides the bribes of the Great King. It is time you smelled blood, youngster; would you like to come?"

"Yes, yes! Can my friends come too?"

"If they like and their fathers let them."

"O King!" said Aristotle.

"What is it, spindle-shanks?"

"I trust thith is not the end of the prince's education. He has much yet to learn."

"No, no; I will send him back when the town falls. But he nears the age when he must learn by doing, not merely by listening to your rarefied wisdom. Who is this?" Philip turned his one eye on me.

"Zandras of India, a barbarian philothopher."

Philip grinned in a friendly way and clapped me on the shoulder. "Rejoice! Come to Pella and tell my generals about India. Who knows? A Macedonian foot may tread there yet."

"It would be more to the point to find out about Persia," said one of Philip's officers, a handsome fellow with a reddish-brown beard. "This man must have just come through there. How about it, man? Is the bloody Artaxerxes still solid on his throne?"

"I know little of such matters," I said, my heart beginning to pound at the threat of exposure. "I skirted the northernmost parts of the Great King's dominions and saw little of the big cities. I know nothing of their politics."

"Is that so?" said Redbeard, giving me a queer look. "We must talk of this again."

They all trooped into the big house, where the cook and the serving wenches were scurrying about. During dinner I found myself between Nearchos, Alexander's little Cretan friend, and a man-at-arms who spoke no Attic. So I did not get much conversation, nor could I follow much of the chatter that went on among the group at the head of the tables. I gathered that they were discussing politics. I asked Nearchos who the generals were.

"The big one at the king's right is the Parmenion," he said, "and the one with the red beard is the Attalos."

When the food was taken away and the drinking had begun, Attalos came over to me. The man-at-arms gave him his place. Attalos had drunk a lot of wine already; but, if it made him a little unsteady, it did not divert him.

"How did you come through the Great King's domain?" he asked. "What route did you follow?"

"I told you, to the north," I said.

"Then you must have gone through Orchoe."

"I—" I began, then stopped. Attalos might be laying a trap for me. What if I said yes and Orchoe was really in the south? Or suppose he had been there and knew all about the place? Many Greeks and Macedonians served the Great King as mercenaries.

"I passed through many places whose names I never got straight," I said. "I do not remember if Orchoe was amongst them."

Attalos gave me a sinister smile through his beard. "Your journey will profit you little, if you cannot remember where you have been. Come, tell me if you heard of unrest among the northern provinces."

I evaded the question, taking a long pull on my wine to

cover my hesitation. I did this again and again until Attalos said: "Very well, perhaps you are really as ignorant of Persia as you profess. Then tell me about India."

"What about it?" I hiccupped; the wine was beginning to affect me, too.

"As a soldier, I should like to know of the Indian art of war. What is this about training elephants to fight?"

"Oh, we do much better than that."

"How so?"

"We have found that the flesh-and-blood elephant, despite its size, is an untrustworthy war-beast because it often takes fright and stampedes back through its own troops. So, the philosophers of Pataliputra make artificial elephants of steel with rapid-fire catapults on their backs."

I was thinking in a confused way of the armored war vehicles of my own world. I do not know what made me tell Attalos such ridiculous lies. Partly, I suppose, it was to keep him off the subject of Persia.

Partly it was a natural antipathy between us. According to history, Attalos was not a bad man, though at times a reckless and foolish one. But it annoyed me that he thought he could pump me by subtle questions, when he was about as subtle as a ton of bricks. His voice and manner said as plainly as words: I am a shrewd, sharp fellow; watch out for me, everybody. He was the kind of man who, if told to spy on the enemy, would don an obviously false beard, wrap himself in a long black cloak, and go slinking about the enemy's places in broad daylight, leering and winking and attracting as much attention as possible. No doubt, too, he had prejudiced me against him by his alarming curiosity about my past.

But the main cause for my rash behavior was the strong wine I had drunk. In my own world, I drank very little and so was not used to these carousals.

Attalos was all eyes and ears at my tale of mechanical elephants. "You do not say!"

"Yes, and we do even better than that. If the enemy's ground forces resist the charge of our iron elephants, we send flying chariots, drawn by gryphons, to drop darts on the foe from above." It seemed to me that never had my imagination been so brilliant.

Attalos gave an audible gasp. "What else?"

"Well—ah—we also have a powerful navy, you know, which controls the lower Ganges and the adjacent ocean. Our ships move by machinery, without oars or sails."

"Do the other Indians have these marvels too?"

"Some, but none is so advanced as the Pataliputrans. When we are outnumbered on the sea, we have a force of tame Tritons who swim under the enemy's ships and bore holes in their bottoms."

Attalos frowned. "Tell me, barbarian, how it is that, with such mighty instruments of war, the Palalal—the Patapata—the people of your city have not conquered the whole world?"

I gave a shout of drunken laughter and slapped Attalos on the back. "We *have*, old boy, we have! You Macedonians have just not yet found out that you are our subjects!"

Attalos digested this, then scowled blackly. "You temple-thief! I think you have been making a fool of me! Of *me!* By Herakles, I ought—"

He rose and swung a fist back to clout me. I jerked an arm up to guard my face.

There came a roar of "Attalos!" from the head of the table. King Philip had been watching us.

Attalos dropped his fist, muttered something like "Flying chariots and tame Tritons, forsooth!" and stumbled back to his own crowd.

40

This man, I remembered, did not have a happy future in store. He was destined to marry his niece to Philip, whose first wife Olympias would have the girl and her baby killed after Philip's assassination. Soon afterwards, Attalos would be murdered by Alexander's orders. It was on the tip of my tongue to give him a veiled warning, but I forebore. I had attracted enough hostile attention already.

Later, when the drinking got heavy, Aristotle came over and shooed his boys off to bed. He said to me: "Let uth walk outside to clear our heads, Zandras, and then go to bed, too. These Makedones drink like sponges. I cannot keep up with them."

Outside, he said: "The Attalos thinks you are a Persian thpy."

"A spy? Me? In Hera's name, why?" Silently I cursed my folly in making an enemy without any need. Would I never learn to deal with this damned human species?

Aristotle said: "He thays nobody could pass through a country and remain as ignorant of it as you theem to be. *Ergo,* you know more of the Persian Empire than you pretend, but wish us to think you have nothing to do with it. And why should you do that, unleth you are yourself a Persian? And being a Persian, why should you hide the fact unleth you are on some hostile mission?"

"A Persian might fear anti-Persian prejudice among the Hellenes. Not that I am one," I hastily added.

"He need not. Many Persians live in Hellas without molestation. Take Artabazos and his sons, who live in Pella, refugees from their own king."

Then the obvious alibi came to me, long after it should have. "The fact is I went even farther north than I said. I went around the northern ends of the Caspian and Euxine seas and so did not cross the Great King's domains save through the Bactrian deserts."

"You did? Then why did you not thay tho? If that is true, you have settled one of our hottest geographical disputes: whether the Caspian is a closed thea or a bay of the Northern Ocean."

"I feared nobody would believe me."

"I am not sure what to believe, Zandras. You are a strange man. I do not think you are a Persian, for no Persian was ever a philothopher. It is good for you that you are not."

"Why?"

"Because I *hate* Persia!" he hissed.

"You do?"

"Yeth. I could list the wrongs done by the Great Kings, but it is enough that they seized my beloved father-in-law by treachery and torture, and crucified him. People like Isokrates talk of uniting the Hellenes to conquer Persia, and Philippos may try it if he lives. I hope he does. However," he went on in a different tone, "I hope he does it without dragging the cities of Hellas into it, for the repositories of civilization have no busineth getting into a brawl between tyrants."

"In India," said I sententiously, "we are taught that a man's nationality means nothing and his personal qualities everything. Men of all nations come good, bad, and indifferent."

Aristotle shrugged. "I have known virtuouth Persians too, but that monstrouth, bloated empire . . . No state can be truly civilized with more than a few thousand citizens."

There was no use telling him that large states, however monstrous and bloated he thought them, would be a permanent feature of the landscape from then on. I was trying to reform, not Aristotle's narrow view of international affairs, but his scientific methodology.

42

Next morning King Philip and his men and Aristotle's six pupils galloped off toward Pella, followed by a train of baggage mules and the boys' personal slaves. Aristotle said:

"Let us hope no chance sling-thtone dashes out Alexandros' brains before he has a chance to show his mettle. The boy has talent and may go far, though managing him is like trying to plow with a wild bull. Now, let us take up the questions of atoms again, my dear Zandras, about which you have been talking thuch utter rubbish. First, you must admit that if a thing exists, parts of it must also exist. Therefore there is no thuch thing as an indivisible particle . . ."

Three days later, while we were still hammering at the question of atoms, we looked up at the clatter of hooves. Here came Attalos and a whole troop of horsemen. Beside Attalos rode a tall swarthy man with a long gray beard. This man's appearance startled me into thinking he must be another time traveler from my own time, for he wore a hat, coat, and pants. The mere sight of these familiar garments filled me with homesickness for my own world, however much I hated it when I lived in it.

Actually, the man's garb was not that of one from my world. The hat was a cylindrical felt cap with earflaps. The coat was a brown knee-length garment, embroidered with faded red and blue flowers, with trousers to match. The whole outfit looked old and threadbare, with patches showing. He was a big craggy-looking fellow, with a great hooked nose, wide cheekbones, and deep-set eyes under bushy, beetling brows.

They all dismounted, and a couple of grooms went around collecting the bridles to keep the horses from running off. The soldiers leaned on their spears in a circle around us.

Attalos said: "I should like to ask your guest some more philosophical questions, O Aristoteles."

"Ask away."

Attalos turned, not to me, but to the tall graybeard. He said something I did not catch, and then the man in trousers spoke to me in a language I did not know.

"I do not understand," I said.

The graybeard spoke again, in what sounded like a different tongue. He did this several times, using a different-sounding speech each time, but each time I had to confess ignorance.

"Now you see," said Attalos. "He pretends not to know Persian, Median, Armenian, or Aramaic. He could not have traversed the Great King's dominions from east to west without learning at least one of these."

"Who are you, my dear sir?" I asked Graybeard.

The old man gave me a small, dignified smile and spoke in Attic with a guttural accent. "I am Artavazda, or Artabazos as the Hellenes say, once governor of Phrygia but now a poor pensioner of King Philippos."

This, then, was the eminent Persian refugee of whom Aristotle had spoken.

"I warrant he does not even speak Indian," said Attalos.

"Certainly," I said, and started off in English: *"Now is the time for all good men to come to the aid of the party. Four score and seven years ago our fathers brought forth—"*

"What would you call that?" Attalos asked Artavazda.

The Persian spread his hands. "I have never heard the like. But then, India is a vast country of many tongues."

"I was not—" I began, but Attalos kept on:

"What race would you say he belonged to?"

"I know not. The Indians I have seen were much darker, but there might be light-skinned Indians for aught I know."

"If you will listen, General, I will explain," I said. "For most of the journey I was not even in the Persian Empire. I crossed through Bactria and went around the north of the Caspian and Euxine seas."

"Oh, so now you tell another story?" said Attalos. "Any educated man knows the Caspian is but a deep bay opening into the Ocean River to the north. Therefore you could not go around it. So, in trying to escape, you do but mire yourself deeper in your own lies."

"Look here," said Aristotle. "You have proved nothing of the sort, O Attalos. Ever thince Herodotos there have been those who think the Caspian a closed thea—"

"Hold your tongue, Professor," said Attalos. "This is a matter of national security. There is something queer about this alleged Indian, and I mean to find out what it is."

"It is not queer that one who comes from unknown distant lands should tell a singular tale of his journey."

"No, there is more to it than that. I have learned that he first appeared in a treetop on the farm of the freeholder Diktys Pisandrou. Diktys remembers looking up into the tree for crows before he cast himself down under it to rest. If the Zandras had been in the tree, Diktys would have seen him, as it was not yet fully in leaf. The next instant there was the crash of a body falling into the branches, and Zandras' staff smote Diktys on the head. Normal mortal men fall not out of the sky into trees."

"Perhaps he flew from India. They have marvelous mechanisms there, he tells me," said Aristotle.

"If he survives our interrogation in Pella, perhaps he can make me a pair of wings," said Attalos. "Or better yet, a pair for my horse, so he shall emulate Pegasos. Meanwhile, seize and bind him, men!"

The soldiers moved. I did not dare submit for fear they

would take my gun and leave me defenceless. I snatched up the hem of my tunic to get at my pistol. It took precious seconds to unsnap the safety strap, but I got the gun out before anybody laid hand on me.

"Stand back or I will blast you with lightning!" I shouted, raising the gun.

Men of my own world, knowing how deadly such a weapon can be, would have given ground at the sight of it. But the Macedonians, never having seen one, merely stared at the device and came on. Attalos was one of the nearest.

I fired at him, then whirled and shot another soldier who was reaching out to seize me. The discharge of the gun produces a lightning-like flash and a sharp sound like a close clap of thunder. The Macedonians cried out, and Attalos fell with a wound in his thigh.

I turned again, looking for a way out of the circle of soldiers, while confused thoughts of taking one of their horses flashed through my head. A heavy blow in the flank staggered me. One of the soldiers had jabbed me with his spear, but my belt kept the weapon from piercing me. I shot at the man but missed him in my haste.

"Do not kill him!" screamed Aristotle.

Some of the soldiers backed up as if to flee; others poised their spears. They hesitated for the wink of an eye, either for fear of me or because Aristotle's command confused them. Ordinarily they would have ignored the philosopher and listened for their general's orders, but Attalos was down on the grass and looking in amazement at the hole in his leg.

As one soldier dropped his spear and started to run, a blow on the head sent a flash of light through my skull and hurled me to the ground, nearly unconscious. A man behind me had swung his spear like a club and struck me on the pate with the shaft.

Before I could recover, they were all over me, raining kicks and blows. One wrenched the gun from my hand. I must have lost consciousness, for the next thing I remember is lying in the dirt while the soldiers tore off my tunic. Attalos stood over me with a bloody bandage around his leg, leaning on a soldier. He looked pale and frightened but resolute. The second man I had shot lay still.

"So that is where he keeps his infernal devices!" said Attalos, indicating my belt. "Take it off, men."

The soldiers struggled with the clasp of the belt until one impatiently sawed through the straps with his dagger. The gold in my money pouch brought cries of delight.

I struggled to get up, but a pair of soldiers knelt on my arms to keep me down. There was a continuous mumble of talk. Attalos, looking over the belt, said:

"He is too dangerous to live. Even stripped as he is, who knows but what he will soar into the air and escape by magic?"

"Do not kill him!" said Aristotle. "He has much valuable knowledge to impart."

"No knowledge is worth the safety of the kingdom."

"But the kingdom can benefit from his knowledge. Do you not agree?" Aristotle asked the Persian.

"Drag me not into this, pray," said Artavazda. "It is no concern of mine."

"If he is a danger to Makedonia, he should be destroyed at once," said Attalos.

"There is but little chance of his doing harm now," said Aristotle, "and an excellent chance of his doing us good."

"Any chance of his doing harm is too much," said Attalos. "You philosophers can afford to be tolerant of interesting strangers. But, if they carry disaster in their baggage, it is on us poor soldiers that the brunt will fall. Is it not so, Artabazos?"

"I have done what you asked and will say no more," said Artavazda. "I am but a simple-minded Persian nobleman who does not understand your Greek subtleties."

"I can increase the might of your armies, General!" I cried to Attalos.

"No doubt, and no doubt you can also turn men to stone with an incantation, as the Gorgons did with their glance." He drew his sword and felt the edge with his thumb.

"You will slay him for mere thuperstition!" wailed Aristotle, wringing his hands. "At least, let the king judge the matter."

"Not superstition," said Attalos, "murder." He pointed to the dead soldier.

"I come from another world! Another age!" I yelled, but Attalos was not to be diverted.

"Let us get this over with," he said. "Set him on his knees, men. Take my sword, Glaukos; I am too unsteady to wield it. Now bow your head, my dear barbarian, and—"

In the middle of Attalos' sentence, he and the others and all my surroundings vanished. Again there came that sharp pain and sense of being jerked by a monstrous catapult . . .

I found myself lying in leaf mold with the pearl-gray trunks of poplars all around me. A brisk breeze was making the poplar leaves flutter and show their silvery bottoms. It was too cool for a man who was naked save for sandals and socks.

I had snapped back to the year 1981 of the calendar of my world, which I had set out from. But where was I? I should be near the site of the Brookhaven National Laboratories in a vastly improved super-scientific world. There was, however, no sign of super-science here; nothing but poplar trees.

I got up, groaning, and looked around. I was covered with bruises and bleeding from nose and mouth.

The only way I had of orienting myself was the boom of a distant surf. Shivering, I hobbled towards the sound. After a few hundred paces, I came out of the forest on a beach. This beach could be the shore of Sewanhaki, or Long Island as we called it, but there was no good way of telling. There was no sign of human life; just the beach curving into the distance and disappearing around headlands, with the poplar forest on one side and the ocean on the other.

What, I wondered, had happened? Had science advanced so fast as a result of my intervention that man had already exterminated himself by scientific warfare? Thinkers of my world had concerned themselves with this possibility, but I had never taken it seriously.

It began to rain. In despair I cast myself down on the sand and beat it with my fists. I may have lost consciousness again.

At any rate, the next thing I knew was the now-familiar sound of hooves. When I looked up, the horseman was almost upon me, for the sand had muffled the animal's footsteps until it was quite close.

I blinked with incredulity. For an instant I thought I must be back in the classical era still. The man was a warrior armed and armored in a style much like that of ancient times. At first he seemed to be wearing a helmet of classical Hellenic type. When he came closer I saw that this was not quite true, for the crest was made of feathers instead of horsehair. The nasal and cheek plates hid most of his face, but he seemed dark and beardless. He wore a shirt of scale mail, long leather trousers, and low shoes. He had a bow and a small shield hung from his saddle and a slender lance slung across his back by a strap. I saw that this could not be ancient times because the horse was fitted with a large, well-molded saddle and stirrups.

As I watched the man stupidly, he whisked the lance out of its boot and couched it. He spoke in an unknown language.

I got up, holding my hands over my head in surrender. The man kept repeating his question, louder and louder, and making jabbing motions. All I could say was "I don't understand" in the languages I knew, none of which seemed familiar to him.

Finally he maneuvered his horse around to the other side of me, barked a command, pointed along the beach the way he had come, and prodded me with the butt of the lance. Off I limped, with rain, blood, and tears running down my hide.

You know the rest, more or less. Since I could not give an intelligible account of myself, the Sachim of Lenape, Wayotan the Fat, claimed me as a slave. For fourteen years I labored on his estate at such occupations as feeding hogs and chopping kindling. When Wayotan died and the present Sachim was elected, he decided I was too old for that kind of work, especially as I was half crippled from the beatings of Wayotan and his overseers. Learning that I had some knowledge of letters (for I had picked up spoken and written Algonkian in spite of my wretched lot) he freed me and made me official librarian.

In theory I can travel about as I like, but I have done little of it. I am too old and weak for the rigors of travel in this world, and most other places are, as nearly as I can determine, about as barbarous as this one. Besides, a few

Lenapes come to hear me lecture on the nature of man and the universe and the virtues of the scientific method. Perhaps I can light a small spark here after I failed in the year 340 B.C.

When I went to work in the library, my first thought was to find out what had happened to bring the world to its present pass.

Wayotan's predecessor had collected a considerable library which Wayotan had neglected, so that some of the books had been chewed by rats and others ruined by dampness. Still, there was enough to give me a good sampling of the literature of this world, from ancient to modern times. There were even Herodotos' history and Plato's dialogues, identical with the versions that existed in my own world.

I had to struggle against more language barriers, as the European languages of this world are different from, though related to, those of my own world. The English of today, for instance, is more like the Dutch of my own world, as a result of England's never having been conquered by the Normans.

I also had the difficulty of reading without eyeglasses. Luckily, most of these manuscript books are written in a large, clear hand. A couple of years ago I did get a pair of glasses, imported from China where the invention of the printing press has stimulated the manufacture. But, as they are a recent invention in this world, they are not so effective as those of mine.

I rushed through all the history books to find out when and how your history diverged from mine. I found that differences appeared quite early. Alexander still marched to the Indus but failed to die at thirty-two on his return. In fact he lived fifteen years longer and fell at last in battle with the Sarmatians in the Caucasus Mountains.

I do not know why that brief contact with me enabled him to avoid the malaria mosquito that slew him in my world. Maybe I aroused in him a keener interest in India than he would otherwise have had, leading him to stay there longer so that all his subsequent schedules were changed. His empire held together for most of a century instead of breaking up right after his death as it did in my world.

The Romans still conquered the whole Mediterranean, but the course of their conquests and the names of the prominent Romans were all different. Two of the chief religions of my world, Christianity and Islam, never appeared at all. Instead we have Mithraism, Odinism, and Soterism, the last an Egypto-Hellenic synthesis founded by that fiery Egyptian prophet whose followers call him by the Greek word for "savior."

Still, classical history followed the same *general* course that it had in my world, even though the actors bore other names. The Roman Empire broke up, as it did in my world, though the details are all different, with a Hunnish emperor ruling in Rome and a Gothic One in Antioch.

It is after the fall of the Roman Empire that profound differences appear. In my world there was a revival of learning that began about nine hundred years ago, followed by a scientific revolution beginning four centuries later. In your history the revival of learning was centuries later, and the scientific revolution has hardly begun. Failure to develop the compass and the full-rigged ship resulted in North America's (I mean Hesperia's) being discovered and settled via the northern route, by way of Iceland, and more slowly than in my world. Failure to invent the gun meant that the natives of Hesperia were not swept aside by the invading Europeans, but held their own against them and gradually learned their arts of iron-working, weaving, cereal-growing, and the like. Now most of the European settlements have been assimilated, though the ruling families of the Abnakis and Mohegans frequently have blue eyes and still call themselves by names like "Sven" and "Eric."

I was eager to get hold of a work by Aristotle, to see what effect I had had on him and to try to relate this effect to the subsequent course of history. From allusions in some of the works in this library I gathered that many of his writings had come down to modern times, though the titles all seemed different from those of his surviving works in my world. The only actual samples of his writings in the library were three essays, *Of Justice*, *On Education*, and *Of Passions and Anger*. None of these showed my influence.

I had struggled through most of the Sachim's collection when I found the key I was looking for. This was an Iberic translation of *Lives of the Great Philosophers*, by one Diomedes of Mazaka. I never heard of Diomedes in the literary history of my own world, and perhaps he never existed. Anyway, he had a long chapter on Aristotle, in which appears the following section:

Now Aristotle, during his sojourn at Mytilene, had been an assiduous student of natural sciences. He had planned, according to Timotheus, a series of works which should correct the errors of Empedokles, Demokritos, and others of his predecessors. But, after he had removed to Macedonia and busied himself with the education of Alexander, there one day appeared before him a traveler, Sandos of Palibothra, a mighty philosopher of India.

The Indian ridiculed Aristotle's attempts at scientific research, saying that in his land these investigations had gone far beyond anything the Hellenes had attempted, and the Indians were still a long way from arriving at satisfactory explanations of the universe. Moreover, he asserted that no real progress could be made in natural philosophy unless the Hellenes abandoned their disdain for physical labor and undertook exhaustive experiments with mechanical devices of the sort which cunning Egyptian and Asiatic craftsmen make.

King Philip, hearing of the presence of this stranger in his land and fearing lest he be a spy sent by some foreign power to harm or corrupt the young prince, came with soldiers to arrest him. But, when he demanded that Sandos accompany him back to Pella, the latter struck dead with thunderbolts all the king's soldiers that were with him. Then, it is said, mounting into his chariot drawn by winged gryphons, he flew off in the direction of India. But other authorities say that the man who came to arrest Sandos was Antipatros, the regent, and that Sandos cast darkness before the eyes of Antipatros and Aristotle, and when they recovered from their swoon he had vanished.

Aristotle, reproached by the king for harboring so dangerous a visitor and shocked by the sanguinary ending of the Indian's visit, resolved to have no more to do with the sciences. For, as he explains in his celebrated treatise *On the Folly of Natural Science*, there are three reasons why no good Hellene should trouble his mind with such matters.

One is that the number of facts which must be mastered before sound theories become possible is so vast that if all the Hellenes did nothing else for centuries, they would still not gather the amount of data required. The task is therefore futile.

Secondly, experiments and mechanical inventions are necessary to progress in science, and such work, though all very well for slavish Asiatics, who have a natural bent for it, is beneath the dignity of a Hellenic gentleman.

And, lastly, some of the barbarians have already surpassed the Hellenes in this activity, wherefore it ill becomes the Hellenes to compete with their inferiors in skills at which the latter have an inborn advantage. They should rather cultivate personal rectitude, patriotic valor, political rationality, and aesthetic sensitivity, leaving to the barbarians such artificial aids to the good and virtuous life as are provided by scientific discoveries.

This was it, all right. The author had gotten some of his facts wrong, but that was to be expected from an ancient historian.

So! My teachings had been too successful. I had so well shattered the naïve self-confidence of the Hellenic philosophers as to discourage them from going on with science at all.

I should have remembered that glittering theories and sweeping generalizations, even when wrong, are the frosting on the cake; they are the carrot that makes the donkey go.

The possibility of pronouncing such universals is the stimulus that keeps many scientists grinding away, year after year, at the accumulation of facts, even seemingly dull and trivial facts. If ancient scientists had realized how much laborious fact-finding lay ahead of them before sound theories would become possible, they would have been so appalled as to drop science altogether. And that is just what happened.

The sharpest irony of all was that I had placed myself where I could not undo my handiwork. If I had ended up in a scientifically advanced world, and did not like what I found, I might have built another time machine, gone back, and somehow warned myself of the mistake lying in wait for me. But such a project is out of the question in a backward world like this one, where seamless columbium tubing, for instance, is not even thought of. All I proved by my disastrous adventure is that space-time has a negative curvature, and who in this world cares about that?

You recall, when you were last here, asking me the meaning of a motto in my native language on the wall of my cell. I said I would tell you in connection with my whole fantastic story. The motto says: "Leave Well Enough Alone," and I wish I had.

Cordially yours,

Sherman Weaver

The Gnarly Man

Dr. Matilda Saddler first saw the gnarly man on the evening of June 14, 1946, at Coney Island.

The spring meeting of the Eastern Section of the American Anthropological Association had broken up, and Dr. Saddler had had dinner with two of her professional colleagues, Blue of Columbia and Jeffcott of Yale. She mentioned that she had never visited Coney, and meant to go there that evening. She urged Blue and Jeffcott to come along, but they begged off.

Watching Dr. Saddler's retreating back, Blue of Columbia cackled: "The Wild Woman from Wichita. Wonder if she's hunting another husband?" He was a thin man with a small gray beard and a who-the-hell-are-you-sir expression.

"How many has she had?" asked Jeffcott of Yale.

"Two to date. Don't know why anthropologists lead the most disorderly private lives of any scientists. Must be that they study the customs and morals of all these different peoples, and ask themselves, 'If the Eskimos can do it, why can't we?' I'm old enough to be safe, thank God."

"I'm not afraid of her," said Jeffcott. He was in his early forties and looked like a farmer uneasy in store clothes. "I'm so very thoroughly married."

"Yeah? Ought to have been at Stanford a few years ago, when she was there. Wasn't safe to walk across the campus with Tuthill chasing all the females and Saddler all the males."

Dr. Saddler had to fight her way off the subway train, as

57

the adolescents who infest the platform of the B.M.T.'s Stillwell Avenue station are probably the worst mannered people on earth, possibly excepting the Dobu Islanders, of the western Pacific. She didn't much mind. She was a tall, strongly built woman in her late thirties, who had been kept trim by the outdoor rigors of her profession. Besides, some of the inane remarks in Swift's paper on acculturation among the Arapaho Indians had gotten her fighting blood up.

Walking down Surf Avenue toward Brighton Beach, she looked at the concessions without trying them, preferring to watch the human types that did and the other human types that took their money. She did try a shooting gallery, but found knocking tin owls off their perch with a .22 too easy to be much fun. Long-range work with an army rifle was her idea of shooting.

The concession next to the shooting gallery would have been called a sideshow if there had been a main show for it to be a sideshow to. The usual lurid banner proclaimed the uniqueness of the two-headed calf, the bearded woman, Arachne the spider girl, and other marvels. The pièce de résistance was Ungo-Bungo, the ferocious ape-man, captured in the Congo at a cost of twenty-seven lives. The picture showed an enormous Ungo-Bungo squeezing a hapless Negro in each hand, while others sought to throw a net over him.

Dr. Saddler knew perfectly well that the ferocious ape-man would turn out to be an ordinary Caucasian with false hair on his chest. But a streak of whimsicality impelled her to go in. Perhaps, she thought, she could have some fun with her colleagues about it.

The spieler went through his leather-lunged harangue. Dr. Saddler guessed from his expression that his feet hurt.

58

The tattooed lady didn't interest her, as her decorations obviously had no cultural significance, as they have among the Polynesians. As for the ancient Mayan, Dr. Saddler thought it in questionable taste to exhibit a poor micro-cephalic idiot that way. Professor Yoki's legerdemain and fire eating weren't bad.

There was a curtain in front of Ungo-Bungo's cage. At the appropriate moment there were growls and the sound of a length of chain being slapped against a metal plate. The spieler wound up on a high note: "—ladies and gentlemen, the one and only UNGO-BUNGO!" The curtain dropped.

The ape-man was squatting at the back of his cage. He dropped his chain, got up, and shuffled forward. He grasped two of the bars and shook them. They were appropriately loose and rattled alarmingly. Ungo-Bungo snarled at the patrons, showing his even, yellow teeth.

Dr. Saddler stared hard. This was something new in the ape-man line. Ungo-Bungo was about five feet three, but very massive, with enormous hunched shoulders. Above and below his blue swimming trunks thick, grizzled hair covered him from crown to ankle. His short, stout-muscled arms ended in big hands with thick, gnarled fingers. His neck projected slightly forward, so that from the front he seemed to have but little neck at all.

His face—well, thought Dr. Saddler, she knew all the living races of men, and all the types of freak brought about by glandular maladjustment, and none of them had a face like *that*. It was deeply lined. The forehead between the short scalp hair and the brows on the huge supraorbital ridges receded sharply. The nose, although wide, was not apelike; it was a shortened version of the thick, hooked Armenoid nose, so often miscalled Jewish. The face ended in a long upper lip and a retreating chin. And the yellowish skin apparently belonged to Ungo-Bungo.

The curtain was whisked up again.

Dr. Saddler went out with the others, but paid another dime, and soon was back inside. She paid no attention to the spieler, but got a good position in front of Ungo-Bungo's cage before the rest of the crowd arrived.

Ungo-Bungo repeated his performance with mechanical precision. Dr. Saddler noticed that he limped a little as he came forward to rattle the bars, and that the skin under his mat of hair bore several big whitish scars. The last joint of his left ring finger was missing. She noted certain things about the proportions of his shin and thigh, of his forearm and upper arm, and his big splay feet.

Dr. Saddler paid a third dime. An idea was knocking at her mind somewhere. If she let it in, either she was crazy or physical anthropology was haywire or—something. But she knew that if she did the sensible thing, which was to go home, the idea would plague her from now on.

After the third performance she spoke to the spieler. "I think your Mr. Ungo-Bungo used to be a friend of mine. Could you arrange for me to see him after he finishes?"

The spieler checked his sarcasm. His questioner was so obviously not a—not the sort of dame who asks to see guys after they finish.

"Oh, him" he said. "Calls himself Gaffney—Clarence Aloysius Gaffney. That the guy you want?"

"Why, yes."

"I guess you can." He looked at his watch. "He's got four more turns to do before we close. I'll have to ask the boss." He popped through a curtain and called, "Hey, Morrie!" Then he was back. "It's okay. Morrie says you can wait in his office. Foist door to the right."

Morrie was stout, bald, and hospitable. "Sure, sure," he

said, waving his cigar. "Glad to be of soivace, Miss Saddler. Chust a min while I talk to Gaffney's manager." He stuck his head out. "Hey, Pappas! Lady wants to talk to your ape-man later. I meant *lady,* O.K." He returned to orate on the difficulties besetting the freak business. "You take this Gaffney, now. He's the best damn ape-man in the business; all that hair rilly grows outa him. And the poor guy rilly has a face like that. But do people believe it? No! I hear 'em going out, saying about how the hair is pasted on, and the whole thing is a fake. It's mawtifying." He cocked his head, listening. "That rumble wasn't no rolly-coaster; it's gonna rain. Hope it's over by tomorrow. You wouldn't believe the way a rain can knock ya receipts off. If you drew a coive, it would be like this." He drew his finger horizontally through space, jerking it down sharply to indicate the effect of rain. "But as I said, people don't appreciate what you try to do for 'em. It's not just the money; I think of myself as an ottist. A creative ottist. A show like this got to have balance and propawtion, like any other ott—"

It must have been an hour later when a slow, deep voice at the door said: "Did somebody want to see me?"

The gnarly man was in the doorway. In street clothes, with the collar of his raincoat turned up and his hat brim pulled down, he looked more or less human, though the coat fitted his great, sloping shoulders badly. He had a thick, knobby walking stick with a leather loop near the top end. A small, dark man fidgeted behind him.

"Yeah," said Morrie, interrupting his lecture. "Clarence, this is Miss Saddler. Miss Saddler, this is Mr. Gaffney, one of our outstanding creative ottists."

"Pleased to meetcha," said the gnarly man. "This is my manager, Mr. Pappas."

61

Dr. Saddler explained, and said she'd like to talk to Mr. Gaffney if she might. She was tactful; you had to be to pry into the private affairs of Naga headhunters, for instance. The gnarly man said he'd be glad to have a cup of coffee with Miss Saddler; there was a place around the corner that they could reach without getting wet.

As they started out, Pappas followed, fidgeting more and more. The gnarly man said: "Oh, go home to bed, John. Don't worry about me." He grinned at Dr. Saddler. The effect would have been unnerving to anyone but an anthropologist. "Every time he sees me talking to anybody, he thinks it's some other manager trying to steal me." He spoke general American, with a suggestion of Irish brogue in the lowering of the vowels in words like "man" and "talk." "I made the lawyer who drew up our contract fix it so it can be ended on short notice."

Pappas departed, still looking suspicious. The rain had practically ceased. The gnarly man stepped along smartly despite his limp.

A woman passed with a fox terrier on a leash. The dog sniffed in the direction of the gnarly man, and then to all appearances went crazy, yelping and slavering. The gnarly man shifted his grip on the massive stick and said quietly, "Better hang onto him, ma'am." The woman departed hastily. "They just don't like me," commented Gaffney. "Dogs, that is."

They found a table and ordered their coffee. When the gnarly man took off his raincoat, Dr. Saddler became aware of a strong smell of cheap perfume. He got out a pipe with a big knobby bowl. It suited him, just as the walking stick did. Dr. Saddler noticed that the deep-sunk eyes under the beetling arches were light hazel.

"Well?" he said in his rumbling drawl.

She began her questions.

"My parents were Irish," he answered. "But I was born in South Boston . . . let's see . . . forty-six years ago. I can get you a copy of my birth certificate. Clarence Aloysius Gaffney, May 2, 1900." He seemed to get some secret amusement out of that statement.

"Were either of your parents of your somewhat unusual physical type?"

He paused before answering. He always did, it seemed. "Uh-huh. Both of 'em. Glands, I suppose."

"Were they both born in Ireland?"

"Yep. County Sligo." Again that mysterious twinkle.

She thought. "Mr. Gaffney, you wouldn't mind having some photographs and measurements made, would you? You could use the photographs in your business."

"Maybe." He took a sip. "Ouch! Gazooks, that's hot!"

"What?"

"I said the coffee's hot."

"I mean, before that."

The gnarly man looked a little embarrassed. "Oh, you mean the 'gazooks'? Well, I . . . uh . . . once knew a man who used to say that."

"Mr. Gaffney, I'm a scientist, and I'm not trying to get anything out of you for my own sake. You can be frank with me."

There was something remote and impersonal in his stare that gave her a slight spinal chill. "Meaning that I haven't been so far?"

"Yes. When I saw you I decided that there was something extraordinary in your background. I still think there is. Now, if you think I'm crazy, say so and we'll drop the subject. But I want to get to the bottom of this."

He took his time about answering. "That would depend." There was another pause. Then he said: "With your connections, do you know any really first-class surgeons?"

"But . . . yes, I know Dunbar."

"The guy who wears a purple gown when he operates? The guy who wrote a book on 'God, Man, and the Universe'?"

"Yes. He's a good man, in spite of his theatrical mannerisms. Why? What would you want of him?"

"Not what you're thinking. I'm satisfied with my . . . uh . . . unusual physical type. But I have some old injuries—broken bones that didn't knit properly—that I want fixed up. He'd have to be a good man, though. I have a couple of thousand dollars in the savings bank, but I know the sort of fees those guys charge. If you could make the necessary arrangements—"

"Why, yes, I'm sure I could. In fact, I could guarantee it. Then I *was* right? And you'll—" She hesitated.

"Come clean? Uh-huh. But remember, I can still prove I'm Clarence Aloysius if I have to."

"Who *are* you, then?"

Again there was a long pause. Then the gnarly man said: "Might as well tell you. As soon as you repeat any of it, you'll have put your professional reputation in my hands, remember.

"First off, I wasn't born in Massachusetts. I was born on the upper Rhine, near Mommenheim. And I was born, as nearly as I can figure out, about the year 50,000 B.C."

Matilda Saddler wondered whether she'd stumbled on the biggest thing in anthropology, or whether this bizarre personality was making Baron Munchausen look like a piker.

He seemed to guess her thoughts. "I can't prove that, of

course. But so long as you arrange about that operation, I don't care whether you believe me or not."

"But . . . but . . . *how?*"

"I think the lightning did it. We were out trying to drive some bison into a pit. Well, this big thunderstorm came up, and the bison bolted in the wrong direction. So we gave up and tried to find shelter. And the next thing I knew I was lying on the ground with the rain running over me, and the rest of the clan standing around wailing about what had they done to get the storm god sore at them, so he made a bull's-eye on one of their best hunters. They'd never said *that* about me before. It's funny how you're never appreciated while you're alive.

"But I was alive, all right. My nerves were pretty well shot for a few weeks, but otherwise I was okay, except for some burns on the soles of my feet. I don't know just what happened, except I was reading a couple of years ago that scientists had located the machinery that controls the replacement of tissue in the medulla oblongata. I think maybe the lightning did something to my medulla to speed it up. Anyway, I never got any older after that. Physically, that is. I was thirty-three at the time, more or less. We didn't keep track of ages. I look older now, because the lines in your face are bound to get sort of set after a few thousand years, and because our hair was always gray at the ends. But I can still tie an ordinary *Homo sapiens* in a knot if I want to."

"Then you're . . . you mean to say you're . . . you're trying to tell me you're—"

"A Neanderthal man? *Homo neanderthalensis?* That's right."

Matilda Saddler's hotel room was a bit crowded, with the gnarly man, the frosty Blue, the rustic Jeffcott, Dr. Saddler herself, and Harold McGannon, the historian. This McGannon was a small man, very neat and pink-skinned. He looked more like a New York Central director than a professor. Just now his expression was one of fascination. Dr. Saddler looked full of pride; Professor Jeffcott looked interested but puzzled; Dr. Blue looked bored—he hadn't wanted to come in the first place. The gnarly man, stretched out in the most comfortable chair and puffing his overgrown pipe, seemed to be enjoying himself.

McGannon was formulating a question. "Well, Mr.— Gaffney? I suppose that's your name as much as any."

"You might say so," said the gnarly man. "My original name meant something like Shining Hawk. But I've gone under hundreds of names since then. If you register in a hotel as 'Shining Hawk,' it's apt to attract attention. And I try to avoid that."

"Why?" asked McGannon.

The gnarly man looked at his audience as one might look at willfully stupid children. "I don't like trouble. The best way to keep out of trouble is not to attract attention. That's why I have to pull up stakes and move every ten or fifteen years. People might get curious as to why I never get any older."

"Pathological liar," murmured Blue. The words were barely audible, but the gnarly man heard them.

"You're entitled to your opinion, Dr. Blue," he said affably. "Dr. Saddler's doing me a favor, so in return I'm letting you all shoot questions at me. And I'm answering. I don't give a damn whether you believe me or not."

McGannon hastily threw in another question. "How is it that you have a birth certificate, as you say you have?"

"Oh, I knew a man named Clarence Gaffney once. He got killed by an automobile, and I took his name."

"Was there any reason for picking this Irish background?"

"Are you Irish, Dr. McGannon?"

"Not enough to matter."

"Okay. I didn't want to hurt any feelings. It's my best bet. There are real Irishmen with upper lips like mine."

Dr. Saddler broke in. "I meant to ask you, Clarence." She put a lot of warmth into his name. "There's an argument as to whether your people interbred with mine, when mine overran Europe at the end of the Mousterian. Some scientists have thought that some modern Europeans, especially along the west coast of Ireland, might have a little Neanderthal blood."

He grinned slightly. "Well—yes and no. There never was any back in the stone age, as far as I know. But these long-lipped Irish are my fault."

"How?"

"Believe it or not, but in the last fifty centuries there have been some women of your species that didn't find me too repulsive. Usually there was no offspring. But in the sixteenth century I went to Ireland to live. They were burning too many people for witchcraft in the rest of Europe to suit me at that time. And there was a woman. The result this time was a flock of hybrids—cute little devils, they were. So the Irishmen who look like me are my descendants."

"What did happen to your people?" asked McGannon. "Were they killed off?"

The gnarly man shrugged. "Some of them. We weren't at all warlike. But then the tall ones, as we called them, weren't either. Some of the tribes of the tall ones looked on us as legitimate prey, but most of them let us severely alone. I guess they were almost as scared of us as we were of them. Savages as primitive as that are really pretty peaceable people. You have to work so hard to keep fed, and there are so few of you, that there's no object in fighting wars. That comes later, when you get agriculture and livestock, so you have something worth stealing.

"I remember that a hundred years after the tall ones had come, there were still Neanderthalers living in my part of the country. But they died out. I think it was that they lost their ambition. The tall ones were pretty crude, but they were so far ahead of us that our things and our customs seemed silly. Finally we just sat around and lived on the scraps we could beg from the tall ones' camps. You might say we died of an inferiority complex."

"What happened to you?" asked McGannon.

"Oh, I was a god among my own people by then, and naturally I represented them in their dealings with the tall ones. I got to know the tall ones pretty well, and they were willing to put up with me after all my own clan were dead. Then in a couple of hundred years they'd forgotten all about my people, and took me for a hunchback or something. I got to be pretty good at flint working, so I could earn my keep. When metal came in, I went into that, and finally into blacksmithing. If you'd put all the horseshoes I've made in a pile, they'd—well, you'd have a damn big pile of horseshoes, anyway."

"Did you . . . ah . . . limp at that time?" asked McGannon.

"Uh-huh. I busted my leg back in the Neolithic. Fell out of a tree, and had to set it myself, because there wasn't anybody around. Why?"

"Vulcan," said McGannon softly.

"Vulcan?" repeated the gnarly man. "Wasn't he a Greek god or something?"

"Yes. He was the lame blacksmith of the gods."

"You mean you think that maybe somebody got the idea from me? That's an interesting theory. Little late to check up on it, though."

Blue leaned forward and said crisply: "Mr. Gaffney, no real Neanderthal man could talk so fluently and entertainingly as you do. That's shown by the poor development of the frontal lobes of the brain and the attachments of the tongue muscles."

The gnarly man shrugged again. "You can believe what you like. My own clan considered me pretty smart, and then you're bound to learn something in fifty thousand years."

Dr. Saddler beamed. "Tell them about your teeth, Clarence."

The gnarly man grinned. "They're false, of course. My own lasted a long time, but they still wore out somewhere back in the Paleolithic. I grew a third set, and they wore out, too. So I had to invent soup."

"You *what?*" It was the usually taciturn Jeffcott.

"I had to invent soup, to keep alive. You know, the bark-dish-and-hot-stones method. My gums got pretty tough after a while, but they still weren't much good for chewing hard stuff. So after a few thousand years I got pretty sick of soup and mushy foods generally. And when metal came in I began experimenting with false teeth. Bone teeth in copper plates. You might say I invented them, too. I tried often to sell them, but they never really caught on until around 1750 A.D. I was living in Paris then, and I built up quite a little business before I moved on." He pulled the handkerchief out of his breast pocket to wipe his forehead; Blue made a face as the wave of perfume reached him.

"Well, Mr. Shining Hawk," snapped Blue with a trace of sarcasm, "how do you like our machine age?"

The gnarly man ignored the tone of the question. "It's not bad. Lots of interesting things happen. The main trouble is the shirts."

"Shirts?"

"Uh-huh. Just try to buy a shirt with a twenty neck and a twenty-nine sleeve. I have to order 'em special. It's almost as bad with hats and shoes. I wear an eight and one half hat and a thirteen shoe." He looked at his watch. "I've got to get back to Coney to work."

McGannon jumped up. "Where can I get in touch with you again, Mr. Gaffney? There's lots of things I'd like to ask you."

The gnarly man told him. "I'm free mornings. My working hours are two to midnight on weekdays, with a couple of hours off for dinner. Union rules, you know."

"You mean there's a union for you show people?"

"Sure. Only they call it a guild. They think they're artists, you know. Artists don't have unions; they have guilds. But it amounts to the same thing."

Blue and Jeffcott saw the gnarly man and the historian walking slowly toward the subway together. Blue said: "Poor old Mac! Always thought he had sense. Looks like he's swallowed this Gaffney's ravings, hook, line, and sinker."

"I'm not so sure," said Jeffcott, frowning. "There's something funny about the business."

"What?" barked Blue. "Don't tell me that *you* believe this story of being alive fifty thousand years? A caveman who uses perfume! Good God!"

"N-no," said Jeffcott. "Not the fifty thousand part. But I don't think it's a simple case of paranoia or plain lying, either. And the perfume's quite logical, if he were telling the truth."

"Huh?"

"Body odor. Saddler told us how dogs hate him. He'd have a smell different from ours. We're so used to ours that we don't even know we have one, unless somebody goes without a bath for a month. But we might notice his if he didn't disguise it."

Blue snorted. "You'll be believing him yourself in a minute. It's an obvious glandular case, and he's made up this story to fit. All that talk about not caring whether we believe him or not is just bluff. Come on, let's get some lunch. Say, see the way Saddler looked at him every time she said 'Clarence'? Like a hungry wolf. Wonder what she thinks she's going to do with him?"

Jeffcott thought. "I can guess. And if he *is* telling the truth, I think there's something in Deuteronomy against it."

The great surgeon made a point of looking like a great surgeon, to pince-nez and Vandyke. He waved the X-ray negatives at the gnarly man, pointing out this and that.

"We'd better take the leg first," he said. "Suppose we do that next Thursday. When you've recovered from that we can tackle the shoulder. It'll all take time, you know."

The gnarly man agreed, and shuffled out of the little private hospital to where McGannon awaited him in his car. The gnarly man described the tentative schedule of operations, and mentioned that he had made arrangements to quit his job. "Those two are the main thing," he said. "I'd like to try professional wrestling again some day, and I can't unless I get this shoulder fixed so I can raise my left arm over my head."

"What happened to it?" asked McGannon.

71

The gnarly man closed his eyes, thinking. "Let me see. I get things mixed up sometimes. People do when they're only fifty years old, so you can imagine what it's like for me.

"In 42 B.C. I was living with the Bituriges in Gaul. You remember that Cæsar shut up Werkinghetorich— Vercingetorix to you—in Alesia, and the confederacy raised an army of relief under Coswollon."

"Coswollon?"

The gnarly man laughed shortly. "I meant Warcaswollon. Coswollon was a Briton, wasn't he? I'm always getting those two mixed up.

"Anyhow, I got drafted. That's all you can call it; I didn't want to go. It wasn't exactly *my* war. But they wanted me because I could pull twice as heavy a bow as anybody else.

"When the final attack on Cæsar's ring fortifications came, they sent me forward with some other archers to provide a covering fire for their infantry. At least, that was the plan. Actually, I never saw such a hopeless muddle in my life. And before I even got within bowshot, I fell into one of the Romans' covered pits. I didn't land on the point of the stake, but I fetched up against the side of it and busted my shoulder. There wasn't any help, because the Gauls were too busy running away from Cæsar's German cavalry to bother about wounded men."

The author of "God, Man, and the Universe" gazed after his departing patient. He spoke to his head assistant: "What do you think of him?"

"I think it's so," said the assistant. "I looked over those X-rays pretty closely. That skeleton never belonged to a human being. And it has more healed fractures than you'd think possible."

"Hm-m-m," said Dunbar. "That's right, he wouldn't be human, would he? Hm-m-m. You know, if anything happened to him—"

The assistant grinned understandingly. "Of course, there's the S.P.C.A."

"We needn't worry about *them*. Hm-m-m." He thought, you've been slipping; nothing big in the papers for a year. But if you published a complete anatomical description of a Neanderthal man—or if you found out why his medulla functions the way it does—Hm-m-m. Of course, it would have to be managed properly—

"Let's have lunch at the Natural History Museum," said McGannon. "Some of the people there ought to know you."

"Okay," drawled the gnarly man. "Only I've still got to get back to Coney afterward. This is my last day. Tomorrow, Pappas and I are going up to see our lawyer about ending our contract. Guy named Robinette. It's a dirty trick on poor old John, but I warned him at the start that this might happen."

"I suppose we can come up to interview you while you're . . . ah . . . convalescing? Fine. Have you ever been to the museum, by the way?"

"Sure," said the gnarly man. "I get around."

"What did you . . . ah . . . think of their stuff in the Hall of the Age of Man?"

"Pretty good. There's a little mistake in one of those big wall paintings. The second horn on the woolly rhinoceros ought to slant forward more. I thought of writing them a letter. But you know how it is. They'd say: 'Were you there?' and I'd say, 'Uh-huh,' and they'd say, 'Another nut.' "

"How about the pictures and busts of Paleolithic men?"

"Pretty good. But they have some funny ideas. They always show us with skins wrapped around our middles. In summer we didn't wear skins, and in winter we hung them around our shoulders, where they'd do some good.

"And then they show those tall ones that you call Cro-Magnon men clean-shaven. As I remember, they all had whiskers. What would they shave with?"

"I think," said McGannon, "that they leave the beards off the busts to . . . ah . . . show the shape of the chins. With the beards they'd all look too much alike."

"Is that the reason? They might say so on the labels." The gnarly man rubbed his own chin, such as it was. "I wish beards would come back into style. I look much more human with a beard. I got along fine in the sixteenth century when everybody had whiskers.

"That's one of the ways I remember when things happened, by the haircuts and whiskers that people had. I remember when a wagon I was driving in Milan lost a wheel and spilled flour bags from hell to breakfast. That must have been in the sixteenth century, before I went to Ireland, because I remember that most of the men in the crowd that collected had beards. Now—wait a minute—maybe that was the fourteenth. There were a lot of beards, then, too."

"Why, why didn't you keep a diary?" asked McGannon with a groan of exasperation.

The gnarly man shrugged characteristically. "And pack around six trunks full of paper every time I moved? No, thanks."

"I . . . ah . . . don't suppose you could give me the real story of Richard III and the princes in the tower?"

"Why should I? I was just a poor blacksmith, or farmer, or something most of the time. I didn't go around with the big shots. I gave up all my ideas of ambition a long time before that. I had to, being so different from other people. As far as I can remember, the only real king I ever got a good look at was Charlemagne, when he made a speech in Paris one day. He was just a big, tall man with Santa Claus whiskers and a squeaky voice."

Next morning McGannon and the gnarly man had a session with Svedberg at the museum. Then McGannon drove Gaffney around to the lawyer's office, on the third floor of a seedy office building in the West Fifties. James Robinette looked something like a movie actor and something like a chipmunk. He looked at his watch and said to McGannon: "This won't take long. If you'd like to stick around, I'd be glad to have lunch with you." The fact was that he was feeling just a trifle queasy about being left with this damn queer client, this circus freak or whatever he was, with his barrel body and his funny slow drawl.

When the business had been completed, and the gnarly man had gone off with his manager to wind up his affairs at Coney, Robinette said: "Whew! I thought he was a half-wit, from his looks. But there was nothing half-witted about the way he went over those clauses. You'd have thought the damn contract was for building a subway system. What is he, anyhow?"

McGannon told him what he knew.

The lawyer's eyebrows went up. "Do you *believe* his yarn? Oh, I'll take tomato juice and filet of sole with tartar sauce— only without the tartar sauce—on the lunch, please."

"The same for me. Answering your question, Robinette, I do. So does Saddler. So does Svedberg up at the museum. They're both topnotchers in their respective fields. Saddler and I have interviewed him, and Svedberg's examined him

75

physically. But it's just opinion. Fred Blue still swears it's a hoax or . . . ah . . . some sort of dementia. Neither of us can prove anything."

"Why not?"

"Well . . . ah . . . how are you going to prove that he was, or was not, alive a hundred years ago?" Take one case: Clarence says he ran a sawmill in Fairbanks, Alaska, in 1906 and '07, under the name of Michael Shawn. How are you going to find out whether there was a sawmill operator in Fairbanks at that time? And if you did stumble on a record of a Michael Shawn, how would you know whether he and Clarence were the same? There's not a chance in a thousand that there'd be a photograph or a detailed description that you could check with. And you'd have an awful time trying to find anybody who remembered him at this late date.

"Then, Svedberg poked around Clarence's face, yesterday, and said that no *Homo sapiens* ever had a pair of zygomatic arches like that. But when I told Blue that, he offered to produce photographs of a human skull that did. I know what'll happen. Blue will say that they're obviously different. So there we'll be."

Robinette mused, "He does seem damned intelligent for an ape-man."

"He's not an ape-man, really. The Neanderthal race was a separate branch of the human stock: they were more primitive in some ways and more advanced in others than we are. Clarence may be slow, but he usually grinds out the right answer. I imagine that he was . . . ah . . . brilliant, for one of his kind, to begin with. And he's had the benefit of so much experience. He knows an incredible lot. He knows us; he sees through us and our motives."

The little pink man puckered up his forehead. "I do hope nothing happens to him. He's carrying around a lot of priceless information in that big head of his. Simply price-less. Not much about war and politics; he kept clear of those as a matter of self-preservation. But little things, about how people lived and how they thought thousands of years ago. He gets his periods mixed up sometimes, but he gets them straightened out if you give him time.

"I'll have to get hold of Pell, the linguist. Clarence knows dozens of ancient languages, such as Gothic and Gaulish. I was able to check him on one of them, like vulgar Latin; that was one of the things that convinced me. And there are archeologists and psychologists—

"If only something doesn't happen to scare him off. We'd never find him. I don't know. Between a man-crazy female scientist and a publicity-mad surgeon—I wonder how it'll work out—"

The gnarly man innocently entered the waiting room of Dunbar's hospital. He, as usual, spotted the most comfortable chair and settled luxuriously into it.

Dunbar stood before him. His keen eyes gleamed with anticipation behind their pince-nez. "There'll be a wait of about half an hour, Mr. Gaffney," he said. "We're all tied up now, you know. I'll send Mahler in; he'll see that you have anything you want." Dunbar's eyes ran lovingly over the gnarly man's stumpy frame. What fascinating secrets mightn't he discover once he got inside it?

Mahler appeared, a healthy-looking youngster. Was there anything Mr. Gaffney would like? The gnarly man paused as usual to let his massive mental machinery grind. A vagrant impulse moved him to ask to see the instruments that were to be used on him.

Mahler had his orders, but this seemed a harmless enough request. He went and returned with a tray full of gleaming steel. "You see," he said, "these are called scalpels."

Presently the gnarly man asked: "What's this?" He picked up a peculiar-looking instrument.

"Oh, that's the boss's own invention. For getting at the mid-brain."

"Mid-brain? What's that doing here?"

"Why, that's for getting at your—That must be there by mistake—"

Little lines tightened around the queer hazel eyes. "Yeah?" He remembered the look Dunbar had given him, and Dunbar's general reputation. "Say, could I use your phone a minute?"

"Why . . . I suppose . . . what do you want to phone for?"

"I want to call my lawyer. Any objections?"

"No, of course not. But there isn't any phone here."

"What do you call that?" The gnarly man got up and walked toward the instrument in plain sight on a table. But Mahler was there before him, standing in front of it.

"This one doesn't work. It's being fixed."

"Can't I try it?"

"No, not till it's fixed. It doesn't work, I tell you."

The gnarly man studied the young physician for a few seconds. "Okay, then I'll find one that does." He started for the door.

"Hey, you can't go out now!" cried Mahler.

"Can't I? Just watch me!"

"Hey!" It was a full-throated yell. Like magic more men in white coats appeared.

Behind them was the great surgeon. "Be reasonable, Mr. Gaffney," he said. "There's no reason why you should go out now, you know. We'll be ready for you in a little while."

"Any reason why I shouldn't?" The gnarly man's big

face swung on his thick neck, and his hazel eyes swiveled. All the exits were blocked. "I'm going."

"Grab him!" said Dunbar.

The white coats moved. The gnarly man got his hands on the back of a chair. The chair whirled, and became a dissolving blur as the men closed on him. Pieces of chair flew about the room, to fall with the dry, sharp *ping* of short lengths of wood. When the gnarly man stopped swinging, having only a short piece of the chair back left in each fist, one assistant was out cold. Another leaned whitely against the wall and nursed a broken arm.

"Go on!" shouted Dunbar when he could make himself heard. The white wave closed over the gnarly man, then broke. The gnarly man was on his feet, and held young Mahler by the ankles. He spread his feet and swung the shrieking Mahler like a club, clearing the way to the door. He turned, whirled Mahler around his head like a hammer thrower, and let the now mercifully unconscious body fly. His assailants went down in a yammering tangle.

One was still up. Under Dunbar's urging he sprang after the gnarly man. The latter had gotten his stick out of the umbrella stand in the vestibule. The knobby upper end went *whoosh* past the assistant's nose. The assistant jumped back and fell over one of the casualties. The front door slammed, and there was a deep roar of "Taxi!"

"Come on!" shrieked Dunbar. "Get the ambulance out!"

James Robinette was sitting in his office, thinking the thoughts that lawyers do in moments of relaxation, when there was a pounding of large feet in the corridor, a startled protest from Miss Spevak in the outer office, and the strange client of the day before was at Robinette's desk, breathing hard.

"I'm Gaffney," he growled between gasps. "Remember me? I think they followed me down here. They'll be up any minute. I want your help."

"They? Who's they?" Robinette winced at the impact of that damn perfume.

The gnarly man launched into his misfortunes. He was going well when there were more protests from Miss Spevak, and Dr. Dunbar and four assistants burst into the office.

"He's ours," said Dunbar, his glasses agleam.

"He's an ape-man," said the assistant with the black eye. "He's a dangerous lunatic," said the assistant with the cut lip.

"We've come to take him away," said the assistant with the torn coat.

The gnarly man spread his feet and gripped his stick like a baseball bat by the small end.

Robinette opened a desk drawer and got out a large pistol. "One move toward him and I'll use this. The use of extreme violence is justified to prevent commission of a felony, to wit: kidnapping."

The five men backed up a little. Dunbar said: "This isn't kidnapping. You can only kidnap a person, you know. He isn't a human being, and I can prove it."

The assistant with the black eye snickered. "If he wants protection, he better see a game warden instead of a lawyer."

"Maybe that's what *you* think," said Robinette. "You aren't a lawyer. According to the law, he's human. Even corporations, idiots, and unborn children are legally persons, and he's a damned sight more human then they are."

"Then he's a dangerous lunatic," said Dunbar.

"Yeah? Where's your commitment order? The only persons who can apply for one are: (a) close relatives and (b) public officials charged with the maintenance of order. You're neither."

Dunbar continued stubbornly: "He ran amuck in my hospital and nearly killed a couple of my men, you know. I guess that gives us some rights."

"Sure," said Robinette. "You can step down to the nearest station and swear out a warrant." He turned to the gnarly man. "Shall we throw the book at 'em, Gaffney?"

"I'm all right," said that individual, his speech returning to its normal slowness. "I just want to make sure these guys don't pester me any more."

"Okay. Now listen, Dunbar. One hostile move out of you and we'll have a warrant out for you for false arrest, assault and battery, attempted kidnapping, criminal conspiracy, and disorderly conduct. *And* we'll slap on a civil suit for damages for sundry torts, to wit: assault, deprivation of civil rights, placing in jeopardy of life and limb, menace, and a few more I may think of later."

"You'll never make that stick," snarled Dunbar. "We have all the witnesses."

"Yeah? And wouldn't the great Evan Dunbar look sweet defending such actions? Some of the ladies who gush over your books might suspect that maybe you weren't such a damn knight in shining armor. We can make a prize monkey of you, and you know it."

"You're destroying the possibility of a great scientific discovery, you know, Robinette."

"To hell with that. My duty is to protect my client. Now beat it, all of you, before I call a cop." His left hand moved suggestively to the telephone.

Dunbar grasped at a last straw. "Hm-m-m. Have you got a permit for that gun?"

"Damn right. Want to see it?"

Dunbar sighed. "Never mind. You *would* have." His greatest opportunity for fame was slipping out of his fingers.

He drooped toward the door.

The gnarly man spoke up. "If you don't mind, Dr. Dunbar, I left my hat at your place. I wish you'd send it to Mr. Robinette here. I have a hard time getting hats to fit me."

Dunbar looked at him silently and left with his cohorts.

The gnarly man was giving the lawyer further details when the telephone rang. Robinette answered: "Yes . . . Saddler? Yes, he's here . . . Your Dr. Dunbar was going to murder him so he could dissect him . . . okay." He turned to the gnarly man. "Your friend Dr. Saddler is looking for you. She's on her way up here."

"Zounds!" said Gaffney. "I'm going."

"Don't you want to see her? She was phoning from around the corner. If you go out now you'll run into her. How did she know where to call?"

"I gave her your number. I suppose she called the hospital and my boardinghouse, and tried you as a last resort. This door goes into the hall, doesn't it? Well, when she comes in the regular door I'm going out this one. And I don't want you saying where I've gone. It's nice to have known you, Mr. Robinette."

"Why? What's the matter? You're not going to run out now, are you? Dunbar's harmless, and you've got friends. I'm your friend."

"You're durn tootin' I'm going to run out. There's too much trouble. I've kept alive all these centuries by staying away from trouble. I let down my guard with Dr. Saddler, and went to the surgeon she recommended. First he plots to take me apart to see what makes me tick. If that brain instrument hadn't made me suspicious, I'd have been on my way to the alcohol jars by now. Then there's a fight, and it's just pure luck I didn't kill a couple of those interns, or whatever they are, and get sent up for manslaughter.

"Now Matilda's after me with a more-than-friendly interest. No. I know what it means when a woman looks at you that way and calls you 'dear.' I wouldn't mind if she weren't a prominent person of the kind that's always in some sort of garboil. That would mean more trouble, sooner or later. You don't suppose I *like* trouble, do you?"

"But look here, Gaffney, you're getting steamed up over a lot of damn—"

"*Ssst!*" The gnarly man took his stick and tiptoed over to the private entrance. As Dr. Saddler's clear voice sounded in the outer office, he sneaked out. He was closing the door behind him when the scientist entered the inner office.

Matilda Saddler was a quick thinker. Robinette hardly had time to open his mouth when she flung herself at and through the private door with a cry of "Clarence!"

Robinette heard the clatter of feet on the stairs. Neither the pursued nor the pursuer had waited for the creaky elevator. Looking out the window, he saw Gaffney leap into a taxi. Matilda Saddler sprinted after the cab, calling: "Clarence! Come back!" But the traffic was light and the chase correspondingly hopeless.

They did hear from the gnarly man once more. Three months later Robinette got a letter whose envelope contained, to his vast astonishment, ten ten-dollar bills. The single sheet was typed, even to the signature.

DEAR MR. ROBINETTE:

I do not know what your regular fees are, but I hope that the inclosed will cover your services to me of last June.

Since leaving New York I have had several jobs. I pushed a hack—as we say—in Chicago, and I tried out as pitcher on a bush league baseball team. Once I made my living by knocking over rabbits and things with stones, and I can still throw fairly well. Nor am I bad at swinging a club, such as a baseball bat. But my lameness makes me too slow for a baseball career, and it will be some time before I try any remedial operations again.

I now have a job whose nature I cannot disclose because I do not wish to be traced. You need pay no attention to the postmark; I am not living in Kansas City, but had a friend post this letter there.

Ambition would be foolish for one in my peculiar position. I am satisfied with a job that furnishes me with the essentials, and allows me to go to an occasional movie, and a few friends with whom I can drink beer and talk.

I was sorry to leave New York without saying good-by to Dr. Harold McGannon, who treated me very nicely. I wish you would explain to him why I had to leave as I did. You can get in touch with him through Columbia University.

If Dunbar sent you my hat as I requested, please mail it to me: General Delivery, Kansas City, Mo. My friend will pick it up. There is not a hat store in this town where I live that can fit me. With best wishes, I remain,

Yours sincerely,

SHINING HAWK
Alias CLARENCE ALOYSIUS GAFFNEY

A Gun for Dinosaur

No, I'm sorry, Mr. Seligman, but I can't take you hunting late-Mesozoic dinosaur.

Yes, I know what the advertisement says.

Why not? How much d' you weigh? Fifty-four kilos? Let's see—that's under sixty kilos, which is my lower limit.

I could take you to other periods, you know. I'll take you to any period in the Cenozoic. I'll get you a shot at an entelodont or a uintathere. They've got fine heads.

I'll even stretch a point and take you to the basal Pleistocene, where you can try for one of the mammoths or the mastodon.

I'll take you back to the Triassic, where you can shoot one of the smaller ancestral dinosaurs. But I will bloody well not take you to the Jurassic or Cretaceous. You're just too small.

What's your size got to do with it? Look here, mate, what did you think you were going to shoot your dinosaur with?

Oh, you hadn't thought, eh?

Well, sit there a minute . . . Here you are: my own private gun for that work, a Continental .600. Does look like a shotgun, doesn't it? But it's rifled, as you can see by looking through the barrels. Shoots a pair of .600 Nitro Express cartridges the size of bananas; weighs nearly seven kilos and has a muzzle energy of over twenty-two hundred KGMs. Costs twenty thousand dollars. Lot of money for a gun, eh?

I have some spares we rent to the sahibs. Designed for knocking down elephant. Not just wounding them, knocking them base-over-apex. That's why they don't make guns like this in America, though I suppose they will if hunting parties keep going back in time.

Now, I've been guiding hunting parties for twenty years. Guided 'em in Africa until the game gave out there except on the preserves. And all that time I've never known a bloke your size who could handle the six-nought-nought. It knocks 'em over, and even when they stay on their feet they get so scared of the bloody cannon after a few shots that they flinch. And they find the gun too heavy to drag around rough Mesozoic country. Wears 'em out.

It's true that lots of people have killed elephant with lighter guns: the .500, .475, and .465 doubles, for instance, or even .375 magnum repeaters. The difference is, with a .375 you have to hit something vital, preferably the heart, and can't depend on simple shock power.

An elephant weighs—let's see—four to six tonnes. You're proposing to shoot reptiles weighing two or three times as much as an elephant and with much greater tenacity of life. That's why the syndicate decided to take no more people dinosaur hunting unless they could handle the .600. We learned the hard way, as you Americans say. There were some unfortunate incidents . . .

I'll tell you, Mr. Seligman. It's after seventeen hundred. Time I closed the office. Why don't we stop at the bar on our way out while I tell you the story?

It was about the Raja's and my fifth safari into time. The Raja? Oh, he's the Aiyar half of Rivers and Aiyar. I call him the Raja because he's the hereditary monarch of Janpur. Means nothing nowadays, of course. Knew him in India and ran into him in New York running the Indian tourist agency. That dark chap in the photograph on my office wall, the one with his foot on the dead sabertooth.

Well, Chandra Aiyar was fed up with handing out brochures about the Taj Mahal and wanted to do a bit of hunting again. I was at loose ends when we heard of Professor Prochaska's time machine at the big University.

Where's the Raja now? Out on safari, in the Early Oligocene after titanothere, while I run the office. We take turn about, but the first few times we went out together.

Anyhow, we caught the next plane to St. Louis. To our mortification, we found we weren't the first. Lord, no! There were other hunting guides and no end of scientists, each with his own idea of the right way to use the machine.

We scraped off the historians and archeologists right at the start. Seems the bloody machine won't work for periods more recent than 100,000 years ago. It works from there up to about a billion years.

Why? Oh, I'm no four-dimensional thinker; but, as I understand it, if people could go back to a more recent time, their actions would affect our own history, which would be a paradox or contradiction of facts. Can't have that in a well-run universe, you know.

But, before 100,000 B.C., more or less, the actions of the expeditions are lost in the stream of time before human history begins. At that, once a stretch of past time has been used, say the month of January, one million B.C., you can't use that stretch over again by sending another party into it. Paradoxes again.

The professor isn't worried, though. With a billion years to exploit, he won't soon run out of eras.

Another limitation of the machine is the matter of size. For technical reasons, Prochaska had to build the transition chamber just big enough to hold four men with their personal gear, and the chamber wallah. Larger parties have to be sent through in relays. That means, you see, it's not practical to take jeeps, launches, aircraft, and other powered vehicles.

On the other hand, since you're going to periods without human beings, there's no whistling up a hundred native bearers to trot along with your gear on their heads. So we usually take a train of asses—burros, they call them here. Most periods have enough natural forage so you can get where you want to go.

As I say, everybody had his own idea for using the machine. The scientists looked down their noses at us hunters and said it would be a crime to waste the machine's time pandering to our sadistic amusements.

We brought up another angle. The machine cost a cool thirty million. I understand this came from the Rockefeller Board and such people, but that accounted for the original cost only, not the cost of operation. And the thing uses fantastic amounts of power. Most of the scientists' projects, while worthy enough, were run on a shoestring, financially speaking.

Now, we guides catered to people with money, a species with which America seems well stocked. No offense, sport. Most of these could afford a substantial fee for passing through the machine into the past. Thus we could help finance the operation of the machine for scientific purposes, provided we got a fair share of its time. In the end, the guides formed a syndicate, one member being the partnership of Rivers and Aiyar, to apportion the machine's time.

We had rush business from the start. Our wives—the Raja's and mine—raised hell with us for a while. They'd hoped that, when the big game gave out in our own era, they'd never have to share us with lions and things again, but you know how women are. Hunting's not really dangerous if you keep your head and take precautions.

★ ★ ★ ★ ★

On the fifth expedition, we had two sahibs to wet-nurse; both Americans in their thirties, both physically sound, and both solvent. Otherwise they were as different as different can be.

Courtney James was what you chaps call a playboy: a rich young man from New York who'd always had his own way and didn't see why that agreeable condition shouldn't continue. A big bloke, almost as big as I am; handsome in a florid way, but beginning to run to fat. He was on his fourth wife and, when he showed up at the office with a blond twist with "model" written all over her, I assumed that this was the fourth Mrs. James.

"Miss Bartram," she corrected me, with an embarrassed giggle.

"She's not my wife," James explained. "My wife is in Mexico, I think, getting a divorce. But Bunny here would like to go along—"

"Sorry," I said, "we don't take ladies. At least, not to the Late Mesozoic."

This wasn't strictly true, but I felt we were running enough risks, going after a little-known fauna, without dragging in people's domestic entanglements. Nothing against sex, you understand. Marvelous institution and all that, but not where it interferes with my living.

"Oh, nonsense!" said James. "If she wants to go, she'll go. She skis and flies my airplane, so why shouldn't she—"

"Against the firm's policy," I said.

"She can keep out of the way when we run up against the dangerous ones," he said.

"No, sorry."

"Damn it!" said he, getting red. "After all, I'm paying you a goodly sum, and I'm entitled to take whoever I please."

"You can't hire me to do anything against my best judgment," I said. "If that's how you feel, get another guide."

"All right, I will," he said. "And I'll tell all my friends you're a God-damned—" Well, he said a lot of things I won't repeat, until I told him to get out of the office or I'd throw him out.

I was sitting in the office and thinking sadly of all that lovely money James would have paid me if I hadn't been so stiff-necked, when in came my other lamb, one August Holtzinger. This was a little slim pale chap with glasses, polite and formal. Holtzinger sat on the edge of his chair and said:

"Uh—Mr. Rivers, I don't want you to think I'm here under false pretences. I'm really not much of an outdoorsman, and I'll probably be scared to death when I see a real dinosaur. But I'm determined to hang a dinosaur head over my fireplace or die in the attempt."

"Most of us are frightened at first," I soothed him, "though it doesn't do to show it." And little by little I got the story out of him.

While James had always been wallowing in the stuff, Holtzinger was a local product who'd only lately come into the real thing. He'd had a little business here in St. Louis and just about made ends meet when an uncle cashed in his chips somewhere and left little Augie the pile.

Now Holtzinger had acquired a fiancée and was building a big house. When it was finished, they'd be married and move into it. And one furnishing he demanded was a ceratopsian head over the fireplace. Those are the ones with the big horned heads with a parrot's beak and a frill over the neck, you know. You have to think twice about collecting them, because, if you put a two-meter *Triceratops* head into a small living room, there's apt to be no room left for anything else.

We were talking about this when in came a girl: a small girl in her twenties, quite ordinary looking, and crying.

"Augie!" she cried. "You can't! You mustn't! You'll be killed!" She grabbed him round the knees and said to me:

"Mr. Rivers, you mustn't take him! He's all I've got! He'll never stand the hardships!"

"My dear young lady," I said, "I should hate to cause you distress, but it's up to Mr. Holtzinger to decide whether he wishes to retain my services."

"It's no use, Claire," said Holtzinger. "I'm going, though I'll probably hate every minute of it."

"What's that, mate?" I said. "If you hate it, why go? Did you lose a bet, or something?"

"No," said Holtzinger. "It's this way. Uh—I'm a completely undistinguished kind of guy. I'm not brilliant or big or strong or handsome. I'm just an ordinary Midwestern small businessman. You never even notice me at Rotary luncheons, I fit in so perfectly.

"But that doesn't say I'm satisfied. I've always hankered to go to far places and do big things. I'd like to be a glamorous, adventurous sort of guy. Like you, Mr. Rivers."

"Oh, come," I said. "Professional hunting may seem glamorous to you, but to me it's just a living."

He shook his head. "Nope. You know what I mean. Well, now I've got this legacy, I could settle down to play bridge and golf the rest of my life, and try to act like I wasn't bored. But I'm determined to do something with some color in it, once at least. Since there's no more real big-game hunting in the present, I'm gonna shoot a dinosaur and hang his head over my mantel if it's the last thing I do. I'll never be happy otherwise."

Well, Holtzinger and his girl argued, but he wouldn't

give in. She made me swear to take the best care of her Augie and departed, sniffling.

When Holtzinger had left, who should come in but my vile-tempered friend Courtney James? He apologized for insulting me, though you could hardly say he groveled.

"I don't really have a bad temper," he said, "except when people won't cooperate with me. Then I sometimes get mad. But so long as they're cooperative I'm not hard to get along with."

I knew that by "cooperate" he meant to do whatever Courtney James wanted, but I didn't press the point. "How about Miss Bartram?" I asked.

"We had a row," he said. "I'm through with women. So, if there's no hard feelings, let's go on from where we left off."

"Very well," I said, business being business.

The Raja and I decided to make it a joint safari to eighty-five million years ago: The Early Upper Cretaceous, or the Middle Cretaceous as some American geologists call it. It's about the best period for dinosaur in Missouri. You'll find some individual species a little larger in the Late Upper Cretaceous, but the period we were going to gives a wider variety.

Now, as to our equipment: The Raja and I each had a Continental .600, like the one I showed you, and a few smaller guns. At this time we hadn't worked up much capital and had no spare .600s to rent.

August Holtzinger said he would rent a gun, as he expected this to be his only safari, and there's no point in spending twenty thousand dollars for a gun you'll shoot only a few times. But, since we had no spare .600s, his choice lay between buying one of those and renting one of our smaller pieces.

We drove into the country and set up a target, to let him try the .600. Holtzinger heaved up the gun and let fly. He missed completely, and the kick knocked him flat on his back.

He got up, looking paler than ever, and handed me back the gun, saying: "Uh—I think I'd better try something smaller."

When his shoulder stopped hurting, I tried him out on the smaller rifles. He took a fancy to my Winchester 70, chambered for the .375 magnum cartridge. This is an excellent all-round gun—perfect for the big cats and bears, but a little light for elephant and definitely light for dinosaur. I should never have given in, but I was in a hurry, and it might have taken months to have a new .600 made to order for him. James already had a gun, a Holland & Holland .500 double express, which is almost in a class with the .600.

Both sahibs had done a bit of shooting, so I didn't worry about their accuracy. Shooting dinosaur is not a matter of extreme accuracy, but of sound judgment and smooth co-ordination so you shan't catch twigs in the mechanism of your gun, or fall into holes, or climb a small tree that the dinosaur can pluck you out of, or blow your guide's head off.

People used to hunting mammals sometimes try to shoot a dinosaur in the brain. That's the silliest thing you can do, because dinosaur haven't got any. To be exact, they have a little lump of tissue the size of a tennis ball on the front end of their spines, and how are you going to hit that when it's imbedded in a two-meter skull?

The only safe rule with dinosaur is: always try for a heart shot. They have big hearts, over fifty kilos in the largest species, and a couple of .600 slugs through the heart will slow them up, at least. The problem is to get the slugs through that mountain of meat around it.

★ ★ ★ ★ ★`

Well, we appeared at Prochaska's laboratory one rainy morning: James and Holtzinger, the Raja and I, our herder Beauregard Black, three helpers, Ming the cook, and twelve jacks.

The transition chamber is a little cubbyhole the size of a small lift. My routine is for the men with the guns to go first, in case a hungry theropod is standing near the machine when it arrives. So the two sahibs, the Raja, and I crowded into the chamber with our guns and packs. The operator, Bruce Cohen, squeezed in after us, closed the door, and fiddled with his dials. He set the thing for April twenty-fourth, eighty-five million B.C., and pressed the red button. The lights went out, leaving the chamber lit by a little battery-operated lamp. James and Holtzinger looked pretty green, but that may have been the lighting. The Raja and I had been through all this before, so the vibration and vertigo didn't bother us.

The little spinning black hands of the dials slowed down and stopped. The operator looked at his ground-level gage and turned the handwheel that raised the chamber so it shouldn't materialize underground. Then he pressed another button, and the door slid open.

No matter how often I do it, I get a frightful thrill out of stepping into a bygone era. The operator had raised the chamber just above ground level, so I jumped down, my gun ready. The others came after.

"Right-o," I said to the chamber wallah, and he closed the door. The chamber disappeared, and we looked around. There weren't any dinosaurs in sight, nothing but lizards.

In this period, the chamber materializes on top of a rocky rise, from which you can see in all directions as far as the haze will let you. To the west, you see the arm of the

Kansas Sea that reaches across Missouri and the big swamp around the bayhead where the sauropods live.

To the north is a low range that the Raja named the Janpur hills, after the Indian kingdom his forebears once ruled. To the east, the land slopes up to a plateau, good for ceratopsians, while to the south is flat country with more sauropod swamps and lots of ornithopod: duckbill and iguanodont.

The finest thing about the Cretaceous is the climate: balmy, like the South Sea Islands, but not so muggy as most Jurassic climates. It was spring, with dwarf magnolias in bloom all over.

A thing about this landscape is that it combines a fairly high rainfall with an open type of vegetation cover. That is, the grasses hadn't yet evolve to the point of forming solid carpets over all the open ground. So the ground is thick with laurel, sassafras, and other shrubs, with bare earth between. There are big thickets of palmettos and ferns. The trees round the hill are mostly cycads, standing singly and in copses. You'd call 'em palms. Down towards the Kansas Sea are more cycads and willows, while the uplands are covered with screw pine and ginkgoes.

Now, I'm no bloody poet—the Raja writes the stuff, not me—but I can appreciate a beautiful scene. One of the helpers had come through the machine with two of the jacks and was pegging them out, and I was looking through the haze and sniffing the air, when a gun went off behind me—
bang! bang!

I whirled round, and there was Courtney James with his .500, and an ornithomime legging it for cover fifty meters away. The ornithomimes are medium-sized running dinosaurs, slender things with long necks and legs, like a cross between a lizard and an ostrich. This kind is over two meters tall and weighs as much as a man. The beggar had wandered out of the nearest copse, and James gave him both barrels. Missed.

I was upset, as trigger-happy sahibs are as much a menace to their party as theropods. I yelled: "Damn it, you idiot! I thought you weren't to shoot without a word from me?"

"And who the hell are you, to tell me when I'll shoot my own gun?" he said.

We had a rare old row until Holtzinger and the Raja got us calmed down. I explained:

"Look here, Mr. James, I've got reasons. If you shoot off all your ammunition before the trip's over, your gun won't be available in a pinch, as it's the only one of its caliber. If you empty both barrels at an unimportant target, what would happen if a big theropod charged before you could reload? Finally, it's not sporting to shoot everything in sight, just to hear the gun go off. Do you understand?"

"Yeah, I guess so," he said.

The rest of the party came through the machine, and we pitched our camp a safe distance from the materializing place. Our first task was to get fresh meat. For a twenty-one-day safari like this, we calculate our food requirements closely, so we can make out on tinned stuff and concentrates if we must, but we count on killing at least one piece of meat. When that's butchered, we go off on a short tour, stopping at four or five camping places to hunt and arriving back at base a few days before the chamber is due to appear.

Holtzinger, as I said, wanted a ceratopsian head, any kind. James insisted on just one head: a tyrannosaur. Then everybody'd think he'd shot the most dangerous game of all time.

Fact is, the tyrannosaur's overrated. He's more a carrion eater than an active predator, though he'll snap you up if he gets the chance. He's less dangerous than some of the other theropods—the flesh eaters, you know—such as the smaller *Gorgosaurus* from the period we were in. But everybody's read about the tyrant lizard, and he does have the biggest head of the theropods.

The one in our period isn't the *rex,* which is later and a bit bigger and more specialized. It's the *trionyches,* with the forelimbs not quite so reduced, though they're still too small for anything but picking the brute's teeth after a meal.

When camp was pitched, we still had the afternoon. So the Raja and I took our sahibs on their first hunt. We had a map of the local terrain from previous trips.

The Raja and I have worked out a system for dinosaur hunting. We split into two groups of two men each and walk parallel from twenty to forty meters apart. Each group had a sahib in front and a guide following and telling him where to go. We tell the sahibs we put them in front so they shall have the first shot. Well, that's true, but another reason is they're always tripping and falling with their guns cocked, and if the guide were in front he'd get shot.

The reason for two groups is that, if a dinosaur starts for one, the other gets a good heart shot from the side.

As we walked, there was the usual rustle of lizards scuttling out of the way: little fellows, quick as a flash and colored like all the jewels in Tiffany's, and big gray ones that hiss at you as they plod off. There were tortoises and a few little snakes. Birds with beaks full of teeth flapped off squawking. And always there was that marvelous mild Cretaceous air. Makes a bloke want to take his clothes off and dance with vine leaves in his hair, if you know what I mean.

Our sahibs soon found that Mesozoic country is cut up into millions of nullahs—gullies, you'd say. Walking is one long scramble, up and down, up and down.

We'd been scrambling for an hour, and the sahibs were soaked with sweat and had their tongues hanging out, when the Raja whistled. He'd spotted a group of bonehead feeding on cycad shoots.

These are the pachycephalosaurs, small ornithopods about the size of men with a bulge on top of their heads that makes them look almost intelligent. Means nothing, because the bulge is solid bone. The males butt each other with these heads in fighting over the females.

These chaps would drop down on all fours, munch up a shoot, then stand up and look around. They're warier than most dinosaurs, because they're the favorite food of the big theropods.

People sometimes assume that, because dinosaur are so stupid, their senses must be dim, too. But it's not so. Some, like the sauropods, are pretty dim-sensed, but most have good smell and eyesight and fair hearing. Their weakness is that, having hardly any minds, they have little memories. Hence, out of sight, out of mind. When a big theropod comes slavering after you, your best defense is to hide in a nullah or behind a bush, and if he can neither see you nor smell you he'll just wander off.

We skulked up behind a patch of palmetto downwind from the bonehead. I whispered to James:

"You've had a shot already today. Hold your fire until Holtzinger shoots, and then shoot only if he misses or if the beast is getting away wounded."

"Uh-huh," said James.

We separated, he with the Raja and Holtzinger with me. This got to be our regular arrangement. James and I got on each other's nerves, but the Raja's a friendly, sentimental sort of bloke nobody can help liking.

We crawled round the palmetto patch on opposite sides, and Holtzinger got up to shoot. You daren't shoot a heavy-caliber rifle prone. There's not enough give, and the kick can break your shoulder.

Holtzinger sighted round the last few fronds of palmetto. I saw his barrel wobbling and waving. Then he lowered his gun and tucked it under his arm to wipe his glasses.

Off went James's gun, both barrels again.

The biggest bonehead went down, rolling and thrashing. The others ran away on their hindlegs in great leaps, their heads jerking and their tails sticking up behind.

"Put your gun on safety," I said to Holtzinger, who'd started forward. By the time we got to the bonehead, James was standing over it, breaking open his gun and blowing out the barrels. He looked as smug as if he'd come into another million and was asking the Raja to take his picture with his foot on the game.

I said: "I thought you were to give Holtzinger the first shot?"

"Hell, I waited," he said, "and he took so long I thought he must have gotten buck fever. If we stood around long enough, they'd see us or smell us."

There was something in what he said, but his way of saying it put my monkey up. I said: "If that sort of thing happens once more, we'll leave you in camp the next time we go out."

"Now, gentlemen," said the Raja. "After all, Reggie, these aren't experienced hunters."

"What now?" said Holtzinger. "Haul him back ourselves or send out the men?"

"We'll sling him under the pole," I said. "He weighs

under one hundred kilos."

The pole was a telescoping aluminium carrying pole I had in my pack, with padded yokes on the ends. I brought it because, in such eras, you can't count on finding saplings strong enough for proper poles on the spot. The Raja and I cleaned our bonehead, to lighten him, and tied him to the pole. The flies began to light on the offal by thousands. Scientists say they're not true flies in the modern sense, but they look and act like flies. There's one huge four-winged carrion fly that flies with a distinctive deep thrumming note.

The rest of the afternoon we sweated under that pole, taking turn about. The lizards scuttled out of the way, and the flies buzzed round the carcass.

We got to camp just before sunset, feeling as if we could eat the whole bonehead at one meal. The boys had the camp running smoothly, so we sat down for our tot of whiskey feeling like lords of creation, while the cook broiled bonehead steaks.

Holtzinger said: "Uh—if I kill a ceratopsian, how do we get his head back?"

I explained: "If the ground permits, we lash it to the patent aluminium roller frame and sled it in."

"How much does a head like that weigh?" he asked.

"Depends on the age and the species," I told him. "The biggest weigh over a tonne, but most run between two and five hundred kilos."

"And all the ground's rough like it was today?"

"Most of it," I said. "You see, it's the combination of the open vegetation cover and the moderately high rainfall. Erosion is frightfully rapid."

"And who hauls the head on its little sled?"

"Everybody with a hand," I said. "A big head would

need every ounce of muscle in this party. On such a job there's no place for side."

"Oh" said Holtzinger. I could see he was wondering whether a ceratopsian head would be worth the effort.

The next couple of days we trekked round the neighborhood. Nothing worth shooting; only a herd of ornithomimes, which went bounding off like a lot of ballet dancers. Otherwise there were only the usual lizards and pterosaurs and birds and insects. There's a big lace-winged fly that bites dinosaurs; so, as you can imagine, its beak makes nothing of a human skin. One made Holtzinger leap and dance like a Red Indian when it bit him through his shirt. James joshed him about it, saying:

"What's all the fuss over one little bug?"

The second night, during the Raja's watch, James gave a yell that brought us all out of our tents with rifles. All that had happened was that a dinosaur tick had crawled in with him and started drilling under his armpit. Since it's as big as your thumb even when it hasn't fed, he was understandably startled. Luckily he got it before it had taken its pint of blood. He'd pulled Holtzinger's leg pretty hard about the fly bite, so now Holtzinger repeated the words:

"What's all the fuss over one little bug, buddy?"

James squashed the tick underfoot with a grunt, not much liking to be hoist by his own what-d'you-call-it.

We packed up and started on our circuit. We meant to take the sahibs first to the sauropod swamp, more to see the wildlife than to collect anything.

From where the transition chamber materializes, the sauropod swamp looks like a couple of hours' walk, but it's really an all-day scramble. The first part is easy, as it's downhill and the brush isn't heavy. Then, as you get near the swamp, the cycads and willows grow so thickly that you have to worm and hack your way among them.

I led the party to a sandy ridge on the border of the swamp, as it was pretty bare of vegetation and afforded a fine view. When we got to the ridge, the sun was about to go down. A couple of crocs slipped off into the water. The sahibs were so tired that they flopped down in the sand as if dead.

The haze is thick round the swamp, so the sun was deep red and weirdly distorted by the atmospheric layers. There was a high layer of clouds reflecting the red and gold of the sun, too, so altogether it was something for the Raja to write one of his poems about. A few little pterosaur were wheeling overhead like bats.

Beauregard Black got a fire going. We'd started on our steaks, and that pagoda-shaped sun was just slipping below the horizon, and something back in the trees was making a noise like a rusty hinge, when a sauropod breathed out in the water. They're the really big ones, you know. If Mother Earth were to sigh over the misdeeds of her children, it would sound like that.

The sahibs jumped up, shouting: "Where is he? Where is he?"

I said: "That black spot in the water, just to the left of that point."

They yammered while the sauropod filled its lungs and disappeared. "Is that all?" said James. "Won't we see any more of him?"

Holtzinger said: "I read that they never come out of the water because they're too heavy to walk."

"No," I explained. "They can walk perfectly well and often do, for egg-laying and moving from one swamp to another. But much of the time they spend in the water, like hippopotamus. They eat hundreds of kilos of soft swamp plants a day, all through those little heads. So they wander about lakes and swamps, chomping away, and stick their heads up to breathe every quarter-hour or so. It's getting dark, so this fellow will soon come out and lie down in the shallows to sleep."

"Can we shoot one?" demanded James.

"I wouldn't," said I.

"Why not?"

I said: "There's no point in it, and it's not sporting. First, they're almost invulnerable. They're even harder to hit in the brain than other dinosaurs because of the way they sway their heads about on those long necks. Their hearts are too deeply buried to reach unless you're awfully lucky. Then, if you kill one in the water, he sinks and can't be recovered. If you kill one on land, the only trophy is that little head. You can't bring the whole beast back because he weighs thirty tonne or more, and we've got no use for thirty tonnes of meat."

Holtzinger said: "That museum in New York got one."

"Yes," said I. "The American Museum of Natural History sent a party of forty-eight to the Early Cretaceous, with a fifty-caliber machine gun. They killed a sauropod and spent two solid months skinning it and hacking the carcass apart and dragging it to the time machine. I know the bloke in charge of that project, and he still has nightmares in which he smells decomposing dinosaur. They had to kill a dozen big theropods attracted by the stench, so they had them lying around and rotting, too. And the theropods ate three men of the party despite the big gun."

Next morning, we were finishing breakfast when one of the helpers said: "Look, Mr. Rivers, up there!"

He pointed along the shoreline. There were six big-crested duckbill, feeding in the shallows. They were the kind called *Parasaurolophus*, with a long spike sticking out the back of their heads and a web of skin connecting this with the back of their necks.

"Keep your voices down!" I said. The duckbill, like the other ornithopods, are wary beasts because they have neither armor nor weapons. They feed on the margins of lakes and swamps, and when a gorgosaur rushes out of the trees they plunge into deep water and swim off. Then when *Phobosuchus*, the super-crocodile, goes for them in the water, they flee to the land. A hectic sort of life, eh?

Holtzinger said: "Uh—Reggie! I've been thinking over what you said about ceratopsian heads. If I could get one of those yonder, I'd be satisfied. It would look big enough in my house, wouldn't it?"

"I'm sure of it, mate," I said. "Now look here. We could detour to come out on the shore near here, but we should have to plow through half a mile of muck and brush, and they'd hear us coming. Or we can creep up to the north end of this sandspit, from which it's three or four hundred meters—a long shot but not impossible. Think you could do it?"

"Hm," said Holtzinger. "With my 'scope sight and a sitting position—okay, I'll try it."

"You stay here, Court," I said to James. "This is Augie's head, and I don't want any argument over your having fired first."

James grunted while Holtzinger clamped his 'scope to his rifle. We crouched our way up the spit, keeping the sand ridge between us and the duckbill. When we got to the end, where there was no more cover, we crept along on hands and knees, moving slowly. If you move slowly enough, directly towards or away from a dinosaur, it probably won't notice you.

The duckbill continued to grub about on all fours, every few seconds rising to look round. Holtzinger eased himself into the sitting position, cocked his piece, and aimed through his 'scope. And then—

Bang! bang! went a big rifle back at the camp.

Holtzinger jumped. The duckbill jerked their heads up and leaped for the deep water, splashing like mad. Holtzinger fired once and missed. I took one shot at the last duckbill before it vanished, too, but missed. The .600 isn't built for long ranges.

Holtzinger and I started back towards the camp, for it had struck us that our party might be in theropod trouble.

What had happened was that a big sauropod had wandered down past the camp under water, feeding as it went. Now, the water shoaled about a hundred meters offshore from our spit, halfway over to the swamp on the other side. The sauropod had ambled up the slope until its body was almost all out of water, weaving its head from side to side and looking for anything green to gobble. This is a species of *Alamosaurus,* which looks much like the well-known *Apatosaurus,* the one they used to call *Brontosaurus.*

When I came in sight of the camp, the sauropod was turning round to go back the way it had come, making horrid groans. By the time we reached the camp, it had disappeared into deep water, all but its head and seven meters of neck, which wove about for some time before they vanished into the haze.

When we came up to the camp, James was arguing with the Raja. Holtzinger burst out:

"You crummy bastard! That's the second time you've spoiled my shots."

"Don't be a fool," said James. "I couldn't let him wander into the camp and stamp everything flat."

"There was no danger of that," said the Raja. "You can see the water is deep offshore. It's just that our trigger-happy Mr. James cannot see any animal without shooting."

I added: "If it did get close, all you needed to do was throw a stick of firewood at it. They're perfectly harmless."

This wasn't strictly true. When the Comte de Lautrec ran after one for a close shot, the sauropod looked back at him, gave a flick of its tail, and took off the Comte's head as neatly as if he'd been axed in the Tower. But, as a rule, they're inoffensive enough.

"How was I to know?" yelled James, turning purple. "You're all against me. What the hell are we on this miserable trip for, except to shoot things? Call yourselves hunters, but I'm the only one who hits anything!"

I got pretty wrothy and said he was just an excitable young skite with more money than brains, whom I should never have brought along.

"If that's how you feel," he said, "give me a burro and some food, and I'll go back to the base by myself. I won't pollute your pure air with my presence!"

"Don't be a bigger ass than you can help," I said. "What you propose is quite impossible."

"Then I'll go alone!" He grabbed his knapsack, thrust a couple of tins of beans and an opener into it, and started off with his rifle.

Beauregard Black spoke up: "Mr. Rivers, we cain't let him go off like that. He'll git lost and starve, or be et by a theropod."

"I'll fetch him back," said the Raja, and started after the runaway.

He caught up with James as the latter was disappearing

106

into the cycads. We could see them arguing and waving their hands in the distance. After a while, they started back with arms around each other's necks like old school pals.

This shows the trouble we get into if we make mistakes in planning such a do. Having once got back in time, we had to make the best of our bargain.

I don't want to give the impression, however, that Courtney James was nothing but a pain in the arse. He had good points. He got over these rows quickly and next day would be as cheerful as ever. He was helpful with the general work of the camp, at least when he felt like it. He sang well and had an endless fund of dirty stories to keep us amused.

We stayed two more days at that camp. We saw crocodile, the small kind, and plenty of sauropod—as many as five at once—but no more duckbill. Nor any of those fifteen-meter super-crocodiles.

So, on the first of May, we broke camp and headed north towards the Janpur Hills. My sahibs were beginning to harden up and were getting impatient. We'd been in the Cretaceous a week, and no trophies.

We saw nothing to speak of on the next leg, save a glimpse of a gorgosaur out of range and some tracks indicating a whopping big iguanodont, eight or ten meters high. We pitched camp at the base of the hills.

We'd finished off the bonehead, so the first thing was to shoot fresh meat. With an eye to trophies, too, of course. We got ready the morning of the third, and I told James:

"See here, cobber, no more of your tricks. The Raja will tell you when to shoot."

"Uh-huh, I get you," he said, meek as Moses.

We marched off, the four of us, into the foothills. There

was a good chance of getting Holtzinger his ceratopsian. We'd seen a couple on the way up, but mere calves without decent horns.

As it was hot and sticky, we were soon panting and sweating. We'd hiked and scrambled all morning without seeing a thing except lizards, when I picked up the smell of carrion. I stopped the party and sniffed. We were in an open glade cut up by those little dry nullahs. The nullahs ran together into a couple of deeper gorges that cut through a slight depression choked with denser growth, cycad and screw pine. When I listened, I heard the thrum of carrion flies.

"This way," I said. "Something ought to be dead— ah, here it is!"

And there it was: the remains of a huge ceratopsian lying in a little hollow on the edge of the copse. Must have weighed six or eight tonne alive; a three-horned variety, perhaps the penultimate species of *Triceratops*. It was hard to tell, because most of the hide on the upper surface had been ripped off, and many bones had been pulled loose and lay scattered about.

Holtzinger said: "Oh, shucks! Why couldn't I have gotten to him before he died? That would have been a darned fine head."

I said: "On your toes, blokes. A theropod's been at this carcass and is probably nearby."

"How d'you know?" said James, with sweat running off his round red face. He spoke in what was for him a low voice, because a nearby theropod is a sobering thought to the flightiest.

I sniffed again and thought I could detect the distinctive rank odor of theropod. I couldn't be sure, though, because the carcass stank so strongly. My sahibs were turning green at the sight and smell of the cadaver. I told James:

"It's seldom that even the biggest theropod will attack a full-grown ceratopsian. Those horns are too much for them. But they love a dead or dying one. They'll hang round a dead ceratopsian for weeks, gorging and then sleeping off their meals for days at a time. They usually take cover in the heat of the day anyhow, because they can't stand much direct hot sunlight. You'll find them lying in copses like this or in hollows, wherever there's shade."

"What'll we do?" asked Holtzinger.

"We'll make our first cast through this copse, in two pairs as usual. Whatever you do, don't get impulsive or panicky."

I looked at Courtney James, but he looked right back and merely checked his gun.

"Should I still carry this broken?" he asked.

"No; close it, but keep the safety on till you're ready to shoot," I said. "We'll keep closer than usual, so we shall be in sight of each other. Start off at that angle, Raja; go slowly, and stop to listen between steps."

We pushed through the edge of the copse, leaving the carcass but not its stench behind us. For a few meters, you couldn't see a thing.

It opened out as we got in under the trees, which shaded out some of the brush. The sun slanted down through the trees. I could hear nothing but the hum of insects and the scuttle of lizards and the squawks of toothed birds in the treetops. I thought I could be sure of the theropod smell, but told myself that might be imagination. The theropod might be any of several species, large or small, and the beast itself might be anywhere within a kilometer's radius.

"Go on," I whispered to Holtzinger. I could hear James and the Raja pushing ahead on my right and see the palm fronds and ferns lashing about as they disturbed them. I suppose they were trying to move quietly, but to me they sounded like an earthquake in a crockery shop.

"A little closer!" I called.

Presently, they appeared slanting in towards me. We dropped into a gully filled with ferns and scrambled up the other side. Then we found our way blocked by a big clump of palmetto.

"You go round that side; we'll go round this," I said. We started off, stopping to listen and smell. Our positions were the same as on that first day, when James killed the bonehead.

We'd gone two-thirds of the way round our half of the palmetto, when I heard a noise ahead on our left. Holtzinger heard it, too, and pushed off his safety. I put my thumb on mine and stepped to one side to have a clear field of fire.

The clatter grew louder. I raised my gun to aim at about the height of a big theropod's heart. There was a movement in the foliage—and a two-meter-high bonehead stepped into view, walking solemnly across our front and jerking its head with each step like a giant pigeon.

I heard Holtzinger let out a breath and had to keep myself from laughing. Holtzinger said: "Uh—"

Then that damned gun of James's went off, *bang! bang!* I had a glimpse of the bonehead knocked arsy-varsy with its tail and hind-legs flying.

"Got him!" yelled James. "I drilled him clean!" I heard him run forward.

"Good God, if he hasn't done it again!" I said.

Then there was a great swishing of foliage and a wild yell from James. Something heaved up out of the shrubbery, and I saw the head of the biggest of the local flesh-eaters,

Tyrannosaurus trionyches himself.

The scientists can insist that *rex* is the bigger species, but I'll swear this blighter was bigger than any *rex* ever hatched. It must have stood six meters high and been fifteen meters long. I could see its big bright eye and twelve-centimeter teeth and the big dewlap that hangs down from its chin to its chest.

The second of the nullahs that cut through the copse ran athwart our path on the far side of the palmetto clump. Perhaps it was two meters deep. The tyrannosaur had been lying in this, sleeping off its last meal. Where its back stuck up above the ground level, the ferns on the edge of the nullah masked it. James had fired both barrels over the theropod's head and woke it up. Then the silly ass ran forward without reloading. Another six meters and he'd have stepped on the tyrannosaur.

James, naturally, stopped when this thing popped up in front of him. He remembered that he'd fired both barrels and that he'd left the Raja too far behind for a clear shot.

At first, James kept his nerve. He broke open his gun, took two rounds from his belt, and plugged them into the barrels. But, in his haste to snap the gun shut, he caught his hand between the barrels and the action. The painful pinch so startled James that he dropped his gun. Then he went to pieces and bolted.

The Raja was running up with his gun at high port, ready to snap it to his shoulder the instant he got a clear view. When he saw James running headlong towards him, he hesitated, not wishing to shoot James by accident. The latter plunged ahead, blundered into the Raja, and sent them both sprawling among the ferns. The tyrannosaur collected what little wits it had and stepped forward to snap them up.

And how about Holtzinger and me on the other side of the palmettos? Well, the instant James yelled and the tyrannosaur's head appeared, Holtzinger darted forward like a rabbit. I'd brought my gun up for a shot at the tyrannosaur's head, in hope of getting at least an eye; but, before I could find it in my sights, the head was out of sight behind the palmettos. Perhaps I should have fired at hazard, but all my experience is against wild shots.

When I looked back in front of me, Holtzinger had already disappeared round the curve of the palmetto clump. I'd started after him when I heard his rifle and the click of the bolt between shots: *bang*—click-click—*bang*—click-click, like that.

He'd come up on the tyrannosaur's quarter as the brute started to stoop for James and the Raja. With his muzzle six meters from the tyrannosaur's hide, Holtzinger began pumping .375s into the beast's body. He got off three shots when the tyrannosaur gave a tremendous booming grunt and wheeled round to see what was stinging it. The jaws came open, and the head swung round and down again.

Holtzinger got off one more shot and tried to leap to one side. As he was standing on a narrow place between the palmetto clump and the nullah, he fell into the nullah. The tyrannosaur continued its lunge and caught him. The jaws went *chomp,* and up came the head with poor Holtzinger in them, screaming like a damned soul.

I came up just then and aimed at the brute's face, but then realized that its jaws were full of my sahib and I should be shooting him, too. As the head went on up, like the business end of a big power shovel, I fired a shot at the heart. The tyrannosaur was already turning away, and I suspect the ball just glanced along the ribs. The beast took a couple of steps when I gave it the other barrel in the back. It staggered on its next step but kept on. Another step, and it was nearly out of sight among the trees, when the Raja fired twice. The stout fellow had untangled himself from James, got up, picked up his gun, and let the tyrannosaur have it.

The double wallop knocked the brute over with a tremendous crash. It fell into a dwarf magnolia, and I saw one of its huge birdlike hind legs waving in the midst of a shower of pink-and-white petals. But the tyrannosaur got up again and blundered off without even dropping its victim. The last I saw of it was Holtzinger's legs dangling out one side of its jaws (he'd stopped screaming) and its big tail banging against the tree trunks as it swung from side to side.

The Raja and I reloaded and ran after the brute for all we were worth. I tripped and fell once, but jumped up again and didn't notice my skinned elbow till later. When we burst out of the copse, the tyrannosaur was already at the far end of the glade. We each took a quick shot but probably missed, and it was out of sight before we could fire again.

We ran on, following the tracks and spatters of blood, until we had to stop from exhaustion. Never again did we see that tyrannosaur. Their movements look slow and ponderous, but with those tremendous legs they don't have to step very fast to work up considerable speed.

When we'd got our breath, we got up and tried to track the tyrannosaur, on the theory that it might be dying and we should come up to it. But, though we found more spoor, it faded out and left us at a loss. We circled round, hoping to pick it up, but no luck.

Hours later, we gave up and went back to the glade.

Courtney James was sitting with his back against a tree,

holding his rifle and Holtzinger's. His right hand was swollen and blue where he'd pinched it, but still usable. His first words were:

"Where the hell have you two been?"

I said: "We've been occupied. The late Mr. Holtzinger. Remember?"

"You shouldn't have gone off and left me; another of those things might have come along. Isn't it bad enough to lose one hunter through your stupidity without risking another one?"

I'd been preparing a warm wigging for James, but his attack so astonished me that I could only bleat: "What? *We* lost . . . ?"

"Sure," he said. "You put us in front of you, so if anybody gets eaten it's us. You send a guy up against these animals undergunned. You—"

"You God-damn stinking little swine!" I said. "If you hadn't been a blithering idiot and blown those two barrels, and then run like the yellow coward you are, this never would have happened. Holtzinger died trying to save your worthless life. By God, I wish he'd failed! He was worth six of a stupid, spoiled, muttonheaded bastard like you—"

I went on from there. The Raja tried to keep up with me, but ran out of English and was reduced to cursing James in Hindi.

I could see by the purple color on James's face that I was getting home. He said: "Why, you—" and stepped forward and sloshed me one in the face with his left fist.

It rocked me a bit, but I said: "Now then, my lad, I'm glad you did that! It gives me a chance I've been waiting for . . ."

So I waded into him. He was a good-sized bod, but between my hundred kilos and his sore right hand he had no

114

chance. I got a few good ones home, and down he went.

"Now get up!" I said. "And I'll be glad to finish you off!"

James raised himself to his elbows. I got set for more fist-icuffs, though my knuckles were skinned and bleeding already. James rolled over, snatched his gun, and scrambled up, swinging the muzzle from one to the other of us.

"You won't finish anybody off!" he panted through swollen lips. "All right, put your hands up! Both of you!"

"Do not be an idiot," said the Raja. "Put that gun away!"

"Nobody treats me like that and gets away with it!"

"There's no use murdering us," I said. "You'd never get away with it."

"Why not? There won't be much left of you after one of these hits you. I'll just say the tyrannosaur ate you, too. Nobody could prove anything. They can't hold you for a murder eighty-five million years old. The statute of limitations, you know."

"You fool, you'd never make it back to the camp alive!" I shouted.

"I'll take a chance—" began James, setting the butt of his .500 against his shoulder, with the barrels pointed at my face. Looked like a pair of bloody vehicular tunnels.

He was watching me so closely that he lost track of the Raja for a second. My partner had been resting on one knee, and now his right arm came up in a quick bowling motion with a rock. The rock bounced off James's head. The .500 went off. The ball must have parted my hair, and the explosion bloody well near broke my eardrums. Down went James again.

"Good work, mate!" I said, gathering up James's gun.

"Yes," said the Raja thoughtfully, as he picked up the rock he'd thrown and tossed it. "Doesn't quite have the balance of a cricket ball, but it is just as hard."

"What shall we do now?" I said. "I'm inclined to leave the beggar here unarmed and let him fend for himself."

The Raja gave a little sigh. "It's a tempting thought, Reggie; but we really cannot, you know. Not done."

"I suppose you're right," I said. "Well, let's tie him up and take him back to camp."

We agreed there was no safety for us unless we kept James under guard every minute until we got home. Once a man has tried to kill you, you're a fool if you give him another chance.

We marched James back to camp and told the crew what we were up against. James cursed everybody.

We spent three dismal days combing the country for that tyrannosaur, but no luck. We felt it wouldn't have been cricket not to make a good try at recovering Holtzinger's remains. Back at our main camp, when it wasn't raining, we collected small reptiles and things for our scientific friends. The Raja and I discussed the question of legal proceedings against Courtney James, but decided we were up a gum tree in that direction.

When the transition chamber materialized, we fell over one another getting into it. We dumped James, still tied, in a corner, and told the chamber operator to throw the switches.

While we were in transition, James said: "You two should have killed me back there."

"Why?" I said. "You don't have a particularly good head."

The Raja added: "Wouldn't look at all well over a mantel."

"You can laugh," said James, "but I'll get you some day. I'll find a way and get off scot-free."

116

"My dear fellow!" I said. "If there were some way to do it, I'd have you charged with Holtzinger's death. Look, you'd best leave well enough alone."

When we came out in the present, we handed him his empty gun and his other gear, and off he went without a word. As he left, Holtzinger's girl, that Claire, rushed up crying:

"Where is he? Where's August?"

There was a bloody heart-rending scene, despite the Raja's skill at handling such situations.

We took our men and beasts down to the old laboratory building that the university has fitted up as a serai for such expeditions. We paid everybody off and found we were broke. The advance payments from Holtzinger and James didn't cover our expenses, and we should have precious little chance of collecting the rest of our fees either from James or from Holtzinger's estate.

And speaking of James, d'you know what that drongo was doing? He went home, got more ammunition, and came back to the university. He hunted up Professor Prochaska and asked him:

"Professor, I'd like you to send me back to the Cretaceous for a quick trip. If you can work me into your schedule right now, you can just about name your own price. I'll offer five thousand to begin with. I want to go to April twenty-third, eighty-five million B.C."

Prochaska answered: "Why do you wish to go back again so soon?"

"I lost my wallet in the Cretaceous," said James. "I figure if I go back to the day before I arrived in that era on my last trip, I'll watch myself when I arrived on that trip and follow myself around till I see myself lose the wallet."

"Five thousand is a lot for a wallet," said the professor.

"It's got some things in it I can't replace," said James.

"Well," said Prochaska, thinking. "The party that was supposed to go out this morning has telephoned that they would be late, so perhaps I can work you in. I have always wondered what would happen when the same man occupied the same stretch of time twice."

So James wrote out a check, and Prochaska took him to the chamber and saw him off. James's idea, it seems, was to sit behind a bush a few meters from where the transition chamber would appear and spot the Raja and me as we emerged.

Hours later, we'd changed into our street clothes and phoned our wives to come and get us. We were standing on Forsythe Boulevard waiting for them when there was a loud crack, like an explosion, and a flash of light not twenty meters from us. The shock wave staggered us and broke windows.

We ran towards the place and got there just as a policeman and several citizens came up. On the boulevard, just off the kerb, lay a human body. At least, it had been that, but it looked as if every bone in it had been pulverized and every blood vessel burst, so it was hardly more than a slimy mass of pink protoplasm. The clothes it had been wearing were shredded, but I recognized an H. & H. .500 double-barreled express rifle. The wood was scorched and the metal pitted, but it was Courtney James's gun. No doubt whatever.

Skipping the investigations and the milling about that ensued, what had happened was this: Nobody had shot at us as we emerged on the twenty-fourth, and that couldn't be changed. For that matter, the instant James started to do anything that would make a visible change in the world of eighty-five million B.C., such as making a footprint in the earth, the space-time forces snapped him forward to Present to prevent a paradox. And the violence of the passage practically tore him to bits.

Now that this is better understood, the professor won't send anybody to a period less than a thousand years prior to the time that some time-traveler has already explored, because it would be too easy to do some act, like chopping down a tree or losing some durable artifact, that would affect the later world. Over longer periods, he tells me, such changes average out and are lost in the stream of time.

We had a rough time after that, with the bad publicity and all, though we did collect a fee from James's estate. Luckily for us, a steel manufacturer turned up who wanted a mastodon's head for his den.

I understand these things better, now, too. The disaster hadn't been wholly James's fault. I shouldn't have taken him when I knew what a spoiled, unstable sort of bloke he was. And, if Holtzinger could have used a really heavy gun, he'd probably have knocked the tyrannosaur down, even if he didn't kill it, and so have given the rest of us a chance to finish it.

So, Mr. Seligman, that's why I won't take you to that period to hunt. There are plenty of other eras, and if you look them over I'm sure you'll find something to suit you. But not the Jurassic or the Cretaceous. You're just not big enough to handle a gun for dinosaur.

The Honeymoon Dragon

Oh, forget the "Sir Reginald," Mr. Saito! Just call me "Reggie," as everyone else does. Of course, in my native Australia it would be "Reg"; but Americans have got it into their heads that it's "Reggie," and I've given up trying to set them right.

Matter of fact, I don't take the title so seriously as do many people, especially Americans. I might even have declined the knighthood offer from London, except that my wife had been salivating over the chance to be "Lady Brenda," and I didn't want to disappoint her.

Let me get the dinkum oil on this, Saito-San. You've been sent here to look into the prospects of Japanese financing of another transition chamber in Ulan Bator, Mongolia. So you wish to know about our experience with the first such chamber, here in St. Louis; and also about my recent visit to the new one in Australia? Of course Professor Prochaska, who invented the bloody thing, can tell you more about the technical features; but you want to know what lessons I have learned in running time safaris from the point of view of the travelers in time, eh?

Until my recent jaunt to Australia, I had never taken my wife on a time safari. Once when my partner, Chandra Aiyar—"the Raja," as I call him—and I were new in the business, I planned to take Brenda on a time trip. But then she got preg, and we didn't want to take a chance. Then, after some unfortunate experiences with parties mixed as to sex, the Raja and I decided to turn down any more such mixed parties. Anyway, Brenda was kept busy for years with a couple of active nippers. The subject has come up since, but there was always some problem that made the time trip impracticable.

When our twentieth wedding anniversary was coming up, I asked Brenda what she would like for a bloody ripper present. She said she would love a time safari. Didn't want to kill anything—she never does—but just go back and have a look round. By coincidence, I had just received an invitation from the new Aussie transition chamber in Darwin, urging me to come and try it out. They would pay the travel expenses—not only mine but also those of any colleagues I brought along.

Well, we decided that I should take Brenda and leave the Raja to run the business in my absence. Of course, I had to invite Professor Prochaska. But he had already been there during the construction and testing of the Darwin chamber, so he begged off. Instead, he urged that I take Bruce Cohen, our chamber wallah, who was eager to have a look at the competition.

I had another reason for wanting to go down-under. Transition-chamber people have a trade journal, *The Time Traveler*, which comes out bimonthly in Darwin, Australia. It was originally published here in St. Louis, but a few years ago it moved to Australia to cut costs. The then editor of this little magazine was one Mark Prendergast. Although I had never met him, for some strange reason he had taken a violent dislike to me from the start. There was never an issue in which he didn't work in a few gibes and insults. Strange, when you consider that we had never seen each other; but there it was. The latest issue of *The Time Traveler* ran a piece stating, among other things, quote:

"I hear that we down-under are about to be blessed with a visit from the Lord of Bull Art, Reginald Rivers—beg pardon, now Sir Reginald. They say he is coming on a second honeymoon. I suppose we common Aussies will have to approach His Lordship on our knees, place our hands between his, and swear fealty in medieval style. He will doubtless have a big bloke standing by with a spiked club, to let any impudent upstart who gets above himself have it on the sconce."

Prendergast had been going on like that ever since the magazine started. This puzzled me, since I had never met the cove or exchanged communications with him. Anyway, I thought it would do no harm to meet the bloke and size him up. If he were laboring under some whopping great misapprehension—let's say, he had confused me with another man who was a convicted thief or child molester—perhaps I could straighten him out.

Labor trouble in the Australian transition chamber? Yes, Mr. Saito, there was, in connection with Prendergast's antics. I'll tell the whole story.

Brenda and I alighted at Darwin, a neat, tidy little green-and-white town. One reason it's rather pretty is that it was twice razed in the last century, once with bombs by your fellow countrymen, and again in 1974 by a hurricane. (They call it a "cyclone" there.) So they rebuilt the city with some care, low to the ground, against future calamities.

The only thing wrong with those parts, aside from their damp tropical climate, is that, although there are fine beaches along the northern coast, nobody in his right mind goes swimming there. The water is infested with the box jellyfish or "sea wasp," whose sting can be fatal; with sea snakes, which are marine members of the cobra family; and with the great white shark, which when it sees a human swimmer says: "Yummy!" If none of these critters gets you, there is also the salt-water crocodile. This croc is the nearest thing in Present to a living dinosaur, ranging up to ten meters long. The name just means that, while it is usually found in fresh-water rivers and lakes, it doesn't mind swimming across stretches of ocean to get where it wants to go. There's a farm nearby where they raise salties for their hides—and for their meat, for people who don't gag at the idea.

The Darwin chamber had a delegation on hand to meet us. As we piled out of the airplane, the Director, Rudy Havens, introduced himself and presented his mates. These included a big black eyeglassed Native Australian, Algernon Malgaru, a professor of anthropology at Northern Territory University; and a little roly-poly bloke with a nervous grin, identified as Mark Prendergast. Meanwhile I was doing likewise for Brenda and Bruce Cohen.

Prendergast gave me a limp-dishrag handshake, muttering about being glad to see me after following my exploits in print for so long. Not a word about the nasty things he had been printing in his trade journal for years. Naturally, I did not bring these matters up in the midst of a ceremonious greeting. Prendergast also stuck out a hand to Brenda; but she only nodded and kept her own hands firmly on her purse and carry-on bag. Havens said:

"Sir Reginald, if you don't object, I shall send Mark and Algy back with you. Mark can't afford to miss recording what is really an historic occasion; while Algernon has already been back to the Pleistocene in our chamber and so gets the picture of the local terrain and biota. He'll take good care of you."

I said: "I hope my visit will be far enough removed in time from Doctor Malgaru's to provide a safety factor against an overlap."

"I'm sure it will," said Havens. "There will be a gap in

time of at least five thousand years."

You see, Mr. Saito, we must be careful not to put two sets of time travelers into the same past period, or the same party twice into the same time slot. This would create a paradox, and an orderly universe just doesn't allow such contradictions. The minute you tried to do that, the space-time forces would snap your travelers back to Present and kill them in the process.

At the dinner in Darwin's best hotel, the new Darwin Hilton on Mitchell Street, Prendergast showed himself a jolly dinner companion, joking and laughing at a great rate. Perhaps he was trying to forestall any embarrassing discussion of those nasty editorials in *The Time Traveler*.

I was seated next to the Native Australian, Algy Malgaru. He was a big bloke with a chocolate-brown skin, the snub nose and beetling brows of the Australoid race, and a bush of Oxford-brown beard beginning to gray. I asked how he came to be, of all things, a professor of anthropology. He chuckled, showing those big Australoid teeth in a wide mouth.

"Sir Reginald, if you're born an Abo—" (he used the old abbreviation for "aborigine," nowadays considered rude for a white Australian to use toward a Native Australian) "—if you're born an Abo but have a bent toward reading and writing, your best bet is the academic life. That's where you'll encounter the least ethnic prejudice. And if you've spent much of your youth in the outback among fellow tribesmen, you might as well capitalize on the experience by going into anthropology, since you've already got a bloody head start."

Since we did not expect to meet any large thick-skinned

game like elephant or dinosaur, I had brought along my new Mannlicher-Schönauer seven-point-five, with an eight-round magazine. I figured it should pack enough punch to take care of anything we might encounter, up to the marsupial lion *Thylacoleo*. Bruce Cohen had borrowed from the Raja's and my armory a Bratislava with similar characteristics.

When Cohen, Brenda, and I approached the van to take us to the chamber, Prendergast and Malgaru already occupied the middle seats, behind those of the driver and his seat mate. Havens, who was driving, said:

"Mark, you and Algy will have to move back to make seats for Sir and Lady Rivers and Mr. Cohen."

"Okay," said Prendergast. "Why don't you blokes hand your guns back here? I'll take care of them."

"Be careful!" I said. "Mine's loaded, with the safety on." I don't usually load so early in the game. But when Havens and his van were over an hour late, I'm sorry to say I got restless and loaded up to give my hands something to do.

Brenda took the front seat next to Havens; Cohen and I took the two middle seats. Malgaru sat on a jump seat behind us, and Prendergast scrunched down in the rear with the guns. Craning my neck, I asked:

"What are you blokes armed with?"

Prendergast spoke up. "I'm relying on you two, since I shall be kept busy working the camera." He pointed to a big video recording apparatus.

Malgaru said: "I was never a good enough shot for guns, because of defective eyesight. That's one reason I never became a real bushie. So I brought along this." He picked up from the floor a boomerang over a meter long. "Whittled it myself. It's not one of those toys that'll spin round in a circle and come back to the thrower. This is a real killer. I practiced with one as a kid until I could knock over a roo at fifty paces."

I said: "If you're determined to use stone-age weapons, Algy, wouldn't a spear be more effective? I've heard you Native Australians can throw spears with such accuracy as to bring down a bird on the wing."

Malgaru shook his head. "Once upon a time, perhaps. But nowadays you won't find any Abos who know how to make a proper spear, let alone throw one accurately. I knew the last Abo flint knapper, before that art died out completely. Now most of them farm or work as stockmen, or as you Yanks call them, cowboys. Or they go into white-collar work, as I did."

"I'm no Yank," I said. "Born and raised in Brisbane."

"Technically I suppose you're not; though you bloody well sound a bit like a Yank."

"It's those years in America, I suppose," I said. "Inside, I'm still a dinkum Aussie."

At last we lined up outside the Australian transition chamber, in the big concrete building they've put up on the outskirts of Darwin. Cohen was deep in conversation with the local chamber wallah, a bloke named Draga Radich.

To my considerable relief, Prendergast handed me back my gun. It had occurred to me during the drive that, if he really felt the way his editorials implied, he might have shot me in the back with it and then said, oh, sorry, that was an accident. But then he unfolded a sketch map, saying:

"This shows the lay of the land about 500,000 B.C., when Algy went back and checked it out. We can hope the topography won't have changed drastically in the interval."

Since we planned to spend only a few hours in the Pleistocene, we did not bring along camp equipment and helpers to set it up. Havens merely shooed us into the transition chamber and waved us off. Radich set his dials for 495,000 B.C. and pushed his buttons.

The vertigo and other symptoms of time travel had Brenda looking like a very dead fish by the time the dials stopped spinning. Radich set the chamber down with scarcely a bump, and out we piled.

The landscape looked pretty much like the present-day Australian bush, dusty green and brown. The timber was mostly eucalyptus and acacia, with some araucaria and pandanus. There was none of that pest, the *Opuntia* or prickly-pear cactus, which some idiot introduced a century or two ago and whose spread the Aussies have been battling ever since. A few birds flew up, but otherwise we saw no animal life, no sign of the marsupial lion or other predators.

Prendergast spread out his map. "I figure, we're just about here," he said. "Now, if the terrain is anything like that of five thousand years ago, the ground drops off west of here into a little dingle or gill, with a billabong at the bottom, and then rises back up on the far side. If you want to see wild life, that's the place for it, since the animals have to come to the billabong for a drink. I'll show you the way."

We set out after Prendergast, with his video recorder on his shoulder. It must have weighed twenty kilos, but the little bloke didn't seem to mind.

After a half-hour scramble, we came to the edge of the depression Prendergast had mentioned. Sure enough, through the bush we could glimpse water at the bottom of the depression. There were also a couple of animals drinking at it. We couldn't tell much about them at that distance and with all the bush in the way, even through the glasses, save that looked to be of pretty good size and clad in brown fur.

"Diprotodons," said Prendergast. "Want to go closer for a look, eh?"

"Oh, yes!" breathed Brenda, stringing the cord of her little camera round her neck. She had stood up under the hike very well. "This is what I've dreamed of."

"You two go down, then," said Prendergast. "I'll stay up here to shoot pictures, if I can find a spot with a better view." To Cohen and Malgaru he said: "You stand by, please, since I need your fire power. As soon as I've shot a good strip, we'll go down and join them." Turning to Brenda and me, he added with a nasty little smirk: "That'll give you two some privacy—that is, if Sir Reg can still rise to the occasion."

As the implications of Prendergast's remark sank in, I felt myself getting as mad as a meat-ax. I started to make a fist to bash the blighter. It wouldn't have been sporting, with my being twice the fellow's size; but at that instant I didn't care.

Then Brenda smiled sweetly in a way that warned me she was going to slip in the stiletto. She said:

"I assure you, *Mister* Prendergast, that Sir Reginald can do all the things he did as a young man—perhaps better if not quite so often. Come on, Reg!"

Away she went, skidding down the slope in her new boots.

Ordinarily I should have been a bit more cautious in my approach; but I couldn't let my life's partner show me up. So I slung my rifle over my back to leave both hands free; and down I went, skidding and stumbling. I took one small tumble, but I grabbed a branch and stopped my fall before it did any harm. I called out to Brenda:

"Watch where you put your feet! Snakes!"

Australia has today a fine assortment of venomous serpents, and we may assume that they slithered around quite as frequently in the Pleistocene. But Brenda bounded on ahead of me as if she were still a schoolgirl. After so many years of dealing with wildlife, I have no irrational horror of snakes, as many have. But I don't take chances with organisms that can kill me with one little bite.

"Slow up!" I called. "You'll scare the critters away from the water hole with a noisy approach." Actually, most of the animals we see in prehistoric times show little or no instinctive fear of human beings, because they have never been hunted by man.

As we neared the bottom of the slope, we began pushing through the bush toward the billabong. Soon we had a good view of the diprotodons, relatives of the present-day wombat but vastly larger. In size this pair resembled a grizzly bear or even a rhinoceros. Otherwise they were rather nondescript creatures, with thick plantigrade limbs and big, bulbous heads with little round ears, and all clad in the same dark-brown fur.

The diprotodons had finished drinking and were just turning away from the pool, when Brenda exclaimed "Hey!" She had her little camera up. "Wait!"

The diprotodons paused at her shout, swiveling those huge heads around. Brenda burst out from cover, ran forward a few steps, dropped to one knee, and focused the camera.

The diprotodons turned away again and lumbered off. Brenda ran a few steps after them, trying for another shot. In so doing, she bumped into—literally bumped into—another patron of the water hole, who had just come out of the bush on its way to the billabong.

The newcomer was a fawn-colored giant kangaroo, so large that it made the biggest present-day kangaroos look like joeys. It had been poling its way forward at the slow-moving gait that modern roos employ in grazing, using its forelimbs as crutches to swing its huge hind limbs forward as a pair. When Brenda brushed against it, the animal reared back and straightened up, raising its head a good three meters above ground. It towered over Brenda, who is a good-sized girl.

I must confess that I had been so busy watching Brenda and the animals that I had forgotten to unsling my rifle, still strapped across my back. I squirmed out of that sling faster than ever before and started to bring the rifle to bear.

At the same time, the giant roo took a swipe with one of its forefeet at this strange little creature that had barged into it. Brenda gave a yelp of pain and swung her camera on its cord so that it banged the roo on its nose. The roo jerked away in a startled manner and cut loose with a huge bound, over some low bush. By the time I had the beast in my sights, it had taken off on a second bound and quickly disappeared.

The whole confrontation lasted only a few seconds. I could, I suppose, have shot the roo before it passed out of sight. But the brute evidently had no intention of bothering us further, and my main concern was for Brenda. I hurried up to find her nursing a single long scratch on her forearm, with little drops of blood forming along it.

I had a bottle of disinfectant in the pocket of my safari vest, and in a few seconds I was swabbing the scratch. It was not serious—the roo's claws had barely penetrated the skin—but we don't take chances with strange infections.

I was bandaging the injured arm when I saw Brenda's eyes, looking past me, widen with apprehension. I spun round as something huge came pouring down the slope after us. A large hole yawned in the side of the slope, and we had passed that gap without noticing it in our carefree descent. The new arrival had popped out of this cave and was headed toward us with evidently unfriendly intent.

This formidable creature stood at the apex of the Australian Pleistocene food chain: not a marsupial or even a mammal, but a reptile, *Megalania*. It was a monitor lizard, related to the Komodo dragon but ranging up to fifteen meters in length. It thus surpassed the biggest crocodiles, the salties; to find a crocodile of such size you would have to go back to the Cretaceous. *Megalania* had larger and stouter limbs, enabling it to get around faster on land than any croc; and crocs can trot along faster than you might think when you see one snoozing after a meal.

One argument among paleontologists has to do with the way the limbs of quadrupeds are joined to the body. In salamanders, the legs protrude sideways and have only limited mobility. In the more primitive reptiles, the shoulder and hip joints still cause the upper part of the limb, the thigh and the upper arm, to project horizontally from the body; but the forearm and lower leg are set vertically, enabling the animal to move in a livelier way.

The final step towards full quadrupedal locomotion is the modification of the hip and shoulder joints to bring the upper limb bones to vertical, as it is in mammals. A completely vertical limb, acting as a column, can obviously support the weight of the body with less muscular effort than a limb that is bent into a right angle.

Back in the Permian, some lines of reptiles made this transition. These included the dinosaurs, the crocodiles, and those that evolved into mammals. But the ancestors of the lizards did not. Well, at the K-T boundary between Cretaceous and Paleocene, all the dinosaurs went *poof,* along with several other orders of reptiles. But the lizards survived, despite this awkward limb arrangement of the upper joints. The dragon that charged Brenda and me was just an over-sized lizard, with the primitive hip and shoulder joints. But that fact did not stop it from being a bloody effective predator, about the nearest thing to the conventional dragon that I had ever seen—

Oh, sorry, Mr. Saito. I sometimes get to lecturing on the wonders of prehistoric life and forget the story I'm telling.

Believe it or not, in setting up this jaunt into the Aussie Pleistocene, I had completely forgotten about *Megalania.* I had read about the animal, of course; but in planning this mini-safari I must have thought only of the larger marsupial carnivores that we might meet. During the Cenozoic, South America had a marsupial sabertooth, *Thylacosmilus,* just as big and bloodthirsty as the more familiar sabertooth cats from other continents.

So here came this super-lizard, scrambling down the slope with its big yellow eyes locked on ours. It was mostly slate gray, like the Komodo dragon; but with faint grayish-green stripes on its flanks instead of those red markings on that model *Megalania* in the Australian Museum in Sydney.

I brought the animal's head into my sights, aimed between the eyes, and pulled the trigger. The gun went—*click!*

I worked the bolt and tried again: another click. The *Magalania* approached within a dozen meters, looking a hell of a lot more dragonny than any Komodo monitor. It was quite as intimidating as any theropod dinosaur I had ever faced, although in a fight between a *Megalania* and a *Tyrannosaurus* or an *Epanterias* I'd bet on the dinosaur. Being a biped, the theropod could simply bend down and grab the lizard by its spine, either the neck or the back.

Sorry, I'm digressing again. You can bloody well bet I

didn't think any such thoughts while the super-lizard was rushing upon us.

A quick check showed that the magazine of the rifle was empty. I felt as that bloke Siegfried in the opera would have felt, as he stood outside the dragon's cave and cocked a snook at the dragon. Then, when Fafnir (I think that was its name) took him up on the challenge and came roaring out, the hero found he had left his sword back in camp.

Brenda threw a stone. It bounced off the dragon's head, but the animal seemed not to notice. On it came, hissing like the whistle of one of those steam-powered excursion boats they run on the Mississippi and some other places for tourists.

I stepped in front of Brenda, fumbling in my safari vest for a cartridge. It was a toss-up whether I could get a round into the chamber before the *Megalania* got its teeth into one of us; it was already gaping and showing the scarlet lining of its gullet. I remember thinking that, if bashing the brute over the head with the butt didn't stop it, perhaps I could jam the gun down its throat.

Then something whirled across the terrain with a swishing noise and struck the dragon in the flank with a boom. It was Malgaru's boomerang. The dragon staggered and swiveled round toward the source of the blow. At that instant, Cohen's Bratislava banged, once, twice, and thrice. The impacts knocked the dragon off its feet, writhing and thrashing in the bush. Three more shots, one from my rifle, which I finally got loaded, quieted the lizard down—though like other reptiles it continued to twitch and snap long after it was officially dead.

The boomerang had not done the dragon much harm, save perhaps to crack a rib. But without the distraction of that blow, the lizard would surely have fleshed its fangs in one or the other of the Riverses before anyone could shoot.

Cohen and Malgaru burst out of the bush and trotted up to see if we were safe. I said:

"Where's Prendergast?"

"Over that way, taking some more shots," said Malgaru. "Told us to go ahead and he'd catch up. Here he comes now."

Prendergast, with the video camera balanced on his shoulder, stepped into view, burbling: "What a marvelous film sequence! This will make a bonzer story for my next issue!"

As he approached, I looked closely at Prendergast's safari vest, and found the pockets bulged suspiciously. I said:

"Mark, let me have a look at those pockets."

"No need for that," he replied airily. "Just spools of extra film."

"Then there's no harm in examining them." Smiling, I took a step toward him.

"No, sir!" he said, backing away. "I won't have you searching my person: that would be an invasion of privacy! I know my rights as an Australian citizen. Go get a warrant from a magistrate!"

"Okay," I said, trading looks with Cohen and Malgaru. "Since there won't be any magistrates for half a million years, we shall have to do it the hard way."

I started for Prendergast. He turned to run, but I brought him down with the kind of tackle they use in American football. Cohen and Malgaru grabbed his arms. In his pockets, as I suspected, I found the missing cartridges for my Mannlicher-Schönauer.

We hauled him back to the chamber, tied him up, and told Radich to return us to Present. There was one delay, when Brenda said:

"Darling, do you know what I'd really love as a souvenir of this trip? The hide of that dragon, to hang on our family-room wall, would make this honeymoon just perfect!"

Well, that's the story, Mr. Saito. When we got back, there was the kind of stink you would expect. We told our story; Prendergast told his. He said my rifle had been fully loaded, but I got buck fever at the sight of the dragon and couldn't shoot. Then we three had ganged up to frame him in revenge for some of the things he had written in his magazine. Since Cohen's, Malgaru's, and my stories tallied, Prendergast's version failed to convince. Havens fired him.

The Australian union of time-chamber employees struck to try to force Doctor Havens to take Prendergast back. Unions have long been a major force in Australia, you know; and these were loyally standing up for a fellow employee regardless of what he had done. Algy Malgaru said with a broad grin:

"What do you expect, Reg? That's simple tribalism, among people who think themselves superior to us Abos because they've evolved beyond that sort of thing."

After a couple of months, the dispute was compromised by the chamber's paying Prendergast some back salary instead of re-hiring him. Prendergast dropped out of sight, and I have no idea of where he is now.

But if you would care to visit us, I'll show you the hide of a fine *Megalania,* spread out on our wall. Of course the tail is bent around, because we have no rooms with walls fifteen meters long!

Why did Prendergast carry on this one-sided feud? Damned if I know, Mr. Saito. I'm no shrink; but if I had to guess, I should say it was simple jealousy, allowed to flower into an obsession. I'm no world shaker; but I have been, and done, and seen a lot of things that I daresay Prendergast wishes he had been and done and seen. Because he is younger than I, and because the paradox tabu stops transition chambers from affecting human history, there is no way he could go back in time a little way and get into the time-safari business ahead of me.

No, I have no idea of how he knew there was a cave in that slope, with a *Megalania* lurking in it. Perhaps he had made an unauthorized time trip just before the one we made—say, within a year of our safari. That's dangerous, because a slight miscalculation can throw you into a paradox, and then—*bam!* you've had it. He must have known the risk but have hated me with sufficient venom to have taken the chance. If that's what the silly galah did, he got away with it on his time trip, but in the long run he lost.

The Mislaid Mastodon

Eh, Mr. Schindler? What has given us the most trouble, not in prehistoric times, but right here in Present? Well, there was that lawsuit by the relatives of the Reverend Hubert after the silly galah got himself pecked to death by a *Diatryma* in the Eocene. Then there were those hearings before the Missouri Senate, where the fringe nuts argued that time safaris were a plot to discredit the Bible, or to change history and make us all go *poof*, or to violate the rights of animals.

The oddest objection, however, came from the hunting ranches. You know, those places where, for a few thousand, some urban bloke who has never taken ten steps off the footpath can shoot a tame lion as it comes up to lick his hand and then pose for photographs with a foot on the carcass. Then he hangs the picture on the wall of his apartment. When he's got a dollybird in, he can use the picture to show what a macho hero he is and soften her up for horizontal sports. If that's sport, I'm a bloody ballet dancer!

These game ranches did well for a while, with the disappearance of all the real wild lands except for parks and preserves, where the beasts are protected. The technique of breeding animals has got to the point where you need only a few of any species and you can keep your breeding group furnishing more specimens indefinitely.

Once Professor Prochaska got his transition chamber working, all the real hunting sahibs wanted to go back in time, shoot some local fauna—especially mammoth and dinosaur—and bring back heads and hides to prove it. So the game ranches had been going broke, and they hired a lobbyist to stop time safaris.

The lobbyist for the Game Ranch Association was a bloody shrewd lawyer named Jason Eckler. He made a pitch against importing fossil fauna to the Present. The Raja and I had brought a couple of stenonychosaurs back from the late Cretaceous. These are man-sized theropods—flesh-eating dinosaurs. That Wildlife Park in San Diego reports that they have bred successfully. The Park people are all of a twitter over a half-dozen little stenos running around and snatching each other's meat rations.

Now there was talk of fetching something more ambitious. Each year the Raja and I find that fewer of our clients want to kill anything and more who prefer just to study, photograph, or watch the beasts, or wish to bring them back to Present alive, as we were trying to do.

This bloke Eckler spoke of the dangers of importing exotic fauna, of which a pair might get loose and fill the country with their descendants. He cited the starling, the walking catfish, the Mediterranean fruitfly, the kudzu vine, and so forth. He pictured America overrun with tyrannosaurs stalking and gobbling citizens.

In my turn, I pointed out that the same objection applied to bringing in any exotic species, as for zoos and circuses. In fact, some game ranches had imported Asian deer, which had got loose and out-competed the native deer. Australia well knows these dangers, as witness our troubles with imported rabbits and foxes.

Then another cove whom I knew took the stand. He was a big bloke with a ruddy complexion, conventionally dressed except for long black hair hanging down his back. He was Norman Blackelk, a Native American of the Crow or Absaroka tribe. He, a lawyer, headed the Redintegration

Society, which was footing the bill for our mastodon hunt. On the stand, he explained that it was a matter of conscience with him to try to restore as much as possible of the North American Pleistocene climax fauna. The theory is that Blackelk's ancestors had come over from Siberia twenty or thirty thousand years ago. Finding the continent swarming with mammoths, mastodons, ground sloths, camels, horses, and other big, edible creatures that had never learned to cope with men, they killed and ate the lot. When the big mammals—the mega-fauna, my scientific friends call it—were nearly all gone, along with the lions and sabertooths that preyed on them, the invaders starved until they learned to grow maize and beans and to trap smaller beasts like marmots—woodchucks, I think you call them.

Another witness was Horace Dunbar, a lean, weather-beaten bloke with a potbelly overhanging his belt and a Texan accent. He owned a game ranch, and he told a pitiful tale of how he had worked long and hard to put his children through college, and now these foreign coves were going to bankrupt him with their devilish time-travel contraption. Had a couple in the audience shedding a tear.

After the hearing, the Raja and I—that dark chap you met when you came in was my partner, Chandra Aiyar. I call him "Raja" because by descent he actually is one, if anybody paid attention to that sort of thing nowadays. We went down with Blackelk to unwind, taking a table for four. Presently Eckler, finding all the stools along the bar taken, asked if he might sit at our table. I said certainly.

"No hard feelings?" he said. "I'm just an advocate, doing what the Game Ranch Association pays me to do."

"I understand," I said. We talked of lightweight matters while our drinks were coming. Then the Raja, who is a near-teetotaler, excused himself and went away to meet his wife. Eckler said:

"May I offer a small piece of advice, Mr. Rivers?"

"Sure, if you like," I said. I looked sharply at him, wondering if the next remark would lead up to a threat or a bribe offer. "Is your meter turned off?"

He laughed. "Oh, I'm not charging for this. I was going to say, next time you're on the witness stand, speak a little more slowly and distinctly than normal. As it is, that Australian accent causes some Americans to miss an occasional word."

"Thanks; I'll try," I said.

Then Eckler, looking round, spotted Dunbar, searching for a place to sit. He called: "Hey, Horace!"

Soon Dunbar, after apologies, occupied our fourth chair. After a bit of persiflage, Dunbar looked at me through narrowed eyes.

"Mr. Rivers," he said, "do I understand rightly that your next Safari won't be for hunting, but to bring back one of them mammoths or mastodons to the present world?"

"That's right," I said. "Mr. Blackelk hopes to get enough of these Pleistocene animals to establish breeding herds."

"We aim," said the Native American, "to start with *Mastodon americanus,* a once very common, successful species. It will have to be young, because the transition chamber isn't large enough for a full-grown specimen; likewise with the three species of mammoth of the North American Pleistocene."

Dunbar gulped his third drink—he was a two-fisted drinker—and said: "I've got a client who'll pay a hefty five-figure sum to shoot one of them mastodons."

"Well then, send him to Rivers and Aiyar, Tame Safaris," I said.

"No, that won't work. This guy's got a phobia, I guess you'd call it, about your time machine. He's mortal afraid it'll get him back to some ancient time and then break down, leaving him stranded millions of years back. He's had a couple of experiences with machines that make him leery—an airplane forced to land in a cow pasture, or a train that ran off the rails, or a ship that went aground. And he figures time travel's the trickiest of all."

"It's always worked for us," I said. "We've made dozens of time trips in it, and it's never failed to fetch us home to Present."

"That don't make no difference. This client's got his mind set and wouldn't listen to you. How about if you was to bring your mastodon back to now and then sell him to us?"

"Hey!" said Blackelk. "You mean so you can stake it out for your client to walk up and shoot?"

"Sure. This guy's crazy mad to kill an elephant, irregardless of how he does it. Only nowadays there ain't no elephants for shooting. The few that still live are all numbered and watched over like so many prize chickens, both the African and the Asiatic kinds. There's no place you're allowed to shoot one. One of my customers tried poaching, and the rangers shot him dead. Well, Mr. Rivers, how about it?"

"I'm not interested in that kind of 'sport,'" I said. "Anyway, the animal will be the property of Mr. Blackelk and his Redintegration Society."

"And you can be damn sure we wouldn't consider any such deal," said Blackelk. "We're trying to restore the species, not exterminate it a second time over."

Dunbar by now had had four or five drinks. He growled: "All right, you snotty sons of bitches! I'll show you! Gonna put me out of business, eh? After I've spent half my life trying to build up an honest sporting establishment—"

Eckler grabbed Dunbar's arm and squeezed hard, saying: "Shut up, Horace! This is your lawyer speaking!" Dunbar subsided, belched, and mumbled: "Sorry, guys. Guess I let my feelings run away with me. Anyways, I gotta go. Put my drinks on your bill, Jason. See y'all." He rose and staggered off.

The first job in our mastodon hunt was to adapt Prochaska's transition chamber. A full-grown American mastodon would stand about two and a quarter meters high at the shoulder and be perhaps five and three-quarters long. That's not so tall as a big modern bull elephant, but it is longer in the body and about as heavy.

Prochaska was dubious about our taking liberties with his precious transition chamber; but he became enthusiastic at the prospect of hauling an endless series of extinct organisms back to Present. That is how it has worked out. He hovered over us while our workmen took out the chairs that the passengers normally sat in during the transition. Then we put a row of stout steel bars round the chamber wallah's corner, so that none of our animal cargo could lay a claw or a fang on Bruce Cohen while he handled his controls.

As usual, these modifications took twice as long and cost twice as much as estimated. For one thing, we needed a pen to hold the animal back in Present until the Redintegration people could come and take it away. Since the local zoo didn't have any vacant pens we could borrow or rent, I rounded up some carpenters and bought some lumber: good, stout ten-by-ten centimeter timbers. The carpenters assembled these on the university grounds and bolted them together, with the sides cross-braced in case the animal tried to push one of his walls over.

As an example of the unforeseen delays that bedevil such a project, we were talking with Joseph Hockersmith, a specialist in catching wild animals uninjured for zoos and scientific institutions. When he saw Cohen's cage being assembled, he cried: "Hey! You've got to put padding on those bars!"

"Eh?" said I. "What for?"

"You want to catch a member of the elephant tribe, don't you?"

"Yes," I said, "though there's a question about calling a mastodon a member of the elephant tribe, since elephants are descended from mastodons."

"But he'll have tusks, won't he?"

"If he's a two-thirds grown one, he will."

"And you'd like to deliver him with tusks undamaged, wouldn't you?"

"Righto!"

"Well, if you put the beast in a cage with iron bars before he's had a chance to get used to you, he'll be so angry and frightened that he'll bang his tusks against the bars hard enough to break them. He'll arrive in the present with only the stumps. I've handled elephants."

So we had to hold up proceedings to pad the bars and also to hang sheets of that quilting that moving men use in their vans to keep the furniture from damage. At last we assembled in the chamber building: the Raja and I, Norman Blackelk, the cook Ming, and our crew. These were Beauregard Black, the crew boss, and his helpers Pancho, Bruno, and Rodrigo. Then there were Hockersmith and his three assistants, and one more man: A young cove, Wilmer Delarue, whom the University of Minnesota had sent us. A graduate student and assistant instructor, Delarue was bucking for his doctorate in paleontology. We were always glad to have a real scientist on these safaris, because it gives certain tax advantages.

There had been a number of such young blokes on our *safariin*, some easy to get along with and some not. Delarue seemed a harmless chap except for a know-it-all tendency to set everybody right on details, such as the pronunciation of words like *Apatosaurus*. When Norman Blackelk pronounced it with the accent on "pat," Delarue picked him up and said the word should be stressed on the "ap."

"Wilmer," said Blackelk, "the most successful lawyer I've known, when a client came in to hire him, if the client mispronounced a word, this lawyer in later conversation used the same mispronunciation, even though he knew better."

"That's why the language goes all to hell," said Delarue.

We hoped to scare up mastodons near enough to the chamber site so as not to need to shift camp. Therefore we did not bring a train of asses to haul our stuff around the outback. We thought that, if we had to move camp, we could send the chamber back to Present with Black and his crew to fetch them.

As a last-minute addition, Hockersmith's boys brought a barrel of apples, which they manhandled into the chamber. Hockersmith explained:

"This is my bait. Don't let any of your people swipe them. With elephant, I never found anything that brings 'em round so fast as ripe yellow apples. They love 'em. The only thing that would fetch them quicker would be the fruit of the umganu tree of Southern Africa. It ferments as it ripens, and the elephants there got drunk on 'em. I didn't have any umganu fruit, and perhaps it's just as well. A sober

144

elephant is problem enough to handle, so you can imagine what it would be like with a drunken one!"

"Bloody good idea," I said. We filed into the chamber, and off we went.

By then, departure was pretty much routine. The dizziness of transition through time caused one of Hockersmith's men to lose his breakfast. He managed to keep it in until the Raja passed an airsickness bag back to him. Cohen had taped envelopes of these bags to the backs of the seats; but then the chairs were taken out, and nobody gave the bags a thought. Bruce Cohen's as fussy about keeping his chamber clean and shipshape as anybody's maiden aunt, so he had laid in his own supply.

I had told Cohen to set his dials for one million years before Present. That was the closest Prochaska's scientists would let users of the chamber come to Present. They didn't want to have time travelers meet Blackelk's ancestors coming over from Siberia. Such a meeting would affect later history and cause a paradox. To prevent that, we should all be thrown back to Present, *boom!*, and killed in the process.

Actually, I am sure that a setting of half a million b.p. would not impose any risk, since all the evidence is that the first Red Indians arrived in North America well after 100,000 b.p. But Prochaska's committee of experts insisted on an extra-wide safety factor.

Cohen found us a nice, soft landing place. He can't move the chamber horizontally, but by hunting back and forth in time he can find a period when the site is flat and hard enough to provide a safe alighting. The landscape of 1,000,000 b.p. looks hardly different from today in those national forests, all named after Mark Twain, across southern Missouri. This state is pretty bloody flat, with a little roll but nothing an American from a western state would call a mountain. The highest place is a hill in Iron County called Taum Sauk Mountain, less than 500 meters. In Colorado they wouldn't bother to name it.

For millions of years, this area has been part of the big temperate-zone forest, which covered the eastern third of the continent until the white men moved in and cut down most of the trees for farmland. It's pretty well out towards the western edge of this forest, and the edge moves back and forth with the weather. In a series of dry centuries, the forest retreats eastward, leaving most of Missouri as grassland; then a sequence of wet centuries brings the forest back again.

We had evidently hit one of the drier periods. There was still plenty of timber around us, mostly maple, hickory, and several kinds of oaks; but it was broken into clumps and copses. In our business, we prefer this to a solid, dense forest. Not only are the animals thicker, since the grass provides them with food down where they can reach it, but also we can better see them. In a real jungle you're bloody lucky to see fifty meters. You never know how many beasts of the kinds you're looking for are just outside that limited radius of vision.

In any case, there were no animals but a couple of squirrels in sight when the Raja and I hopped out with guns ready. After a trip by the chamber back to Present to fetch our equipment, setting up the camp kept us all busy for the first couple of hours.

One of our preparations was to spread a big sheet of canvas away from the camp. This sheet was attached by a steel cable to a power winch, and the winch in turn was belayed to the bars of the chamber and plugged in to the chamber's power point. If we could get our mastodon to stand on the sheet, we could tranquilize it and use the winch to haul it into the chamber. I had the boys build a little earthen ramp from the ground of our landing place to the sill of the chamber door. But the canvas could be carried only as far from the chamber as the length of the cable allowed.

I was about to call time for tucker when we heard crashing from a clump of trees south of us.

"Hey!" said Hockersmith. "Maybe that's our mastodon, right to hand! Fred, get out the apples!"

Hockersmith's boys rolled out the barrel, while the Raja and I cautiously approached the grove. As we slunk around the clump of trees, the cause of the disturbance came in sight. It was a big ground sloth, which had hooked its claws under the roots of a young maple and pulled it out of the ground. Now it was sitting up on its hind legs and tail, holding the uprooted sapling in its forepaws and eating its way down the tree. It had already eaten all the leaves and twigs, branch by branch, most of the distance from top to base.

Imagine an animal like an oversized bear with a big, bushy tail, or better yet a wolverine scaled up to the bulk of a small elephant. The hind feet had heels that stuck out to the rear almost as far as the rest of the foot did forwards, which certainly gave the animal a solid stance.

The ground sloth looked at us in a vague sort of way and went back to its feeding. Hockersmith asked:

"What d'you call that critter, Reggie?"

"Ground sloth," I said. "First discovered by your President Jefferson, who got hold of a fossil claw and named the animal *Megalonyx*. He thought it some sort of lion."

"Excuse me, Reggie," said young Delarue. "I'm sure that one belongs to the genus *Mylodon*, not *Megalonyx*."

"Okay, call it what you like."

147

"Are we going to do anything about it?" asked Delarue.

"I see no reason to. Some clients would shoot it just to hear the gun bang and see the animal drop dead. But we shan't have room in the chamber for it and our mastodon, too, assuming we catch one. So I would leave it be."

"It doesn't seem afraid of us," said Hockersmith.

"Has never seen creatures like us," I said. "If the books are right, the only predator it seriously had to fear was the sabertooth. The ground sloth has an armor of little round bones embedded in its skin, and it would take those saberfangs to reach a vital organ. We don't look or smell like sabertooths. Even the American lion might have found it too tough to handle, since a swipe with those big claws could take your head off."

We watched; but all the ground sloth did was just eat, eat, eat. From what I've seen of large plant eaters, especially those who live on leaves or grass, that is what they mostly do. They have to spend their time eating, because grass and leaves have a bloody low nutritional value.

Soon the *Mylodon* had cleaned that sapling of every last leaf. It dropped the trunk, came down on all fours, and ambled into the grove, looking for another sapling. It walked on the knuckles of its forefeet, somewhat as a gorilla does, and paid us no more heed.

In looking for animals to shoot, photograph, or just gawk at, one must be prepared for the unpredictability of their appearance. During the following days we saw other Pleistocene mammals—deer, bear, ground sloth, horse, a bear-sized beaver, and a glimpse of a lion at long distance—but no mastodon. Hockersmith explained:

"It's the same with elephants. They are always migratory, because they have such enormous appetites that a herd soon strips all the greenery from any place they inhabit, even the bark of the trees. So they have to move on, leaving the area they have devastated to recover. That may take years, and this fact complicates trying to preserve them."

More time passed without sight of mastodons. One of Hockersmith's men shot a deer, so the camp had fresh meat for a while. One day Hockersmith and the Raja came in from a hike in considerable excitement.

"There's something of the elephant kind near here!" said Hockersmith. "We passed a fine pile of elephant turds; no mistake!"

We got up a safari to look into the matter. After some hours of tracking, we heard a rumble ahead.

"We're getting close!" said Delarue. "That's the proboscidean borborygmus."

"The *what?*" said Blackelk, turning his coppery face to me. "What does he mean?"

I said: "That's technical for the rumble that gases make in an elephant's guts."

We went ahead cautiously until we could hear the sound of breaking branches. At last we sighted our quarry, about seventy meters off and pulling the branches from a basswood tree to eat the twigs and leaves.

It proved a big mammoth, a good four meters at the shoulder. It was rather short in the body but long-legged, covered with reddish-brown fur, nowhere near so long as that of the smaller true or woolly mammoth further north. It also bore a fine pair of long, spirally curved tusks, crossing at the tips, which would have driven any of my trophy-hunting sahibs into ecstasies. There was once a lot of argument over what use such crossed tusks could be, since the points could not be applied to anything. Then it was figured out that the bulls used them as snow shovels to get at food in winter, the cows and young following behind. Time travel has confirmed the theory.

"Columbian mammoth," I said. "*Paraloxodon jeffersoni,* if I remember the textbooks."

"Oh, that terminology's obsolete," said young Delarue in his irritating way. "Nowadays most specialists lump it in with the woolly mammoth as *Mammuthus.* Some even want to cram them all back in Linnaeus's *Elephas,* but I wouldn't go that far."

We watched the mammoth; but just looking at an animal eat, eat, eat gets pretty bloody boring after a while. Hockersmith asked:

"Shall we try to capture it, Reggie?"

I shook my head. "He's too tall to fit into the chamber, unless we could get him to go down on knees and elbows and crawl in. I don't see much prospect of that."

"You could shoot him with a tranquilizer charge," said Delarue. "He'd fit in lying down, I'm sure."

"Yes? And suppose I did give him a tranquilizer shot. He'd just lie down and doze; and then how should we get him to the chamber? We must be a kilometer from the camp, and almost as far from the pallet." That was what we called the canvas sheet attached to the chamber. "Besides, he must weigh at least five or six tons. Anybody want those tusks for trophies?"

"Not I," said Blackelk. "My ancestors did enough of that."

"Then let's return to camp."

"Hey, wait!" said Delarue, fiddling with his camera. "I want a close-up shot."

Off he trotted, right towards that bull mammoth. I had read that lone males of the elephant tribe are likely to be short-tempered; lack of regular sexual outlets, I suppose. I called:

"Hey, come back here!" But Delarue just gave a vague wave and kept on towards the mammoth.

When he had covered half the distance, the mammoth noticed him with its rather dim eyesight, I suppose; or perhaps it caught his smell. It dropped the branch it was eating and started towards Delarue with its trunk up and waving about, sniffing. Delarue, who had no gun, kept his eyes glued to the camera finder.

The mammoth gave a squealing grunt and kept coming. I got ready to shoot. Delarue at last caught on to what was happening and rose to his feet. As he turned to run back to us, with the mammoth looming over him, the silly galah tripped over his own feet and fell sprawling. Now I dared not shoot for fear that the mammoth would fall on Delarue and squash him.

Then, to one side, the Raja's gun went off. The mammoth staggered as if from a tremendous blow. It regained its balance and shuffled away, shaking its head.

"I shot him through that bump on top of his skull," said the Raja. "Knowing you didn't want him killed. The bullet just went through that spongy mass of bony cavities. He may have a headache for a while, but the holes should soon heal up." That dome atop the heads of mammoths provides anchorage for the huge neck muscles, which have to be bloody powerful to support those tusks.

"You should have killed him," said Delarue. "I could have gotten a paper out of a study of its head, or even my thesis."

"You didn't speak up," said the Raja.

"But I should think anyone with brains—" began Delarue.

My own temper was getting frazzled, and I did my lolly: "Look, God damn it, you almost got us into serious trouble by going close to the mammoth when I told you not to, and then falling over your own stupid feet in the animal's path. The next stunt of that kind you pull, we'll hogtie you, put you in the chamber, and tell Cohen to drop you off at Present."

"I—I'm sorry," he mumbled.

More days passed without a sign of mastodon, although all the paleontological finds indicated that at this time the place should swarm with them. The Raja and I began to worry, since the charges for keeping the chamber back in the Pleistocene were mounting up. Norman Blackelk worried, too, saying:

"I don't know, Reggie, how much more money the directors of the Redintegration Society are willing to sink in this trip. Perhaps we ought to shift camp after all."

"That would run the charges up pretty fast, too," I said. "We should have to go back to Present and round up some extra crew and our train of asses—burros, if you prefer—to help with the move."

Hockersmith said: "Why don't we try to catch one of the smaller mammals: say, a Pleistocene horse or beaver; or even that ground sloth."

Blackelk looked dubious. "We may come to that; but first I'd have to consult the exec committee of the Society. They were pretty definite that they wanted a young mastodon. They already have a breeding stock of several other Pleistocene species, and they want to spend their money where it'll do the most good."

"Hey, Norm!" said Hockersmith. "Just had an idea. You're a real Native American, aren't you?"

"So they tell me," said Blackelk. "Less than one-quarter white genes."

"Well, the Indians used to put on ceremonies, with dances, to encourage animals of the kinds they hunted to come around and let themselves be killed. I seem to recall that the Ghost Dance, which got poor old Sitting Bull killed, was supposed to bring back the buffalo. It didn't, of course, since by then the whites had shot most of the buffalo with repeating rifles."

Delarue cleared his throat. "Don't you mean 'bring back the bison'?"

"No; I said 'buffalo' and I meant 'buffalo.' That's what the animal was always called in that time and place. A 'bison' is something an Aussie like Reggie here uses to wash his hands in."

"Oh, bulsh!" I said. "A dinkum Aussie does *not* pronounce 'basin' and 'bison' alike. Unless you're hearing-impaired, you can hear the difference: 'basin,' 'bison,' 'basin,' 'bison.' "

"I see," said Delarue. "You move 'basin' halfway to 'bison,' and 'bison' halfway to 'boyson.' "

Blackelk asked: "Is there such a word as 'boyson'?"

Delarue shrugged. "I once knew a Mr. Boysen." He turned to Blackelk. "What did the Crows call it, Norm?"

Blackelk spread his hands. "Don't know. I learned Absaroka in school, although all the tribes are Anglophones now. The theory was that the language mustn't be allowed to die out, because it was a priceless cultural heritage or something. I never became fluent in it. Actually, 'bison' and 'buffalo' are both names for several kinds of Old World wild cattle. The white invaders carelessly applied both Old World names to the one American species, since they couldn't pronounce the Native American words for the animal."

Hockersmith said: "We're getting away from the subject.

153

Norm, we want you to do a ghost dance to bring back the mastodon. It may not work, but what have we got to lose?"

"Don't know that I could do that," said Blackelk. "Even if I could remember enough Absaroka, the language has no word for 'mastodon.' Maybe it did once, but if so it must have been forgotten soon after the animal went extinct."

"Well then, simply call it 'mastodon.' Your Native American gods would understand."

"I'll see what I can think up—"

"Don't do it, Norm!" said Delarue. "It's just pandering to primitive superstition. The world will never be able to manage its affairs in a rational manner as long as people go in for irrational, unscientific cults and sects, with gods and other spooks."

Delarue's cocksureness even got under the skin of Joe Hockersmith, usually an even-tempered, self-controlled man. "Look, squirt," he said. "We'll make it a sporting proposition. If Norman comes up with a ghost dance, what'll you bet the mastodon don't appear in a reasonable time, say ten days? How about ten bucks?"

"Make it fifty," said Delarue. "I don't ordinarily bet, but against a silly superstition it's a sure thing."

They shook hands. Blackelk said: "The first thing I need is a drum. Too bad we didn't bring one."

After much yabber, we decided to convert Hockersmith's barrel of apples into a drum. We dumped the apples out in the chamber, took a sheet of plastic used as a tarpaulin, and with much tugging and grunting got it pulled tight over the empty barrel and dogged down. It gave a satisfactory *boom* when Blackelk slapped it. He said:

"Now I need some dancers. Reggie, you and Joe ought to do."

"Me, dance?" said Hockersmith. "Never have in my life.

My wife's been after me for years to take lessons—"

"You thought up this project," said Blackelk, "so you can damn well play your part in it."

"What steps have we got to learn?" asked Hockersmith.

"I'll show you." The steps proved simple enough, with much stamping and raising the knees, as in that British parade step the Commonwealth armies used to practice.

After tucker that night, when full dark came, we cleared a space and went to work. Blackelk sat on a camp chair with the barrel between his knees. Stripped to the waist, he had a necktie knotted around his forehead for a headband and some feathers, which Ming supplied from a fresh turkey in our commissariat, stuck in the band. He began a chant in Absaroka. I can't reproduce any of it. It had a rather monotonous little tune with about three notes, while Blackelk slapped his drum. Hockersmith and I hopped and stamped around him in circles, as Blackelk had taught us. The rest of the crew, standing about in the firelight, kept time by clapping. After a while the rhythm and the pounding got into our blood, as they got into mine when I once took part in a corroboree with some Native Australians in the outback.

When Blackelk ran out of song and Hockersmith and I out of wind, we paused. From the dark woods came a squeal, and then another. Then several proboscidean throats let loose with that sound called 'trumpeting,' because it does sound like some sort of trumpet, only a horn with spit in it.

Everybody turned to look while the Raja and I got our guns. Presently an animal hove into view, near enough so that we could dimly make it out by firelight. It stared at us and turned away; the light showed it to be an American mastodon. I guessed it to be a female from its slender tusks. I had read that elephant herds are commonly bossed by the oldest cow; they have alpha females instead of alpha males.

After this first mastodon came another, then a couple of little ones no more than waist high; then another big one, following the track of the first. More went by until at least a dozen had passed. All, as nearly as I could judge, were cows and young. At the tail of the procession, a big bull ambled along. This one looked our way, hoisted his trunk to sniff, and flapped his ears. Then we heard a loud toot, which seemed to come from the head of the line. The bull turned away and single-footed it after the herd like a Bondi tram. It must, I thought, have been the big cow who headed the line, the matriarch, telling the bull:

"Hurry up, you stupid male! Close up!"

With his hand out, Hockersmith walked up to Delarue. "Fifty bucks, please!"

"Damned coincidence!" grumbled Delarue. But he paid.

Did I think our ghost dance had anything to do with the herd's appearance? Not really; but I try to keep an open mind in such matters. There is so much that human beings don't yet understand.

It did not seem practical to go after the herd that night. We got up extra early next morning and set out with our helpers and equipment. Hockersmith carried not only his gun but also a big bag of apples hanging round his neck. He explained:

"In my experience, you can train almost any animal of the smarter kinds, such as elephant or bear, to come for a free handout. The trouble starts when you run out of goodies. Then the animal may decide to take you apart to see where you've got the rest of the stuff hidden."

Trailing the herd presented no problem. I am not the trailsman that some black trackers are down-under. Some claim these Native Australians can track an animal across bare rock. I don't believe that; but what they can do is remarkable enough. However, between the big, round footprints wherever the soil was a little soft, and the droppings, following that herd needed no Native Australians. We could tell when we came near the herd by the sound of breaking branches.

We scouted round to get up-wind and stole up on them. Everybody was told to keep quiet. Hockersmith warned that if startled, the animals might charge, forcing us to slaughter them, or all run off along their migration route and not be seen again in this area for a year.

"All right, Joe," I said. "Your turn."

"Which one do you want?" asked Hockersmith.

"That young bull," said I, pointing to an animal not quite old enough to have gone off on its own yet. It stood about two meters at the shoulder, with thick male-mastodon tusks only about half as long as those of the herd bull, and a coat of golden-brown fur like that on the mammoth that Delarue had bothered. I asked:

"Where is the big bull now?"

"Don't see him," murmured Hockersmith. "Ah, here he comes. Seems to have something on his mind."

Out from behind some trees came a young female mastodon and, right behind her, the big bull. This last obviously had something on his mind, for his huge penis, the size of a big man's arm with the fist clenched, was fully extended. It seemed, though, that his lady love did not want any just now. After her came the bull with squeaking sounds, which I suppose were mastodontic endearments. She single-footed away fast, weaving among the trees and other members of the herd with the bull behind her. Soon the two passed out of sight, so we never did learn whether the bull consummated his passion.

It took self-control not to burst out laughing. In fact, young Delarue did emit a sputter until the Raja shushed him.

"Okay, here goes!" said Hockersmith.

He stole in Red Indian style towards the young bull I had pointed out. When there was nothing between him and the juvenile male but a big bush, he took an apple from his bag and tossed it. It bounced off the flank of the mastodon, which was munching a shrub it had uprooted. The mastodon jerked up its head and turned this way and that to see what had disturbed it.

Hockersmith tossed another apple, so that it landed on the ground a couple of meters from the mastodon's head, in the direction of the pallet.

The mastodon stood weaving this way and that and sniffing in all directions. It located the second apple, walked to it, and ate it. This brought it in sight of Joe Hockersmith. It gave him a suspicious stare but otherwise followed the trail of apples that Hockersmith was laying down by tossing them ahead of the beast.

An hour of this brought us to the canvas pallet. When, by the use of more apples, Hockersmith had maneuvered all four of the mastodon's feet on the canvas, he slipped a tranquilizer charge into his rifle and fired. Tranquilizers nowadays work much faster than those of the last century, when this method of immobilizing animals began. The mastodon squealed, gave a prodigious yawn, and sank down on the canvas. I called the camp on my communicator and told Beauregard to start the winch.

The rest of that capture was routine. With the help of the winch, we got the mastodon, still tranquilized, into the chamber. The transition back to Present went off without a hitch, save that the beast crapped on the floor. This led Cohen to put on one of his expositions of high-class cursing.

Thank Aljira that Prochaska's transition chamber was on the ground floor of its building! Otherwise I don't know how we should ever have got a couple of tons of mastodon down a flight of stairs and round corners. With all members of the safari pulling and heaving on the canvas, we got the tranquilized beast to the exit. By detaching the winch from inside the chamber and rigging it with extension cords in our timber pen, we gave the winch a clear shot at hauling the mastodon into the inclosure.

During a break in this chore, Norman Blackelk telephoned Redintegration headquarters and told them to send a lorry to pick up their specimen. He also told them to bring a few hundred kilos of lettuce and cabbages to feed the creature on its way to California.

The lorry took a week to reach us. Meanwhile we got better acquainted with the animal, for which someone suggested the name 'Lancelot.' Once a day we opened his cage door to shove in a hundred-kilo bundle of hay and a few cabbages. Lancelot gobbled the cabbages but did not much like hay. He let the bundle sit for hours before starting to eat it. Delarue explained that, while the mastodon would eat anything vegetable, it was really more of a browser than a grazer. What he would really have liked was an equal weight of cuttings from the branch ends of trees and bushes; but we lacked the time to arrange for that.

When the cage door was opened, Lancelot backed away, snorting and grumbling. If I could sum up his attitude towards us, I should call it 'surly,' although I know better than to attribute human emotions and attitudes to an animal of another species. The only one for whom Lancelot seemed to have slightly warmer feelings was Joe Hockersmith. Every day he came to the cage with a couple of apples, which Lancelot learned to take from Hockersmith's outstretched hand. When Hockersmith went away, you could see regret in the mastodon's stance, with drooping head, trunk, and eyelids.

At last the lorry arrived. It was not a semi-trailer rig but a one-piece ten-wheeler. Still, its body was just about the dimensions of the transition chamber, so there should be no problem with fitting Lancelot into it.

My crew wrestled the timber ramp into place outside the door of the cage, and the driver backed the lorry up against its high end. At its rear, the lorry had a pair of swinging doors. When closed, they were secured by a pair of big vertical bolts, running from top to bottom. When the lorry was buttoned up, these bolts were held down by a couple of hinged latches, which in turn were secured by padlocks.

Lancelot plainly did not like the looks of the lorry. He backed into the farthest corner of his pen and, whenever one of us tried to coax him to climb the ramp into the lorry, he trumpeted and swiped at us with his trunk and tusks.

"Think we'll have to tranquilize him again?" said Blackelk.

"I hope not," I said. "He's had so much of that already that it might impair his health."

"Let me try," said Hockersmith. He came back soon with the bag of apples round his neck.

In the cage, Hockersmith approached Lancelot with an apple, talking in friendly, man-to-mastodon tones. Lancelot took the apple, ate it, and began sniffing round until he located the bag. Hockersmith pulled the bag open and let

Lancelot extract an apple. Then he moved slowly towards the open gate. Lancelot took another apple, and another, and another. Soon Hockersmith had him up the ramp and inside the lorry. I heard a shout:

"Hey, you dumb brute, let go! I'll give you the god-dam bag!"

Peering round the door frame, I saw that Lancelot, having figured out where the apples were coming from, had wrapped his trunk around the bag and was trying to pull it away from Hockersmith. The latter ducked and slid out of the loop just in time to keep Lancelot from breaking his neck. Hockersmith came out, saying:

"Okay, Mr. Barnes, close her up!"

The sun was setting; getting the equipment in place and Lancelot into the lorry had taken us all day, and we were bloody tired. So it was decided not to send Barnes off with the lorry that night but to let him get a good night's sleep.

"Lancelot won't really mind being in the dark," said Hockersmith. "In the elephant tribe, the sense of sight is weak, while those of smell and hearing are very keen. He will sniff out the rest of those apples."

Barnes pulled down the door-holding bolts into their bolt holes. But he did not bother to fasten the padlocks.

Next morning, my wife drove me to the University grounds early. Instead of the Redintegration Society s lorry, hacked up to the timber pen outside the transition-chamber building, there was no lorry but a lot of people talking excitedly and a couple of coppers. One of these troopers was taking down statements from Norman Blackelk on a pad. I hurried up, saying:

"What's happened? Has Barnes left already?"

"Hell, no!" said Hockersmith. "Lancelot's been hijacked!"

"Eh? What happened?"

"When people came to work this morning, they found poor old Fitz bound and gagged, with a story of having been held up after midnight by masked men with an assault rifle." FitzHerbert was the University's night watchman. "They tied him up, hot-wired the truck, and drove away."

That is how, a couple of hours later, I found myself riding a police helicopter over the southern suburbs. We quartered back and forth over a huge area, looking for our lorry, with another vehicle nearby. Alarms had been sent out for our lorry, of course, and there was little chance of its even getting to the state line. With its description and known license number, it would easily be picked up: the mastodonnappers had not had time to disguise it.

Since the drongos would probably have figured this out, it seemed likely that they would have brought another lorry to which to transfer Lancelot. I thought they might not have an easy time with this. Lancelot had got used to the Raja's and my people to the point of tolerating us; but any lot of strangers who confronted him might suffer difficulties.

At last I pointed down and told the pilot policeman: "That looks like it." I tried to read the license number with my binoculars, but the aircraft's vibration made this impossible.

A lorry just like the Redintegrationists' stood in a clear space in a bushy area that the cockies had abandoned but that developers had not yet cut up and built over. That was not all; a big semi-trailer rig was backing towards the rear of the smaller lorry. I could understand why the hijackers would bring a larger vehicle, since they would not know how big a Pleistocene animal we should fetch back to Present.

The cop spoke on his radio to headquarters. He had to study a map to give the exact location. Then he circled and went to a small airfield, used by private-aeroplane owners. He got permission to land, and down we went.

More cops drove up, and one of their cars took me. The cop who was driving said: "Mr. Rivers, I don't think we can go busting in shooting like it was a show. They got one of them assault rifles, and all we got is pistols. Have to wait for more artillery."

"Too bad I haven't got my dinosaur gun," I said. "Didn't have a chance to pick it up."

"Okay, but it don't spray bullets like an assault rifle does. So keep your head well down when we get near these perps."

Eventually we found a little rise from which with glasses we could sweep the area where the lorries were parked. There seemed to be three in that push: one carrying the gun, while two others worked to erect a movable platform between the two lorries. This was one of those steel contraptions on wheels, where the platform is raised on scissor legs by a hydraulic jack. One man was turning a crank to pump up the platform, now about halfway up to the lorries' doorsills. The other of that pair I recognized as Horace Dunbar, the game-ranch owner.

"Don't you blokes keep rifles handy for such occasions?" I asked my cop.

"Yeah," he said "but you gotta go through red tape to take 'em out. Takes time." He spoke in low tones into his handset, then back to me: "Keep your shirt on, Mr. Rivers. They're sending some of the boys with more fire power."

We left the car to creep up a little closer to the lorries. When I looked through the glasses again, I saw that the platform wallah now had the thing all the way up to the lorry sills.

The man who had worked the hydraulic jack climbed up on the platform. He undogged the bolts that secured the doors of the smaller lorry. I saw that Barnes had made a mistake in not closing the padlocks. Even if he had, that would only have delayed things a bit, provided the hijackers had brought a bolt cutter or some such implement with them.

The fellow hoisted the two long bolts out of their sockets and dogged them in the raised position. Then he climbed down to the ground again and went to the tractor unit of the eighteen-wheel semi. He climbed up into the cab, and soon the door at the arse end of the trailer began to rise. It had one of those roll-up doors in sections, which rises like a window shade and stows itself against the roof of the trailer. Soon the end of the trailer yawned wide open.

Then this bloke climbed down, came aft again, and climbed back on the platform. Meanwhile Dunbar stood watching and giving orders, while the cove with the rifle stood with his back to the lorry, looking in all directions.

The man on the platform took hold of the door handles and pulled the doors open. Dunbar handed him up a dowel rod about a meter and a half long, with a steel hook in the end. I recalled seeing a circus man control an elephant by catching his ear with such a hook. I had a feeling that Lancelot would not take kindly to such treatment.

Then Dunbar climbed into the cab of the smaller lorry. I could not see what the ratbag did; I suppose he opened the window in the back of the cab, and that in front of the lorry body, and poked something through. At any rate, Lancelot gave a shrill toot and emerged on the platform between the vehicles. The man with the goad leaped off the platform when Lancelot took a swipe at him.

It's a comfort to know that we were not the only ones to make mistakes. I suppose the man who jacked up the platform neglected to turn the handle that locked the platform in the raised position. As soon as Lancelot put his full weight on the device, it started to sink slowly back to ground level, while the crank handle spun in reverse.

Even at that distance, we could hear the shouts of the three men. As the platform neared the bottom of its travel, Lancelot stepped down to the ground. He trumpeted, lashed the air with his trunk, and started off.

Dunbar, who had come down from the lorry cab, yelled and put himself in front of that mastodon, waving his arms, like those people who stand in front of tanks when a government tries to put down an insurrection. Lancelot gave a swipe of his trunk, brushing Dunbar to one side but not quite knocking him down.

Dunbar yelled, stepped back to the mastodon, and grabbed the animal round the foreleg. I suppose he had counted on Lancelot to keep him out of bankruptcy, by the money he would get by letting his rich client shoot the beast; and he couldn't bear to see his last financial hope shuffle away. Desperate, he did one of the most foolish things you can do, which is to try to match muscle with a big wild animal. Even a fifty-kilo chimp is much stronger than any mere human being. But desperate men often go a bit nuts.

Lancelot just gave a kind of sideways kick, which sent Dunbar flying into a bush. Then cops with rifles sprouted from the shrubbery, yelling to the remaining two. The one with the assault rifle dropped it and raised his hands. With the leader of the push down and out of action, there was no reason for the subordinates to make it a fight to the death.

Joe Hockersmith appeared with another bag of apples. The mastodon gave a happy squeal and grabbed it.

There's little more to tell. Horace Dunbar died on his way to the hospital in the ambulance. He was in his sixties, and that kick had broken some things inside him. Blackelk and his Society got their mastodon, and Lancelot is growing into a fine big tusker. But the only one who can safely approach him on foot is Joe Hockersmith, provided he brings some apples with him.

You asked what had caused us the most trouble in Present. I think this case, the only one where we brought an extinct form forward to Present and had it hijacked, qualifies, eh, Mr. Schindler?

Nothing in the Rules

Not many spectators turn out for a meet between two minor women's swimming clubs, and this one was no exception. Louis Connaught, looking up at the balcony, thought casually that the single row of seats around it was about half full, mostly with the usual bored-looking assortment of husbands and boy friends, and some of the Hotel Creston's guests who had wandered in for want of anything better to do. One of the bellboys was asking an evening-gowned female not to smoke, and she was showing irritation. Mr. Santalucia and the little Santalucias were there as usual to see mamma perform. They waved down at Connaught.

Connaught—a dark devilish-looking little man—glanced over to the other side of the pool. The girls were coming out of the shower rooms, and their shrill conversation was blurred by the acoustics of the pool room into a continuous buzz. The air was faintly steamy. The stout party in white duck pants was Laird, coach of the Knickerbockers and Connaught's archrival. He saw Connaught and boomed: "Hi, Louie!" The words rattled from wall to wall with a sound like a stick being drawn swiftly along a picket fence. Wambach of the A.A.U. Committee, who was refereeing, came in with his overcoat still on and greeted Laird, but the booming reverberations drowned his words before they got over to Connaught.

Then somebody else came through the door; or rather, a knot of people crowded through it all at once, facing inward, some in bathing suits and some in street clothes. It was a few seconds before Coach Connaught saw what they were looking at. He blinked and looked more closely, standing with his mouth half open.

But not for long. *"Hey!"* he yelled in a voice that made the pool room sound like the inside of a snare drum in use. "Protest! PROTEST! *You can't do that!"*

It had been the preceding evening when Herbert Laird opened his front door and shouted, "H'lo, Mark, come on in." The chill March wind was making a good deal of racket but not as much as all that. Laird was given to shouting on general principles. He was stocky and bald.

Mark Vining came in and deposited his briefcase. He was younger than Laird—just thirty, in fact—with octagonal glasses and rather thin severe features that made him look more serious than he was, which was fairly serious.

"Glad you could come, Mark," said Laird. "Listen, can you make our meet with the Crestons tomorrow night?"

Vining pursed his lips thoughtfully. "I guess so. Loomis decided not to appeal, so I don't have to work nights for a few days anyhow. Is something special up?"

Laird looked sly. "Maybe. Listen, you know that Mrs. Santalucia that Louie Connaught has been cleaning up with for the past couple of years? I think I've got that fixed. But I want you along to think up legal reasons why my scheme's O.K."

"Why," said Vining cautiously, "what's your scheme?"

"Can't tell you now. I promised not to. But if Louie can win by entering a freak—a woman with webbed fingers—"

"Oh, look here, Herb, you know those webs don't really help her—"

"Yes, yes, I know all the arguments. You've already got more water-resistance to your arms than you've got muscle

168

to overcome it with, and so forth. But I know Mrs. Santalucia has webbed fingers, and I know she's the best woman swimmer in New York. And I don't like it. It's bad for my prestige as a coach." He turned and shouted into the gloom: "Iantha!"

"Yes?"

"Come here, will you please? I want you to meet my friend Mr. Vining. Here, we need some light."

The light showed the living room as usual buried under disorderly piles of boxes of bathing suits and other swimming equipment, the sale of which furnished Herbert Laird with most of his income. It also showed a young woman coming in in a wheel chair.

One look gave Vining a feeling that, he knew, boded no good for him. He was unfortunate in being a pushover for any reasonably attractive girl, and at the same time being cursed with an almost pathological shyness where women were concerned. The facts that both he and Laird were bachelors and took their swimming seriously were the main ties between them.

This girl was more than reasonably attractive. She was, thought the dazzled Vining, a wow, a ten-strike, a direct sixteen-inch hit. Her smooth, rather flat features and high cheekbones had a hint of Asian or American Indian, and went oddly with her light-gold hair, which, Vining could have sworn, had a faint greenish tinge. A blanket was wrapped around her legs.

He came out of his trance as Laird introduced the exquisite creature as "Miss Delfoiros."

Miss Delfoiros didn't seem exactly overcome. As she extended her hand, she said with a noticeable accent: "You are not from the newspapers, Mr. Vining?"

"No," said Vining. "Just a lawyer. I specialize in wills

169

and probates and things. Not thinking of drawing up yours, are you?"

She relaxed visibly and laughed. "No. I 'ope I shall not need one for a long, long time."

"Still," said Vining seriously, "you never know—"

Laird bellowed: "Wonder what's keeping that sister of mine. Dinner ought to be ready. *Martha!*" He marched out, and Vining heard Miss Laird's voice, something about "—but Herb, I had to let those things cool down—"

Vining wondered with a great wonder what he should say to Miss Delfoiros. Finally he said, "Smoke?"

"Oh, no, thank you very much. I do not do it."

"Mind if I do?"

"No, not at all."

"Whereabouts do you hail from?" Vining thought the question sounded both brusque and silly. He never did get the hang of talking easily under these circumstances.

"Oh, I am from Kip—Cyprus, I mean. You know, the island."

"Really? That makes you a British subject, doesn't it?"

"Well . . . no, not exactly. Most Cypriots are, but I am not."

"Will you be at this swimming meet?"

"Yes, I think so."

"You don't"—he lowered his voice—"know what scheme Herb's got up his sleeve to beat La Santalucia?"

"Yes . . . no . . . I do not . . . what I mean is, I must not tell."

More mystery, thought Vining. What he really wanted to know was why she was confined to a wheel chair; whether the cause was temporary or permanent. But you couldn't ask a person right out, and he was still trying to concoct a leading question when Laird's bellow wafted in: "All right, folks, soup's on!" Vining would have pushed the wheel chair in, but before he had a chance, the girl had spun the chair around and was halfway to the dining room.

Vining said: "Hello, Martha, how's the school-teaching business?" But he wasn't really paying much attention to Laird's capable spinster sister. He was gaping at Miss Delfoiros, who was quite calmly emptying a teaspoonful of salt into her water glass and stirring.

"What . . . what?" he gulped.

"I 'ave to," she said. "Fresh water makes me—like what you call drunk."

"Listen, Mark!" roared his friend. "Are you sure you can be there on time tomorrow night? There are some questions of eligibility to be cleared up, and I'm likely to need you badly."

"Will Miss Delfoiros be there?" Vining grinned, feeling very foolish inside.

"Oh, sure. Iantha's out . . . say, listen, you know that little eighteen-year-old Clara Havranek? She did the hundred in one-o-five yesterday. She's championship material. We'll clean the Creston Club yet—" He went on, loud and fast, about what he was going to do to Louie Connaught's girls. The while, Mark Vining tried to concentrate on his own food, which was good, and on Iantha Delfoiros, who was charming but evasive.

There seemed to be something special about Miss Delfoiros's food, to judge by the way Martha Laird had served it. Vining looked closely and saw that it had the peculiarly dead and clammy look that a dinner once hot but now cold has. He asked about it.

"Yes," she said, "I like it cold."

"You mean you don't eat *anything* hot?"

171

She made a face. " 'ot food? No, I do not like it. To us it is—"

"Listen, Mark! I hear the W.S.A. is going to throw a post-season meet in April for novices only—"

Vining's dessert lay before him a full minute before he noticed it. He was too busy thinking how delightful Miss Delfoiros's accent was.

When dinner was over, Laird said, "Listen, Mark, you know something about these laws against owning gold? Well, look here—" He led the way to a candy box on a table in the living room. The box contained, not candy, but gold and silver coins. Laird handed the lawyer several of them. The first one he examined was a silver crown, bearing the inscription "Carolus II Dei Gra" encircling the head of England's Merry Monarch with a wreath in his hair—or, more probably, in his wig. The second was an eighteenth-century Spanish dollar. The third was a Louis d'Or.

"I didn't know you went in for coin collecting, Herb," said Vining. "I suppose these are all genuine?"

"They're genuine all right. But I'm not collecting 'em. You might say I'm taking 'em in trade. I have a chance to sell ten thousand bathing caps, if I can take payment in those things."

"I shouldn't think the U.S. Rubber Company would like the idea much."

"That's just the point. What'll I do with 'em after I get 'em? Will the government put me in jail for having 'em?"

"You needn't worry about that. I don't think the law covers old coins, though I'll look it up to make sure. Better call up the American Numismatic Society—they're in the phone book—and they can tell you how to dispose of them. But look here, what the devil is this? Ten thousand bathing caps to be paid for in pieces-of-eight? I never heard of such a thing."

"That's it exactly. Just ask the little lady here." Laird turned to Iantha, who was nervously trying to signal him to keep quiet. "The deal's her doing."

"I did . . . did—" She looked as if she were going to cry. " 'Erbert, you should not have said that. You see," she said to Vining, "we do not like to 'ave a lot to do with people. Always it causes us troubles."

"Who," asked Vining, "do you mean by 'we'?"

She shut her mouth obstinately. Vining almost melted. But his legal instincts came to the surface. If you don't get a grip on yourself, he thought, you'll be in love with her in another five minutes. And that might be a disaster. He said firmly: "Herb, the more I see of this business the crazier it looks. Whatever's going on, you seem to be trying to get me into it. But I won't let you before I know what it's all about."

"Might as well tell him, Iantha," said Laird. "He'll know when he sees you swim tomorrow, anyhow."

She said: "You will not tell the newspaper men, Mr. Vining?"

"No. I won't say anything to anybody."

"You promise?"

"Of course. You can depend on a lawyer to keep things under his hat."

"Under his—I suppose you mean not to tell. So, look." She reached down and pulled up the lower end of the blanket.

Vining looked. Where he expected to see feet, there was a pair of horizontal flukes, like those of a porpoise.

Louis Connaught's having kittens, when he saw what his

rival coach had sprung on him, can thus be easily explained. First he doubted his own senses. Then he doubted whether there was any justice in the world.

Meanwhile Mark Vining proudly pushed Iantha's wheel chair in among the cluster of judges and timekeepers at the starting end of the pool. Iantha herself, in a bright green bathing cap, held her blanket around her shoulders, but the slate-gray tail with its flukes was smooth and the flukes were horizontal; artists who show mermaids with scales and a vertical tail fin, like a fish's, simply don't know their zoology.

"All right, all right," bellowed Laird. "Don't crowd around. Everybody get back to where they belong. Everybody, please."

One of the spectators, leaning over the rail of the balcony to see, dropped a fountain pen into the pool. One of the Connaught's girls, a Miss Black, dove in after it. Ogden Wambach, the referee, poked a finger at the skin of the tail. He was a well-groomed, gray-haired man.

"Laird," he said, "is this a joke?"

"Not at all. She's entered in the backstroke and all the freestyles, just like any other club member. She's even registered with the A.A.U."

"But . . . but . . . I mean, is it alive? Is it real?"

Iantha spoke up. "Why do you not ask me those questions, Mr. . . . Mr. . . . I do not know you—"

"Good grief," said Wambach. "It talks! I'm the referee, Miss—"

"Delfoiros. Iantha Delfoiros."

"My word. Upon my word. That means—let's see—Violet Porpoise-tail, doesn't it? *Delphis* plus *oura*—"

"You know Greek? Oh, 'ow nice!" She broke into a string of Romaic.

Wambach gulped a little. "Too fast for me, I'm afraid. And that's *modern* Greek, isn't it?"

"Why, yes. I am modern, am I not?"

"Dear me. I suppose so. But is that tail really real? I mean, it's not just a piece of costumery?"

"Oh, but yes." Iantha threw off the blanket and waved her flukes.

"Dear me," said Ogden Wambach. "Where are my glasses? You understand, I just want to make sure there's nothing spurious about this."

Mrs. Santalucia, a muscular-looking lady with a visible mustache and fingers webbed down to the first joint, said, "You mean I gotta swim against *her*?"

Louis Connaught had been sizzling like a dynamite fuse. "You can't do it!" he shrilled. "This is a woman's meet! I protest!"

"So what?" said Laird.

"But you can't enter a fish in a woman's swimming meet! Can you, Mr. Wambach?"

Mark Vining spoke up. He had just taken a bunch of papers clipped together out of his pocket, and was running through them.

"Miss Delfoiros," he asserted, "is not a fish. She's a mammal."

"How do you figure that?" yelled Connaught.

"*Look* at her."

"Um-m-m," said Ogden Wambach. "I see what you mean."

"But," howled Connaught, "she still ain't human!"

"There is a question about that, Mr. Vining," said Wambach.

"No question at all. There's nothing in the rules against entering a mermaid, and there's nothing that says the competitors have to be human."

175

L. Sprague de Camp

Connaught was hopping about like an overwrought cricket. He was now waving a copy of the current A.A.U. swimming, diving and water polo rules. "I still protest! Look here! All through here it only talks about two kinds of meets, men's and women's. She ain't a woman, and she certainly ain't a man. If the Union had wanted to have meets for mermaids they'd have said so."

"Not a woman?" asked Vining in a manner that juries learned meant a rapier thrust at an opponent. "I beg your pardon, Mr. Connaught. I looked the question up." He frowned at his sheaf of papers. "Webster's International Dictionary, Second Edition, defines a woman as 'any female person.' And it further defines 'person' as 'a being characterized by conscious apprehension, rationality and a moral sense.'" He turned to Wambach. "Sir, I think you'll agree that Miss Delfoiros has exhibited conscious apprehension and rationality during her conversation with you, won't you?"

"My word . . . I really don't know what to say, Mr. Vining . . . I suppose she has, but I couldn't say—"

Horowitz, the scorekeeper, spoke up. "You might ask her to give the multiplication table." Nobody paid him any attention.

Connaught exhibited symptoms alarmingly suggestive of apoplexy. "But you can't—What are you talking about . . . conscious ap-ap—"

"Please, Mr. Connaught!" said Wambach. "When you shout that way I can't understand you because of the echoes."

Connaught mastered himself with a visible effort. Then he looked crafty. "How do I know she's got a moral sense?"

Vining turned to Iantha. "Have you ever been in jail, Iantha?"

176

Iantha laughed. "What a funny question, Mark! But of course, I have not."

"That's what *she* says," sneered Connaught. "How you gonna prove it?"

"We don't have to," said Vining loftily. "The burden of proof is on the accuser, and the accused is legally innocent until proved guilty. That principle was well established by the time of King Edward the First."

"That wasn't the kind of moral sense I meant," cried Connaught. "How about what they call moral turp-turp— You know what I mean."

"Hey," growled Laird, "what's the idea? Are you trying to cast—What's the word, Mark?"

"Aspersions?"

"—Cast aspersions on one of my swimmers? You watch out, Louie. If I hear you be—What's the word, Mark?"

"Besmirching her fair name?"

"—Besmirching her fair name I'll drown you in your own tank."

"And after that," said Vining, "we'll slap a suit on you for slander."

"Gentlemen! Gentlemen!" said Wambach. "Let's not have any more personalities, please. This is a swimming meet, not a lawsuit. Let's get to the point."

"We've made ours," said Vining with dignity. "We've shown that Iantha Delfoiros is a woman, and Mr. Connaught has stated, himself, that this is a woman's meet. Therefore, Miss Delfoiros is eligible. Q.E.D."

"Ahem," said Wambach. "I don't quite know—I never had a case like this to decide before."

Louis Connaught almost had tears in his eyes; at least he sounded as if he did. "Mr. Wambach, you can't let Herb do this to me. I'll be a laughingstock."

Laird snorted. "How about your beating me with your Mrs. Santalucia? I didn't get any sympathy from you when people laughed at me on account of that. And how much good did it do me to protest against her fingers?"

"But," wailed Connaught, "if he can enter this Miss Delfurrus, what's to stop somebody from entering a trained sea lion or something? Do you want to make competitive swimming into a circus?"

Laird grinned. "Go ahead, Louie. Nobody's stopping you from entering anything you like. How about it, Ogden? Is she a woman?"

"Well . . . really . . . oh, dear—"

"Please!" Iantha Delfoiros rolled her violet-blue eyes at the bewildered referee. "I should so like to swim in this nice pool with all these nice people!"

Wambach sighed. "All right, my dear, you shall!"

"Whoopee!" cried Laird, the cry being taken up by Vining, the members of the Knickerbocker Swimming Club, the other officials, and lastly the spectators. The noise in the enclosed space made sensitive eardrums wince.

"Wait a minute," yelped Connaught when the echoes had died. "Look here, page nineteen of the rules. 'Regulation Costume, Women: Suits must be of dark color, with skirt attached. Leg is to reach—' and so forth. Right here it says it. She can't swim the way she is, not in a sanctioned meet."

"That's true," said Wambach. "Let's see—"

Horowitz looked up from his little score-sheet-littered table. "Maybe one of the girls has a halter she could borrow," he suggested. "That would be *something*."

"Halter, phooey!" snapped Connaught. "This means a regular suit with legs and skirt, and everybody knows it."

"But she hasn't got any legs!" cried Laird. "How could she get into—"

"That's just the point! If she can't wear a suit with legs, and the rules say you gotta have legs, she can't wear the regulation suit, and she can't compete! I gotcha that time! Haha, I'm sneering!"

"I'm afraid not, Louie," said Vining, thumbing his own copy of the rulebook. He held it up to the light and read: " 'Note.—These rules are approximate, the idea being to bar costumers which are immodest, or will attract undue attention and comment. The referee shall have the power'— et cetera, et cetera. If we cut the legs out of a regular suit, and she pulled the rest of it on over her head, that would be modest enough for all practical purposes. Wouldn't it, Mr. Wambach?"

"Dear me—I don't know—I suppose it would."

Laird hissed to one of his pupils, "Hey, listen, Miss Havranek! You know where my suitcase is? Well, you get one of the extra suits out of it, and there's a pair of scissors in with the first-aid things. You fix that suit up so Iantha can wear it."

Connaught subsided. "I see now," he said bitterly, "why you guys wanted to finish with a 300-yard freestyle instead of a relay. If I'd'a' known what you were planning—and, you, Mark Vining, if I ever get in a jam, I'll go to jail before I hire you for a lawyer, so help me."

Mrs. Santalucia had been glowering at Iantha Delfoiros. Suddenly she turned to Connaught. "Thissa no fair. I swim against people. I no gotta swim against moimaids."

"Please, Maria, don't *you* desert me," wailed Connaught.

"I no swim tonight."

Connaught looked up appealingly to the balcony. Mr.

Santalucia and the little Santalucias, guessing what was happening, burst into a chorus of: "Go on, mamma! You show them, mamma!"

"Aw right. I swim one, maybe two races. If I see I no got a chance, I no swim no more."

"That's better, Maria. It wouldn't really count if she beat you any way." Connaught headed for the door, saying something about "telephone" on the way.

Despite the delays in starting the meet, nobody left the pool room through boredom; in fact the empty seats in the balcony were full by this time and people were standing up behind them. Word had got around the Hotel Creston that something was up.

By the time Louis Connaught returned, Laird and Vining were pulling the altered bathing suit on over Iantha's head. It didn't reach quite as far as they expected, having been designed for a slightly slimmer swimmer. Not that Iantha was fat. But her human part, if not exactly plump, was at least comfortably upholstered, so that no bones showed. Iantha squirmed around in the suit a good deal, and threw a laughing remark in Greek to Wambach, whose expression showed that he hoped it didn't mean what he suspected it did.

Laird said, "Now listen, Iantha, remember not to move till the gun goes off. And remember that you swim directly over the line on the bottom, not between two lines."

"Are they going to shoot a gun? Oh, I am afraid of shooting!"

"It's nothing to be afraid of; just blank cartridges. They don't hurt anybody. And it won't be so loud inside that cap."

"Herb," said Vining, "won't she lose time getting off,

not being able to make a flat dive like the others?"

"She will. But it won't matter. She can swim a mile in *four* minutes, without really trying."

Ritchey, the starter, announced the 50-yard freestyle. He called: "All right, everybody, line up." Iantha slithered off her chair and crawled over to the starting platform. The other girls were all standing with feet together, bodies bent forward at the hips, and arms pointing backward. Iantha got into a curious position of her own, with her tail under her and her weight resting on her hands and flukes.

"Hey! Protest!" shouted Connaught. "The rules say that all races, except backstrokes, are started with dives. What kind of a dive do you call that?"

"Oh, dear," said Wambach. "What—"

"That," said Vining urbanely, "is a mermaid dive. You couldn't expect her to stand upright on her tail."

"But that's just it!" cried Connaught. "First you enter a nonregulation swimmer. Then you put a nonregulation suit on her. Then you start her off with a nonregulation dive. Ain't there anything you guys do like other people?"

"But," said Vining, looking through the rule book, "it doesn't say—here it is. 'The start in all races shall be made with a dive.' But there's nothing in the rules about what kind of dive shall be used. And the dictionary defines a dive simply as a 'plunge into water.' So if you jump in feet first holding your nose, that's a dive for the purpose of the discussion. And in my years of watching swimming meets I've seen some funnier starting-dives than Miss Delfoiros's."

"I suppose he's right," said Wambach.

"O.K., O.K.," snarled Connaught. "But the next time I have a meet with you and Herb, I bring a lawyer along too, see?"

Ritchey's gun went off. Vining noticed that Iantha

flinched a little at the report, and perhaps was slowed down a trifle in getting off by it. The other girls' bodies shot out horizontally to smack the water loudly, but Iantha slipped in with the smooth, unhurried motion of a diving seal. Lacking the advantage of feet to push off with, she was several yards behind the other swimmers before she really got started. Mrs. Santalucia had taken her usual lead, foaming along with the slow strokes of her webbed hands.

Iantha didn't bother to come to the surface except at the turn, where she had been specifically ordered to come up so the judge of the turns wouldn't raise arguments as to whether she had touched the end, and at the finish. She hardly used her arms at all, except for an occasional flip of her trailing hands to steer her. The swift up-and-down flutter of the powerful tail-flukes sent her through the water like a torpedo, her wake appearing on the surface six or eight feet behind her. As she shot through the as yet unruffled waters at the far end of the pool on the first leg, Vining, who had gone around to the side to watch, noticed that she had the power of closing her nostrils tightly under water, like a seal or hippopotamus.

Mrs. Santalucia finished the race in the very creditable time of 29.8 seconds. But Iantha Delfoiros arrived, not merely first, but in the time of 8.0 seconds. At the finish she didn't reach up to touch the starting-platform, and then hoist herself out by her arms the way human swimmers do. She simply angled up sharply, left the water like a leaping trout, and came down with a moist smack on the concrete, almost bowling over a timekeeper. By the time the other contestants had completed the turn she was sitting on the platform with her tail curled under her. As the girls foamed laboriously down the final leg, she smiled dazzlingly at Vining, who had had to run to be in at the finish.

"That," she said, "was much fun, Mark. I am so glad you an 'Erbert put me in these races."

Mrs. Santalucia climbed out and walked over to Horowitz's table. That young man was staring in disbelief at the figures he had just written.

"Yes," he said, "that's what it says. Miss Iantha Delfoiros, 8.0; Mrs. Maria Santalucia, 29.8. Please don't drip on my score sheets, lady. Say, Wambach, isn't this a world's record or something?"

"My word!" said Wambach. "It's less than half the existing short-course record. Less than a third, maybe; I'd have to check it. Dear me. I'll have to take it up with the Committee. I don't know whether they'd allow it; I don't think they will, even though there isn't any specific rule against mermaids."

Vining spoke up. "I think we've complied with all the requirements to have records recognized, Mr. Wambach. Miss Delfoiros was entered in advance like all the others."

"Yes, yes, Mr. Vining, but don't you see, a record's a serious matter. No ordinary human being could ever come near a time like that."

"Unless he used an outboard motor," said Connaught. "If you allow contestants to use tail fins like Miss Delfurrus, you ought to let 'em use propellers. I don't see why these guys should be the only ones to be let bust rules all over the place, and then think up lawyer arguments why it's O.K. I'm gonna get me a lawyer, too."

"That's all right, Ogden," said Laird. "You take it up with the Committee, but we don't really care much about the records anyway, so long as we can lick Louie here." He smiled indulgently at Connaught, who sputtered with fury.

"I no swim," announced Mrs. Santalucia. "This is all crazy business. I no get a chance."

183

"Now, Maria," said Connaught, taking her aside, "just once more, won't you please? My reputation—" The rest of his words were drowned in the general reverberation of the pool room. But at the end of them the redoubtable female appeared to have given in to his entreaties.

The 100-yard freestyle started in much the same manner as the 50-yard. Iantha didn't flinch at the gun this time, and got off to a good start. She skimmed along just below the surface, raising a wake like a tuna-clipper. These waves confused the swimmer in the adjacent lane, who happened to be Miss Breitenfeld of the Creston Club. As a result, on her first return leg, Iantha met Miss Breitenfeld swimming athwart her—Iantha's—lane, and rammed the unfortunate girl amidships. Miss Breitenfeld went down without even a gurgle, spewing bubbles.

Connaught shrieked: "Foul! Foul!" though in the general uproar it sounded like "Wow, wow!" Several swimmers who weren't racing dove in to the rescue, and the race came to a stop in general confusion and pandemonium. When Miss Breitenfeld was hauled out it was found that she had merely had the wind knocked out of her and had swallowed considerable water.

Mark Vining, looking around for Iantha, found her holding on to the edge of the pool and shaking her head. Presently she crawled out, crying: "Is she 'urt? Is she 'urt? Oh, I am so sorree! I did not think there would be anybody in my lane, so I did not look ahead."

"See?" yelled Connaught. "See, Wambach? See what happens? They ain't satisfied to walk away with the races with their fish-woman. No, they gotta try to cripple my swimmers by butting their slats in. Herb," he went on nastily, "why dontcha get a pet swordfish? Then when you rammed one of my poor girls she'd be out of competition for good."

"Oh," said Iantha. "I did not mean . . . it was an accident!"

"Accident my foot!"

"But it was. Mr. Referee, I do not want to bump people. My 'ead 'urts, and my neck also. You think I try to break my neck on purpose?" Iantha's altered suit had crawled up under her armpits, but nobody noticed particularly.

"Sure it was an accident," bellowed Laird. "Anybody could see that. And, listen, if anybody was fouled it was Miss Delfoiros."

"Certainly," chimed in Vining. "She was in her own lane, and the other girl wasn't."

"Oh, dear me," said Wambach. "I suppose they're right again. This'll have to be reswum anyway. Does Miss Breitenfeld want to compete?"

Miss Breitenfeld didn't but the others lined up again. This time the race went off without untoward incident. Iantha again made a spectacular leaping finish, just as the other three swimmers were halfway down the second of their four legs.

When Mrs. Santalucia emerged this time, she said to Connaught: "I swim no more. That is final."

"Oh, but Maria—" It got him nowhere. Finally he said, "Will you swim in the races that she don't enter?"

"Is there any?"

"I think so. Hey, Horowitz, Miss Delfurrus ain't entered in the breaststroke, is she?"

Horowitz looked. "No, she isn't," he said.

"That something. Say, Herb, how come you didn't put your fish-woman in the breaststroke?"

Vining answered for Laird. "Look at your rules, Louie. 'The feet shall be drawn up simultaneously, the knees bent and open,' et cetera. The rules for backstroke and freestyle don't say anything about how the legs shall be used, but those for breaststroke do. So no legs, no breaststroke. We aren't giving you a chance to make any legitimate protests."

"Legitimate protests!" Connaught turned away, sputtering.

While the dives were being run off, Vining, watching, became aware of an ethereal melody. First he thought it was in his head. Then he was sure it was coming from one of the spectators. He finally located the source; it was Iantha Delfoiros, sitting in her wheel chair and singing softly. By leaning nearer he could make out the words:

> *"Die schonstte Jungfrau sitzet*
> *Dort ober wunderbar;*
> *Ihr goldenes Geschmeide blitzet;*
> *Sie kaemmt ihr goldenes Haar."*

Vining went over quietly. "Iantha," he said. "Pull your bathing suit down, and don't sing."

She complied, looking up at him with a giggle. "But that is a nice song! I learn it from a wrecked German sailor. It is about one of my people."

"I know, but it'll distract the judges. They have to watch the dives closely, and the place is too noisy as it is."

"Such a nice man you are, Mark, but so serious!" She giggled again.

Vining wondered at the subtle change in the mermaid's manner. Then a horrible thought struck him.

"Herb!" he whispered. "Didn't she say something last night about getting drunk on fresh water?"

Laird looked up. "Yes. She— The water in the pool's fresh! I never thought of that. Is she showing signs?"

"I think she is."

"Listen, Mark, what'll we do?"

"I don't know. She's entered in two more events, isn't she? backstroke and 300-yard freestyle?"

"Yes."

"Well, why not withdraw her from the backstroke, and give her a chance to sober up before the final event?"

"Can't. Even with all her firsts we aren't going to win by any big margin. Louie has the edge on us in the dives, and Mrs. Santalucia'll win the breaststroke. In the events Iantha's in, if she takes first and Louie's girls take second and third, that means five points for us but four for him, so we have an advantage of only one point. And her world's record times don't give us any more points."

"Guess we'll have to keep her in and take a chance," said Vining glumly.

Iantha's demeanor was sober enough in lining up for the backstroke. Again she lost a fraction of a second in getting started by not having feet to push off with. But once she got started, the contest was even more one-sided than the freestyle races had been. The human part of her body was practically out of water, skimming the surface like the front half of a speedboat. She made paddling motions with her arms, but that was merely for technical reasons; the power was all furnished by the flukes. She didn't jump out onto the starting-platform this time; for a flash Vining's heart almost stopped as the emerald-green bathing cap seemed about to crash into the tiles at the end of the pool. But Iantha had judged the distance to a fraction of an inch, and braked to a stop with her flukes just before striking.

The breaststroke was won easily by Mrs. Santalucia, though her slow plodding stroke was less spectacular than the butterfly of her competitors. The shrill cheers of the little Santalucias could be heard over the general hubbub. When the winner climbed out, she glowered at Iantha and said to Connaught: "Louie, if you ever put me in a meet wit' moimaids again, I no swim for you again, never. Now I go home." With which she marched off to the shower room.

Ritchey was just about to announce the final event, the 300-yard freestyle, when Connaught plucked his sleeve. "Jack," he said, "wait a second. One of my swimmers is gonna be delayed a coupla minutes." He went out a door.

Laird said to Vining: "Wonder what Louie's grinning about. He's got something nasty, I bet. He was phoning earlier, you remember."

"We'll soon see—What's that?" A hoarse bark wafted in from somewhere and rebounded from the walls.

Connaught reappeared carrying two buckets. Behind him was a little round man in three sweaters. Behind the little round man galumphed a glossy California sea lion. At the sight of the gently rippling, jade-green pool the animal barked joyously and skidded the water, swam swiftly about, and popped out onto the landing-platform, barking. The bark had a peculiarly nerve-racking effect in the echoing pool room.

Ogden Wambach seized two handfuls of his sleek gray hair and tugged. "Connaught!" he shouted. "What is that?"

"Oh, that's just one of my swimmers, Mr. Wambach."

"Hey, listen!" rumbled Laird. "We're going to protest this time. Miss Delfoiros is at least a woman, even if she's a kind of peculiar one. But you can't call *that* a woman."

Connaught grinned like Satan looking over a new shipment of sinners. "Didn't you just say to go ahead and enter a sea lion if I wanted to?"

"I don't remember saying—"

"Yes, Herbert," said Wambach, looking haggard. "You did say it. There didn't used to be any trouble in deciding whether a swimmer was a woman or not. But now that you've brought in Miss Delfoiros, there doesn't seem to be any place we can draw a line."

"But look here, Ogden, there is such a thing as going too far—"

"That's just what I said about you!" shrilled Connaught.

Wambach took a deep breath. "Let's not shout, please. Herbert, technically you may have an argument. But after we allowed Miss Delfoiros to enter, I think it would be only sporting to let Louis have his sea lion. Especially after you told him to get one if he could."

Vining spoke up. "Oh, we're always glad to do the sporting thing. But I'm afraid the sea lion wasn't entered at the beginning of the meet as is required by the rules. We don't want to catch hell from the Committee—"

"Oh, yes, she was," said Connaught. "See!" He pointed to one of Horowitz's sheets. "Her name's Alice Black, and there it is."

"But," protested Vining, "I thought *that* was Alice Black." He pointed to a slim dark girl in a bathing suit who was sitting on a window ledge.

"It is," grinned Connaught. "It's just a coincidence that they both got the same name."

"You don't expect us to believe *that?*"

"I don't care whether you believe or not. It's so. Ain't the sea lion's name Alice Black?" He turned to the little fat man, who nodded.

"Let it pass," moaned Wambach. "We can't take time off to get this animal's birth certificate."

"Well, then," said Vining, "how about the regulation suit? Maybe you'd like to try to put a suit on your sea lion?"

"Don't have to. She's got one already. It grows on her. Yah, yah, yah, gotcha that time."

"I suppose," said Wambach, "that you *could* consider a natural sealskin pelt as equivalent to a bathing suit."

"Sure you could. That's the pernt. Anyway the idea of suits is to be modest, and nobody gives a care about a sea lion's modesty."

Vining made a final point. "You refer to the animal as 'her,' but how do we know it's a female? Even Mr. Wambach wouldn't let you enter a male sea lion in a women's meet."

Wambach spoke: "How do you tell on a sea lion?"

Connaught looked at the little fat man. "Well, maybe we had better not go into that here. How would it be if I put up a ten-dollar bond that Alice is a female, and you checked on her sex later?"

"That seems fair," said Wambach.

Vining and Laird looked at each other. "Shall we let 'em get away with that, Mark?" asked the latter.

Vining rocked on his heels for a few seconds. Then he said, "I think we might as well. Can I see you outside a minute, Herb? You people don't mind holding up the race a couple of minutes more, do you? We'll be right back."

Connaught started to protest about further delay, but thought better of it. Laird presently reappeared looking unwontedly cheerful.

" 'Erbert!" said Iantha.

"Yes?" he put his head down.

"I'm afraid—"

"You're afraid Alice might bite you in the water? Well, I wouldn't want that—"

"Oh, no, not afraid that way. Alice, poof! If she gets

190

nasty I give her one with the tail. But I am afraid she can swim faster than me."

"Listen, Iantha, you just go ahead and swim the best you can. Twelve legs, remember. And don't be surprised, no matter what happens."

"What you two saying?" asked Connaught suspiciously.

"None of your business, Louie. Whatcha got in that pail? *Fish?* I see how you're going to work this. Wanta give up and concede the I meet now?"

Connaught merely snorted.

The only competitors in the 300-yard freestyle race were Iantha Delfoiros and the sea lion, allegedly named Alice. The normal members of both clubs declared that nothing would induce them to get into the pool with the animal. Not even the importance of collecting a third-place point would move them.

Iantha got into her usual starting position. Beside her the little round man maneuvered Alice, holding her by an improvised leash made of a length of rope. At the far end, Connaught had placed himself and one of the buckets.

Ritchey fired his gun; the little man slipped the leash and said: "Go get 'em, Alice!" Connaught took a fish out of his bucket and waved it. But Alice, frightened by the shot, set up a furious barking and stayed where she was. Not till Iantha had almost reached the far end of the pool did Alice sight the fish at the other end. Then she slid off and shot down the water like a streak. Those who have seen sea lions merely loafing about a pool in a zoo or aquarium have no conception of how fast they can go when they try. Fast as the mermaid was, the sea lion was faster. She made two bucking jumps out of water before she arrived and oozed out onto the concrete. One gulp and the fish had vanished.

Alice spotted the bucket and tried to get her head into it. Connaught fended her off as best he could with his feet. At the starting end, the little round man had taken a fish out of the other bucket and was waving it, calling: "Here, Alice!" Alice didn't get the idea until Iantha had finished her second leg. Then she went like the proverbial bat from hell.

The same trouble occurred at the starting end of the pool; Alice didn't see why she should swim twenty-five yards for a fish when there were plenty of them a few feet away. The result was that at the halfway mark Iantha was two legs ahead. But then Alice, who was no dope as sea lions go, caught on. She caught up with and passed Iantha in the middle of her eighth leg, droozling out of the water at each end long enough to gulp a fish and then speeding down to the other end. In the middle of the tenth leg she was ten yards ahead of the mermaid.

At that point Mark Vining appeared through the door, running. In each hand he held a bowl of goldfish by the edge. Behind him came Miss Havranek and Miss Tufts, also of the Knickerbockers, both similarly burdened. The guests of the Hotel Creston had been mildly curious when a dark, severe-looking young man and two girls in bathing suits had dashed into the lobby and made off with the six bowls. But they had been too well bred to inquire directly about the rape of the goldfish.

Vining ran down the side of the pool to a point near the far end. There he extended his arms and inverted the bowls. Water and fish cascaded into the pool. Miss Havranek and Miss Tufts did likewise at other points along the edge of the pool.

Results were immediate. The bowls had been large, and each had contained about six or eight fair-sized goldfish. The forty-odd bright-colored fish, terrified by their rough handling, darted hither and thither about the pool, or at least went as fast as their inefficient build would permit them. Alice, in the middle of her ninth leg, angled off sharply. Nobody saw her snatch the fish; one second it was there, and the next it wasn't. Alice doubled with a swirl of flippers and shot diagonally across the pool. Another fish vanished. Forgotten were her master and Louis Connaught and their buckets. This was much more fun. Meanwhile, Iantha finished her race, narrowly avoiding a collision with the sea lion on her last leg.

Connaught hurled the fish he was holding as far as he could. Alice snapped it up and went on hunting. Connaught ran toward the starting-platform, yelling: "Foul! Foul! Protest! Protest! Foul! Foul!"

He arrived to find the timekeepers comparing watches on Iantha's swim, Laird and Vining doing a kind of war dance, and Ogden Wambach looking like the March Hare on the twenty-eighth of February. "Stop!" cried the referee. "Stop, Louie! If you shout like that you'll drive me mad! I'm almost mad now! I know what you're going to say."

"Well . . . well . . . why don't you do something, then? Why don't you tell these crooks where to head in? Why don't you have 'em expelled from the Union? Why don't you—"

"Relax, Louie," said Vining. "We haven't done anything illegal."

"*What?* Why, you dirty—"

"Easy, easy." Vining looked speculatively at his fist. The little man followed his glance and quieted somewhat. "There's nothing in the rules about putting fish into a pool. Intelligent swimmers, like Miss Delfoiros, know enough to ignore them when they're swimming a race."

"But . . . what . . . why you—"

Vining walked off, leaving the two coaches and the referee to fight it out. He looked for Iantha. She was sitting on the edge of the pool, paddling in the water with her flukes. Beside her were four feebly flopping goldfish laid out in a row on the tiles. As he approached, she picked one up and put the front end of it in her mouth. There was a flash of pearly teeth and a spasmodic flutter of the fish's tail, and the front half of the fish was gone. The other half followed immediately.

At that instant Alice spotted the three remaining fish. The sea lion had cleaned out the pool, and was now slithering around on the concrete, barking and looking for more prey. She galumphed past Vining toward the mermaid.

Iantha saw her coming. The mermaid hoisted her tail out of water, pivoted where she sat, swung the tail up in a curve, brought the flukes down on the sea lion's head with a loud *spat*. Vining, who was twenty feet off, could have sworn he felt the wind of the blow.

Alice gave a squawk of pain and astonishment and slithered away, shaking her head. She darted past Vining again, and for reasons best known to herself hobbled over to the center of the argument and bit Ogden Wambach in the leg. The referee screeched and climbed up on Horowitz's table.

"Hey," said the scorekeeper. "You're scattering my papers!"

"I still say they're publicity-hunting crooks!" yelled Connaught, waving his copy of the rulebook at Wambach.

"Bunk!" bellowed Laird. "He's just sore because we can think up more stunts than he can. He started it, with his web-fingered woman."

"I'm going mad!" screamed Wambach. "You hear? Mad,

mad, mad! One more word out of either of you and I'll have you suspended from the Union!"

"*Ow, ow, ow!*" barked Alice.

Iantha had finished her fish. She started to pull the bathing suit down again; changed her mind, pulled it off over her head, rolled it up, and threw it across the pool. Halfway across it unfolded and floated down onto the water. The mermaid then cleared her throat, took a deep breath, and, in a clear singing soprano, launched into the heart-wrenching strains of:

> *"Rheingold!*
> *Reines Gold,*
> *Wie lauter und hell*
> *Leuchtest hold du uns!*
> *Urn dich, du klares—"*

"*Iantha!*"

"What is it, Markee?" she giggled.

"I said, it's getting time to go home!"

"Oh, but I do not want to go home. I am having much fun.

> *"Nun wir klagen!*
> *Gebt uns das Gold—"*

"No, really, Iantha, we've got to go." He laid a hand on her shoulder. The touch made his blood tingle. At the same time it was plain that the remains of Iantha's carefully husbanded sobriety had gone where the woodbine twineth. The last race in fresh water had been like three oversized Manhattans. Through Vining's head ran an absurd but apt paraphrase of an old song:

*"What shall we do with a drunken mermaid
At three o'clock in the morning?"*

"Oh, Markee, always you are so serious when people are
'aving fun. But if you say 'please' I will come."

"Very well, please come. Here, put your arm around my
neck, and I'll carry you to your chair."

Such, indeed was Mark Vining's intention. He got one
hand around her waist and another under her tail. Then he
tried to straighten up. He had forgotten that Iantha's tail
was a good deal heavier than it looked. In fact, that long
and powerful structure of bone, muscle, and cartilage ran
the mermaid's total weight up to the surprising figure of
over two hundred and fifty pounds. The result of his attempt was to send himself and his burden headlong into the
pool. To the spectators it looked as though he picked Iantha
up and then deliberately dived in with her.

He came up and shook the water out of his head. Iantha
popped up in front of him.

"So!" she gurgled. "You are 'aving fun with Iantha! I
think you are serious, but you want to play games! All right,
I show you! She brought her palm down smartly, filling
Vining's mouth and nose with water. He struck out blindly
for the edge of the pool. He was a powerful swimmer, but
his street clothes hampered him. Another splash cascaded
over his luckless head. He got his eyes clear in time to see
Iantha's head go down and her flukes up.

"Markeeee!" The voice was behind him. He turned, and
saw Iantha holding a large black block of soft rubber. This
object was a plaything for users of the Hotel Creston's pool,
and it had been left lying on the bottom during the meet.

"Catch!" cried Iantha gaily, and let drive. The block
took Vining neatly between the eyes.

The next thing he knew he was lying on the wet concrete. He sat up and sneezed. His head seemed to be full of ammonia. Louis Connaught put away the smelling-salts bottle, and Laird shoved a glass containing a snort of whiskey at him. Beside him was Iantha, sitting on her curled-up tail. She was actually crying.

"Oh, Markee, you are not dead? You are all right? Oh, I am so sorry! I did not mean to 'it you."

"I'm all right, I guess," he said thickly. "Just an accident. Don't worry."

"Oh, I am so glad!" She grabbed his neck and gave it a hug that made its vertebrae creak alarmingly.

"Now," he said, "if I could dry out my clothes. Louie, could you . . . uh—"

"Sure," said Connaught, helping him up. "We'll put your clothes on the radiator in the men's shower room, and I can lend you a pair of pants and a sweatshirt while they're drying."

When Vining came out in his borrowed garments, he had to push his way through the throng that crowded the starting end of the pool room. He was relieved to note that Alice had disappeared. In the crowd, Iantha in her wheel chair was holding court. In front of her stood a large man in a dinner jacket and a black coat, with his back to the pool.

"Permit me," he was saying. "I am Joseph Clement. Under my management nothing you wished in the way of a dramatic or musical career would be beyond you. I heard you sing, and I know that with but little training even the doors of the Metropolitan would fly open at your approach."

"No, Mr. Clement. It would be nice, but tomorrow I 'ave to leave for 'ome." She giggled.

197

"But my dear Miss Delfoiros—where is your home, if I may presume to ask?"

"Cyprus."

"Cyprus? Hm-m-m—let's see, where's that?"

"You do not know where Cyprus is? You are not a nice man. I do not like you. Go away."

"Oh, but my dear, dear Miss Del—"

"Go away I said. Scram."

"But—"

Iantha's tail came up and lashed out, catching the cloaked man in the solar plexus.

Little Miss Havranek looked at her teammate, Miss Tufts, as she prepared to make her third rescue of the evening. "Poisonally," she said, "I am getting sick of pulling dopes out of this pool."

The sky was just turning gray the next morning when Laird drove his huge old town car out into the driveway of his house in the Bronx. Although he always drove himself, he couldn't resist the dirt-cheap prices at which second-hand town cars can be obtained. Now the car had the detachable top over the driver's seat in place, with good reason; the wind was driving a heavy rain almost horizontally.

He got out and helped Vining carry Iantha into the car. Vining got in the back with the mermaid. He spoke into the voice tube: "Jones Beach, Chauncey."

"Aye, aye, sir," came the reply. "Listen, Mark, you sure we remembered everything?"

"I made a list and checked it." He paused. "I could have done with some more sleep last night. Are you sure you won't fall asleep at the wheel?"

"Listen, Mark, with all the coffee I got sloshing around

in me, I won't get to sleep for a week."

"We certainly picked a nice time to leave."

"I know we did. In a coupla hours the place'll be covered six deep with reporters. If it weren't for the weather, they might be arriving now. When they do, they'll find the horse has stolen the stable door—that isn't what I mean, but you get the idea. Listen, you better pull down some of those curtains until we get out on Long Island."

"Righto, Herb."

Iantha spoke up in a small voice. "Was I very bad last night when I was drunk, Mark?"

"Not very. At least, not worse than I'd be if I went swimming in a tank of sherry."

"I am so sorry—always I try to be nice, but the fresh water gets me out of my head. And that poor Mr. Clement, that I pushed into the water—"

"Oh, he's used to temperamental people. That's his business. But I don't know that it was such a good idea on the way home to stick your tail out of the car and biff that cop under the chin with it."

She giggled. "But he looked so surprised!"

"I'll say he did! But a surprised cop is sometimes a tough customer."

"Will that make trouble for you?"

"I don't think so. If he's a wise cop, he won't report it at all. You know how the report would read: 'Attacked by mermaid at corner Broadway and Ninety-eighth Street, 11:45 P.M.' And *where* did you learn the unexpurgated version of 'Barnacle Bill the Sailor'?"

"Greek sponge diver I met in Florida told me. 'E is a friend of us mer-folk, and he taught me my first English. 'E used to joke about my Cypriot accent when we talked

199

Greek. It is a pretty song, is it not?"

"I don't think 'pretty' is exactly the word I'd use."

" 'Oo won the meet? I never die 'ear."

"Oh, Louie and Herb talked it over, and decided they'd both get so much publicity out of it that it didn't much matter. They're leaving it up to the A.A.U., who will get a first-class headache. For instance, we'll claim we didn't foul Alice, because Louie had already disqualified her by his calling and fish waving. You see, that's coaching, and coaching a competitor during an event is illegal. But, look here, Iantha, why do you have to leave so abruptly?"

She shrugged. "My business with 'Erbert is over, and I promised to get back to Cyprus before my sister's baby was born."

"You don't lay eggs? But of course you don't. Didn't I just prove last night you were mammals?"

"Markee, what an idea! Anyway, I do not want to stay around. I like you and I like 'Erbert, but I do not like living on land. You just imagine living in water for yourself, and you get an idea. And if stay, the newspapers come, and soon all New York knows about me. We mer-folk do not believe in letting the land men know about us."

"Why?"

"We used to be friends with them sometimes, and always it made trouble. And now they 'ave guns and go around shooting things a mile away, to collect them, my great-uncle was shot in the tail last year by some aviator man who thought he was a porpoise or something. We don't like being collected. So when we see a boat or an airplane coming, we duck down and swim away quick."

"I suppose," said Vining slowly, "that that's why there were plenty of reports of mer-folks up to a few centuries ago, and then they stopped, so that now people don't believe they exist."

"Yes. We are smart, and we can see as far as the land men can. So you do not catch us very often. That is why this business with 'Erbert, to buy ten thousand caps for the mer-folk, 'as to be secret. Not even his company will know about it. But they will not care if they get their money. And we shall not 'ave to sit on rocks drying our 'air so much. Maybe later we can arrange to buy some good knives and spears the same way. They would be better than the shell things we use now."

"I suppose you get all these old coins out of wrecks?"

"Yes. I know of one just off . . . no, I must not tell you. If the land men know about a wreck, they come with divers. Of course, the very deep ones we do not care about, because we cannot dive down that far. We 'ave to come up for air, like a whale."

"How did Herb happen to sack you in on that swimming meet?"

"Oh, I promised him when he asked—when I did not know 'ow much what-you-call-it fuss there would be. When I found out he would not let me go back on my promise. I think he 'as a conscience about that, and that is why he gave me that nice fish spear."

"Do you ever expect to get back this way?"

"No, I do not think so. We 'ad a committee to see about the caps, and they chose me to represent them. But now that is arranged, and there is no more reason for me going out on land again."

He was silent for a while. Then he burst out: "Iantha, I just can't believe that you're starting off this morning to swim the Atlantic, and I'll never see you again."

She patted his hand. "Maybe you cannot, but that is so. Remember, friendships between my folks and yours always make people un'appy. I shall remember you a long time, but that is all there will ever be to it."

He growled something in his throat, looking straight in front of him.

She said: "Mark, you know I like you, and I think you like me. 'Erbert 'as a moving-picture machine in his house, and he showed me some pictures of 'ow the land folk live.

"These pictures showed a custom of the people in this country, when they like each other. It is called—kissing, I think. I should like to learn that custom."

"Huh? You mean *me?*" To a man of Vining's temperament, the shock was almost physically painful. But her arms were already sliding around his neck. Presently twenty firecrackers, six Roman candles, and a skyrocket seemed to go off inside him.

"Here we are, folks," called Laird. Getting no response, he repeated the statement more loudly. A faint and unenthusiastic "Yeah" came through the voice tube.

Jones Beach was bleak under the lowering March clouds. The wind drove the rain against the car windows.

They drove down the beach road a way, till the tall tower was lost in the rain. Nobody was in sight.

The men carried Iantha down onto the beach and brought the things she was taking. These consisted of a boxful of cans of sardines, with a strap to go over the shoulders; a similar but smaller container with her personal belongings; and the fish spear, with which she might be able to pick up lunch on the way.

Iantha peeled off her land-woman's clothes and pulled on the emerald bathing cap. Vining, watching her with the skirt of his overcoat whipping about his legs, felt as if his heart were running out of his damp shoes onto the sand.

They shook hands, and Iantha kissed them both. She squirmed down the sand and into the water. Then she was gone. Vining thought he saw her wave back from the crest of a wave, but in that visibility he couldn't be sure.

They walked back to the car, squinting against the drops. Laird said: "Listen, Mark, you look as if you'd just taken a right to the button."

Vining merely grunted. He had got in front with Laird, and was drying his glasses with his handkerchief, as if that were an important and delicate operation.

"Don't tell me you're hooked?"

"So what?"

"Well, I suppose you know there's absolutely nothing you can do about it."

"Herb!" Vining snapped angrily. "Do you have to point out the obvious?"

Laird, sympathizing with his friend's feelings, did not take offense. After they had driven awhile, Vining spoke on his own initiative. "That," he said, "is the only woman I've ever known that made me feel at ease. I could talk to her."

Later, he said, "I never felt so mixed up in my life. I doubt whether anybody else ever did, either. Maybe I ought to feel relieved it's over. But I don't."

Pause. Then: "You'll drop me in Manhattan on your way back, won't you?"

"Sure, anywhere you say. Your apartment?"

"Anywhere near Times Square will do. There's a bar there I like."

So, thought Laird, at least the normal male's instincts were functioning correctly in the crisis.

When he let Vining out on Forty-sixth Street, the young

203

lawyer walked off into the rain whistling. The whistle surprised Laird. Then he recognized the tune as one that was written for one of Kipling's poems. But he couldn't, at the moment, think which one.

Two Yards of Dragon

Eudoric Damberton, Esquire, rode home from his courting of Lusina, daughter of the enchanter Baldonius, with a face as long as an olifant's nose. Eudoric's sire, Sir Dambert, said:

"Well, how fared thy suit, boy? Ill, eh?"

"I—" began Eudoric.

"I told you 'twas an asinine notion, eh? Was I not right? When Baron Emmerhard has more daughters than he can count, any one of which would fetch a pretty parcel of land with her, eh? Well, why answerest not?"

"I—" said Eudoric.

"Come on, lad, speak up!"

"How can he, when ye talk all the time?" said Eudoric's mother, the Lady Aniset.

"Oh," said Sir Dambert. "Your pardon, son. Moreover and furthermore, as I've told you, an' ye were Emmerhard's son-in-law, he'd use his influence to get you your spurs. Here ye be, a strapping youth of three-and-twenty, not yet knighted. 'Tis a disgrace to our lineage."

"There are no wars toward, to afford opportunity for deeds of knightly dought," said Eudoric.

"Aye, 'tis true. Certes, we all hail the blessings of peace, which the wise governance of our sovran emperor hath given us for lo these thirteen years. Howsomever, to perform a knightly deed, our young men must needs waylay banditti, disperse rioters, and do suchlike fribbling feats."

As Sir Dambert paused, Eudoric interjected, "Sir, that problem now seems on its way to solution."

"How meanest thou?"

"If you'll but hear me, Father! Doctor Baldonius has set me a task, ere he'll bestow Lusina on me, which should fit me for knighthood in any jurisdiction."

"And that is?"

"He's fain to have two square yards of dragon hide. Says he needs 'em for his magical mummeries."

"But there have been no dragons in these parts for a century or more!"

"True; but, quoth Baldonius, the monstrous reptiles still abound far to eastward, in the lands of Pathenia and Pantorozia. Forsooth, he's given me a letter of introduction to his colleague, Doctor Raspiudus, in Pathenia."

"What?" cried the Lady Aniset. "Thou, to set forth on some year-long journey to parts unknown, where, 'tis said, men hop on a single leg or have faces in their bellies? I'll not have it! Besides, Baldonius may be privy wizard to Baron Emmerhard, but 'tis not to be denied that he is of no gentle blood."

"Well," said Eudoric, "so who was gentle when the Divine Pair created the world?"

"Our forebears were, I'm sure, whate'er were the case with those of the learned Doctor Baldonius. You young people are always full of idealistic notions. Belike thou'lt fall into heretical delusions, for I hear that the Easterlings have not the true religion. They falsely believe that God is one, instead of two as we truly understand."

"Let's not wander into the mazes of theology," said Sir Dambert, his chin in his fist. "To be sure, the paynim Southrons believe that God is three, an even more pernicious notion than that of the Easterlings."

"An' I meet God in my travels, I'll ask him the truth o't," said Eudoric.

"Be not sacrilegious, thou impertinent whelp! Still and all and notwithstanding, Doctor Baldonius were a man of influence to have in the family, be his origin never so humble. Methinks I could prevail upon him to utter spells to cause my crops, my neat, and my villeins to thrive, whilst casting poxes and murrains on my enemies. Like that caitiff Rainmar, eh? What of the bad seasons we've had? The God and Goddess know we need all the supernatural help we can get to keep us from penury. Else we may some fine day awaken to find that we've lost the holding to some greasy tradesman with a purchased title, with pen for lance and tally sheet for shield."

"Then I have your leave, sire?" cried Eudoric, a broad grin splitting his square, bronzed young face.

The Lady Aniset still objected, and the argument raged for another hour. Eudoric pointed out that it was not as if he were an only child, having two younger brothers and a sister. In the end, Sir Dambert and his lady agreed to Eudoric's quest, provided he return in time to help with the harvest, and take a manservant of their choice.

"Whom have you in mind?" asked Eudoric.

"I fancy Jillo the trainer," said Sir Dambert.

Eudoric groaned. "That old mossback, ever canting and haranguing me on the duties and dignities of my station?"

"He's but a decade older than ye," said Sir Dambert. "Moreover and furthermore, ye'll need an older man, with a sense of order and propriety, to keep you on the path of a gentleman. Class loyalty above all, my boy! Young men are wont to swallow every new idea that flits past, like a frog snapping at flies. Betimes they find they've engulfed a wasp, to their scathe and dolor."

"He's an awkward wight, Father, and not overbrained."

"Aye, but he's honest and true, no small virtues in our

degenerate days. In my sire's time there was none of this newfangled saying the courteous 'ye' and 'you' even to mere churls and scullions. 'Twas always 'thou' and 'thee.' "

"How you do go on, Dambert dear," said the Lady Aniset.

"Aye, I ramble. 'Tis the penalty of age. At least, Eudoric, the faithful Jillo knows horses and will keep your beasts in prime fettle." Sir Dambert smiled. "Moreover and furthermore, if I know Jillo Godmarson, he'll be glad to get away from his nagging wife for a spell."

So Eudoric and Jillo set forth to eastward, from the knight's holding of Arduen, in the barony of Zurgau, in the county of Treveria, in the kingdom of Locania, in the New Napolitanian Empire. Eudoric—of medium height, powerful build, dark, with square-jawed but otherwise undistinguished features—rode his palfrey and led his mighty destrier Morgrim. The lank, lean Jillo bestrode another palfrey and led a sumpter mule. Morgrim was piled with Eudoric's panoply of plate, carefully nested into a compact bundle and lashed down under a canvas cover. The mule bore the rest of their supplies.

For a fortnight they wended uneventfully through the duchies and counties of the Empire. When they reached lands where they could no longer understand the local dialects, they made shift with Helladic, the tongue of the Old Napolitanian Empire, which lettered men spoke everywhere.

They stopped at inns where inns were to be had. For the first fortnight, Eudoric was too preoccupied with dreams of his beloved Lusina to notice the tavern wenches. After that, his urges began to fever him, and he bedded one in Zerbstat, to their mutual satisfaction. Thereafter, however, he forebore, not as a matter of sexual morals but as a matter of thrift.

When benighted on the road, they slept under the stars—or, as befell them on the marches of Avaria, under a rain-dripping canopy of clouds. As they bedded down in the wet, Eudoric asked his companion:

"Jillo, why did you not remind me to bring a tent?"

Jillo sneezed. "Why, sir, come rain, come snow, I never thought that so sturdy a springald as ye be would ever need one. The heroes in the romances never travel with tents."

"To the nethermost hell with heroes of the romances! They go clattering around on their destriers for a thousand cantos. Weather is ever fine. Food, shelter, and a change of clothing appear, as by magic, whenever desired. Their armor never rusts. They suffer no tisics and fluxes. They pick up no fleas or lice at the inns. They're never swindled by merchants, for none does aught so vulgar as buying and selling."

"If ye'll pardon me, sir," said Jillo, "that were no knightly way to speak. It becomes not your station."

"Well, to the nethermost hells with my station, too! Wherever these paladins go, they find damsels in distress to rescue, or have other agreeable, thrilling and sanitary adventures. What adventures have we had? The time we fled from robbers in the Turonian Forest. The time I fished you out of the Albis half drowned. The time we ran out of food in the Asciburgi Mountains and had to plod fodderless over those hair-raising peaks for three days on empty stomachs."

"The Divine Pair do but seek to try the mettle of a valorous aspirant knight, sir. Ye should welcome these petty adversities as a chance to prove your manhood."

Eudoric made a rude noise with his mouth. "That for my manhood! Right now, I'd fainer have a stout roof overhead, a warm fire before me, and a hot repast in my belly. An' ever I go on such a silly jaunt again, I'll find one of those versemongers—like that troubadour, Landwin of Kromnitch, that visited us yesteryear—and drag him along, to show him how little real adventures are like those of the romances. And if he fall into the Albis, he may drown, for all of me. Were it not for my darling Lusina—"

Eudoric lapsed into gloomy silence, punctuated by sneezes.

They plodded on until they came to the village of Liptai, on the border of Pathenia. After the border guards had questioned and passed them, they walked their animals down the deep mud of the main street. Most of the slatternly houses were of logs or of crudely hewn planks, innocent of paint.

"Heaven above!" said Jillo. "Look at that, sir!"

"That" was a gigantic snail shell, converted into a small house.

"Knew you not of the giant snails of Pathenia?" asked Eudoric. "I've read of them in Doctor Baldonius' encyclopedia. When full grown, they—or rather their shells—are ofttimes used for dwellings in this land."

Jillo shook his head. " 'Twere better had ye spent more of your time on your knightly exercises and less on reading. Your sire hath never learnt his letters, yet he doth his duties well enow."

"Times change, Jillo. I may not clang rhymes so featly as Doctor Baldonius, or that ass Landwin of Kromnitch; but in these days a stroke of the pen were oft more fell than the slash of a sword. Here's a hostelry that looks not too slummocky. Do you dismount and inquire within as to their tallage."

"Why, sir?"

"Because I am fain to know, ere we put our necks in the

noose! Go ahead. An' I go in, they'll double the scot at sight of me."

When Jillo came out and quote prices, Eudoric said, "Too dear. We'll try the other."

"But, Master! Mean ye to put us in some flea-bitten hovel, like that which we suffered in Bitava?"

"Aye. Didst not prate to me on the virtues of petty adversity in strengthening one's knightly mettle?"

" 'Tis not that, sir."

"What, then?"

"Why, when better quarters are to be had, to make do with the worse were an insult to your rank and station. No gentleman—"

"Ah, here we are!" said Eudoric. "Suitably squalid, too! You see, good Jillo, I did but yester'een count our money, and lo! more than half is gone, and our journey not yet half completed."

"But, noble Master, no man of knightly mettle would so debase himself as to tally his silver, like some base-born commercial—"

"Then I must needs lack true knightly mettle. Here we be!"

For a dozen leagues beyond Liptai rose the great, dense Motolian Forest. Beyond the forest lay the provincial capital of Velitchovo. Beyond Velitchovo, the forest thinned out *gradatim* to the great grassy plains of Pathenia. Beyond Pathenia, Eudoric had been told, stretched the boundless deserts of Pantorozia, over which a man might ride for months without seeing a city.

Yes, the innkeeper told them, there were plenty of dragons in the Motolian Forest. "But fear them not," said Kasmar in broken Helladic. "From being hunted, they have become wary and even timid. An' ye stick to the road and move yarely, they'll pester you not unless ye surprise or corner one."

"Have any dragons been devouring maidens fair lately?" asked Eudoric.

Kasmar laughed. "Nay, good Master. What were maidens fair doing, traipsing round the woods to stir up the beasties? Leave them be, I say, and they'll do the same by you."

A cautious instinct warned Eudoric not to speak of his quest. After he and Jillo had rested and had renewed their equipment, they set out, two days later, into the Motolian Forest. They rode for a league along the Velitchovo road. Then Eudoric, accoutered in full plate and riding Morgrim, led his companion off the road into the woods to southward. They threaded their way among the trees, ducking branches, in a wide sweep around. Steering by the sun, Eudoric brought them back to the road near Liptai.

The next day they did the same, except that their circuit was to the north of the highway.

After three more days of this exploration, Jillo became restless. "Good Master, what do we, circling round and about so bootlessly? The dragons dwell farther east, away from the haunts of men, they say."

"Having once been lost in the woods," said Eudoric, "I would not repeat the experience. Therefore do we scout our field of action, like a general scouting a future battlefield."

" 'Tis an arid business," said Jillo with a shrug. "But then, ye were always one to see further into a millstone than most."

At last, having thoroughly committed the byways of the nearer forest to memory, Eudoric led Jillo farther east. After casting about, they came at last upon the unmistakable tracks of a dragon. The animal had beaten a path through the brush, along which they could ride almost as well as on the road. When they had followed this track for above an hour, Eudoric became aware of a strong, musky stench.

"My lance, Jillo!" said Eudoric, trying to keep his voice from rising with nervousness.

The next bend in the path brought them into full view of the dragon, a thirty-footer facing them on the trail.

"Ha!" said Eudoric. "Meseems 'tis a mere cockadrill, albeit longer of neck and of limb than those that dwell in the rivers of Agisymba—if the pictures in Doctor Baldonius' books lie not. Have at thee, vile worm!"

Eudoric couched his lance and put spurs to Morgrim. The destrier bounded forward.

The dragon raised its head and peered this way and that, as if it could not see well. As the hoofbeats drew nearer, the dragon opened its jaws and uttered a loud, hoarse, groaning bellow.

At that, Morgrim checked his rush with stiffened forelegs, spun ponderously on his haunches, and veered off the trail into the woods. Jillo's palfrey bolted likewise, but in another direction. The dragon set out after Eudoric at a shambling trot.

Eudoric had not gone fifty yards when Morgrim passed close aboard a massive old oak, a thick limb of which jutted into their path. The horse ducked beneath the bough. The branch caught Eudoric across the breastplate, flipped him backward over the high cantle of his saddle, and swept him to earth with a great clatter.

Half stunned, he saw the dragon trot closer and closer— and then lumber past him, almost within arm's length, and disappear on the trail of the fleeing horse. The next that Eudoric knew, Jillo was bending over him, crying:

213

"Alas, my poor heroic Master! Be any bones broke, sir?"

"All of them, methinks," groaned Eudoric. "What's be-fallen Morgrim?"

"That I know not. And look at this dreadful dent in your beauteous cuirass!"

"Help me out of the thing. The dent pokes most sorely into my ribs. The misadventures I suffer for my dear Lusina!"

"We must get your breastplate to a smith to have it ham-mered out and filed smooth again."

"Fiends take the smiths! They'd charge half the cost of a new one. I'll fix it myself, if I can find a flat rock to set it on and a big stone wherewith to pound it."

"Well, sir," said Jillo, "ye were always a good man of your hands. But the mar will show, and that were not suit-able for one of your quality."

"Thou mayst take my quality and stuff it!" cried Eudoric. "Canst speak of nought else? Help me up, pray." He got slowly to his feet, wincing, and limped a few steps.

"At least," he said, "nought seems fractured. But I mis-doubt I can walk back to Liptai."

"Oh, sir, that were not to be thought of! Me allow you to wend afoot whilst I ride? Fiends take the thought!" Jillo un-hitched the palfrey from the tree to which he had tethered it and led it to Eudoric.

"I accept your courtesy, good Jillo, only because I must. To plod the distance afoot were but a condign punishment for so bungling my charge. Give me a boost, will you?" Eudoric grunted as Jillo helped him into the saddle.

"Tell me, sir," said Jillo, "why did the beast ramp on past you without stopping to devour you as ye lay helpless? Was't that Morgrim promised a more bounteous repast? Or that the monster feared that your plate would give him a disorder of the bowels?"

"Meseems 'twas neither. Marked you how gray and milky appeared its eyes? According to Doctor Baldonius' book, dragons shed their skins from time to time, like serpents. This one neared the time of its skin change, wherefore the skin over its eyeballs had become thickened and opaque, like glass of poor quality. Therefore it could not plainly discern objects lying still, and pursued only those that moved."

They got back to Liptai after dark. Both were barely able to stagger, Eudoric from his sprains and bruises and Jillo footsore from the unaccustomed three-league hike.

Two days later, when they had recovered, they set out on the two palfreys to hunt for Morgrim. "For," Eudoric said, "that nag is worth more in solid money than all the rest of my possessions together."

Eudoric rode unarmored save for a shirt of light mesh mail, since the palfrey could not carry the extra weight of the plate all day at a brisk pace. He bore his lance and sword, however, in case they should again encounter a dragon.

They found the site of the previous encounter, but no sign either of the dragon or of the destrier. Eudoric and Jillo tracked the horse by its prints in the soft mold for a few bowshots, but then the slot faded out on harder ground.

"Still, I misdoubt Morgrim fell victim to the beast," said Eudoric. "He could show clean heels to many a steed of lighter build, and from its looks the dragon was no courser."

After hours of fruitless searching, whistling, and calling, they returned to Liptai. For a small fee, Eudoric was allowed to post a notice in Helladic on the town notice board, offering a reward for the return of his horse.

No words, however, came of the sighting of Morgrim. For all that Eudoric could tell, the destrier might have run clear to Velitchovo.

"You are free with advice, good Jillo," said Eudoric. "Well, rede me this riddle. We've established that our steeds will bolt from the sight and smell of dragon, for which I blame them little. Had we all the time in the world, we could doubtless train them to face the monsters, beginning with a stuffed dragon, and then, perchance, one in a cage in some monarch's menagerie. But our lucre dwindles like the snow in spring. What's to do?"

"Well, if the nags won't stand, needs we must face the worms on foot," said Jillo.

"That seems to me to throw away our lives to no good purpose, for these vasty lizards can outrun and outturn us and are well harnessed to boot. Barring the luckiest of lucky thrusts with the spear—as, say, into the eye or down the gullet—that fellow we erst encountered could make one mouthful of my lance and another of me."

"Your knightly courage were sufficient defense, sir. The Divine Pair would surely grant victory to the right."

"From all I've read of battles and feuds," said Eudoric, "methinks the Holy Couple's attention oft strays elsewhither when they should be deciding the outcome of some mundane fray."

"That is the trouble with reading; it undermines one's faith in the True Religion. But ye could be at least as well armored as the dragon, in your panoply of plate."

"Aye, but then poor Daisy could not bear so much weight to the site—or, at least, bear it thither and have breath left for a charge. We must be as chary of our beasts' welfare as of our own, for without them 'tis a long walk back to Trevaria. Nor do I deem that we should like to pass our lives in Liptai."

"Then, sir, we could pack the armor on the mule, for you to do on in dragon country."

"I like it not," said Eudoric. "Afoot, weighted down by that lobster's habit, I could move no more spryly than a tortoise. 'Twere small comfort to know that if the dragon ate me, he'd suffer indigestion afterward."

Jillo sighed. "Not the knightly attitude, sir, if ye'll pardon my saying so."

"Say what you please, but I'll follow the course of what meseems were common sense. What we need is a brace of those heavy steel crossbows for sieges. At close range, they'll punch a hole in a breastplate as 'twere a sheet of papyrus."

"They take too long to crank up," said Jillo. "By the time ye've readied your second shot, the battle's over."

"Oh, it would behoove us to shoot straight the first time; but better one shot that pierces the monster's scales than a score that bounce off. Howsomever, we have these fell little hand catapults not, and they don't make them in this barbarous land."

A few days later, while Eudoric still fretted over the lack of means to his goal, he heard a sudden sound like a single thunderclap from close at hand. Hastening out from Kasmar's Inn, Eudoric and Jillo found a crowd of Pathenians around the border guard's barracks.

In the drill yard, the guard was drawn up to watch a man demonstrate a weapon. Eudoric, whose few words of Pathenian were not up to conversation, asked among the crowd for somebody who could speak Helladic. When he found one, he learned that the demonstrator was a Pantorozian. The man was a stocky, snub-nosed fellow in a bulbous fur hat, a jacket of coarse undyed wool, and baggy trousers tucked into soft boots.

"He says the device was invented by the Sericans," said the villager. "They live half a world away, across the Pantorozian deserts. He puts some powder into that thing, touches a flame to it, and *boom!* it spits a leaden ball through the target as neatly as you please."

The Pantorozian demonstrated again, pouring black powder from the small end of a horn down his brass barrel. He placed a wad of rag over the mouth of the tube, then a leaden ball, and pushed both ball and wad down the tube with a rod. He poured a pinch of powder into a hole on the upper side of the tube near its rear, closed end.

Then he set a forked rest in the ground before him, rested the barrel in the fork, and took a small torch that a guardsman handed him. He pressed the wooden stock of the device against his shoulder, sighted along the tube, and with his free hand touched the torch to the touchhole. Ffft, *bang!* A cloud of smoke, and another hole appeared in the target.

The Pantorozian spoke with the captain of the guard, but they were too far for Eudoric to hear, even if he could have understood their Pathenian. After a while, the Pantorozian picked up his tube and rest, slung his bag of powder over his shoulder, and walked with downcast air to a cart hitched to a shade tree.

Eudoric approached the man, who was climbing into his cart.

"God den, fair sir!" began Eudoric, but the Pantorozian spread his hands with a smile of incomprehension.

"Kasmar!" cried Eudoric, sighting the innkeeper in the crowd. "Will you have the goodness to interpret for me and this fellow?"

"He says," said Kasmar, "that he started out with a

wainload of these devices and has sold all but one. He hoped to dispose of his last one in Liptai, but our gallant Captain Boriswaf will have nought to do with it."

"Why?" asked Eudoric. "Meseems 'twere a fell weapon in practiced hands."

"That is the trouble, quoth Master Vlek. Boriswaf says that should so fiendish a weapon come into use, 'twill utterly extinguish the noble art of war, for all men will down weapons and refuse to fight rather than face so devilish a device. Then what should he, a lifelong soldier, do for his bread? Beg?"

"Ask Master Vlek where he thinks to pass the night."

"I have already persuaded him to lodge with us, Master Eudoric."

"Good, for I would fain have further converse with him."

Over dinner, Eudoric sounded out the Pantorozian on the price he asked for his device. Acting as translator, Kasmar said, "If ye strike a bargain on this, I should get ten per centum as a broker's commission, for ye were helpless without me."

Eudoric got the gun, with thirty pounds of powder and a bag of leaden balls and wadding, for less than half of what Vlek had asked of Captain Boriswaf. As Vlek explained, he had not done badly on this peddling trip and was eager to get home to his wives and children.

"Only remember," he said through Kasmar, "overcharge it not, lest it blow apart and take your head off. Press the stock firmly against your shoulder, lest it knock you on your arse like a mule's kick. And keep fire away from the spare powder, lest it explode all at once and blast you to gobbets."

Later, Eudoric told Jillo, "That deal all but wiped out our funds."

"After the tradesmanlike way ye chaffered that barbarian down?"

"Aye. The scheme had better work, or we shall find ourselves choosing betwixt starving and seeking employment as collectors of offal or diggers of ditches. Assuming, that is, that in this reeky place they even bother to collect offal."

"Master Eudoric!" said Jillo. "Ye would not really lower yourself to accept menial wage labor?"

"Sooner than starve, aye. As Helvolius the philosopher said, no rider wears sharper spurs than Necessity."

"But if 'twere known at home, they'd hack off your gilded spurs, break your sword over your head, and degrade you to base varlet!"

"Well, till now I've had no knightly spurs to hack off, but only the plain silvered ones of an esquire. For the rest, I count on you to see that they don't find out. Now go to sleep and cease your grumbling."

The next day found Eudoric and Jillo deep into the Motolian Forest. At the noonday halt, Jillo kindled a fire. Eudoric made a small torch of a stick whose end was wound with a rag soaked in bacon fat. Then he loaded the device as he had been shown how to do and fired three balls at a mark on a tree. The third time, he hit the mark squarely, although the noise caused the palfreys frantically to tug and rear.

They remounted and went on to where they had met the dragon. Jillo rekindled the torch, and they cast up and down the beast's trail.

For two hours they saw no wildlife save a fleeing sow with a farrow of piglets and several huge snails with boulder-sized shells.

Then the horses became unruly. "Methinks they scent our quarry," said Eudoric.

When the riders themselves could detect the odor and the horses became almost unmanageable, Eudoric and Jillo dismounted.

"Tie the nags securely," said Eudoric. " 'Twould never do to slay our beast and then find that our horses had fled, leaving us to drag this land cockadrill home afoot."

As if in answer, a deep grunt came from ahead. While Jillo secured the horses, Eudoric laid out his new equipment and methodically loaded his piece.

"Here it comes," said Eudoric. "Stand by with that torch. Apply it not ere I give the word!"

The dragon came in sight, plodding along the trail and swinging its head from side to side. Having just shed its skin, the dragon gleamed in a reticular pattern of green and black, as if it had been freshly painted. Its great, golden, slit-pupiled eyes were now keen.

The horses screamed, causing the dragon to look up and speed its approach.

"Ready?" said Eudoric, setting the device in its rest.

"Aye, sir. Here goeth!" Without awaiting further command, Jillo applied the torch to the touchhole.

With a great boom and a cloud of smoke, the device discharged, rocking Eudoric back a pace. When the smoke cleared, the dragon was still rushing upon them, unharmed.

"Thou idiot!" screamed Eudoric. "I told thee not to give fire until I commanded! Thou has made me miss it clean!"

"I'm s-sorry, sir. I was palsied with fear. What shall we do now?"

"Run, fool!" Dropping the device, Eudoric turned and fled.

Jillo also ran. Eudoric tripped over a root and fell sprawling. Jillo stopped to guard his fallen master and turned to face the dragon. As Eudoric scrambled up, Jillo hurled the torch at the dragon's open maw.

The throw fell just short of its target. It happened, how-ever, that the dragon was just passing over the bag of black powder in its charge. The whirling torch, descending in its flight beneath the monster's head, struck this sack.

BOOM!

When the dragon hunters returned, they found the dragon writhing in its death throes. Its whole underside had been blown open, and blood and guts spilled out.

"Well!" said Eudoric, drawing a long breath. "That is enough knightly adventure to last me for many a year. Fall to; we must flay the creature. Belike we can sell that part of the hide that we take not home ourselves."

"How do ye propose to get it back to Liptai? Its hide alone must weigh in the hundreds."

"We shall hitch the dragon's tail to our two nags and lead them, dragging it behind. 'Twill be a weary swink, but we must needs recover as much as we can to recoup our losses."

An hour later, blood-splattered from head to foot, they were still struggling with the vast hide. Then, a man in for-ester's garb, with a large gilt medallion on his breast, rode up and dismounted. He was a big, rugged-looking man with a rattrap mouth.

"Who slew this beast, good my sirs?" he inquired.

Jillo spoke: "My noble master, the squire Eudoric Dambertson here. He is the hero who hath brought this ac-cursed beast to book."

"Be that sooth?" said the man to Eudoric.

"Well, ah," said Eudoric, "I must not claim much credit for the deed."

"But ye were the slayer, yea? Then, sir, ye are under ar-rest."

"What? But wherefore?"

"Ye shall see." From his garments, the stranger produced a length of cord with knots at intervals. With this he measured the dragon from nose to tail. Then the man stood up again.

"To answer your question, on three grounds: *imprimis,* for slaying a dragon out of lawful season; *secundus,* for slaying a dragon below the minimum size permitted; and *tertius,* for slaying a female dragon, which is protected the year round."

"You say this is a female?"

"Aye, 'tis as plain as the nose on your face."

"How does one tell with dragons?"

"Know, knave, that the male hath small horns behind the eyes, the which this specimen patently lacks."

"Who are you anyway?" demanded Eudoric.

"Senior game warden Voytsik of Prath, at your service. My credentials." The man fingered his medallion. "Now, show me your licenses, pray!"

"Licenses?" said Eudoric blankly.

"Hunting licenses, oaf!"

"None told us that such were required, sir," said Jillo.

"Ignorance of the law is no pretext; ye should have asked. That makes four counts of illegality."

Eudoric said, "But why—why in the name of the God and Goddess—"

"Pray, swear not by your false, heretical deities."

"Well, why should you Pathenians wish to preserve these monstrous reptiles?"

"*Imprimis,* because their hides and other parts have commercial value, which would perish were the whole race extirpated. *Secundus,* because they help to maintain the balance of nature by devouring the giant snails, which otherwise would issue forth nightly from the forest in such numbers as to strip bare our crops, orchards, and gardens and reduce our folk to hunger. And *tertius,* because they add a picturesque element to the landscape, thus luring foreigners to visit our land and spend their gold therein. Doth that explanation satisfy you?"

Eudoric had a fleeting thought of assaulting the stranger and either killing him or rendering him helpless while Eudoric and Jillo salvaged their prize. Even as he thought, three more tough-looking fellows, clad like Voytsik and armed with crossbows, rode out of the trees and formed up behind their leader.

"Now come along, ye two," said Voytsik.

"Whither?" asked Eudoric.

"Back to Liptai. On the morrow, we take the stage to Velitchovo, where your case will be tried."

"Your pardon, sir; we take the what?"

"The stagecoach."

"What's that, good my sir?"

"By the only God, ye must come from a barbarous land indeed! Ye shall see. Now come along, lest we be benighted in the woods."

The stagecoach made a regular round trip between Liptai and Velitchovo thrice a sennight. Jillo made the journey sunk in gloom, Eudoric kept busy viewing the passing countryside and, when opportunity offered, asking the driver about his occupation: pay, hours, fares, the cost of the vehicle, and so forth. By the time the prisoners reached their destination, both stank mightily because they had had no chance to wash the dragon's blood from their blood-soaked garments.

As they neared the capital, the driver whipped up his

team to a gallop. They rattled along the road beside the muddy river Pshora until the river made a bend. Then they thundered across the planks of a bridge.

Velitchovo was a real city, with a roughly paved main street and an onion-domed, brightly colored cathedral of the One God. In a massively timbered municipal palace, a bewhiskered magistrate asked, "Which of you two aliens truly slew the beast?"

"The younger, hight Eudoric," said Voytsik.

"Nay, Your Honor, 'twas I!" said Jillo.

"That is not what he said when we came upon them red-handed from their crime," said Voytsik. "This lean fellow plainly averred that his companion had done the deed, and the other denied it not."

"I can explain that," said Jillo. "I am the servant of the most worshipful squire Eudoric Dambertson of Arduen. We set forth to slay the creature, thinking this a noble and heroic deed that should redound to our glory on earth and our credit in Heaven. Whereas we both had a part in the act, the fatal stroke was delivered by your humble servant here. Howsomever, wishing like a good servant for all the glory to go to my master, I gave him the full credit, not knowing that this credit should be counted as blame."

"What say ye to that, Master Eudoric?" asked the judge.

"Jillo's account is essentially true," said Eudoric. "I must, however, confess that my failure to slay the beast was due to mischance and not want of intent."

"Methinks they utter a pack of lies to confuse the court," said Voytsik. "I have told Your Honor of the circumstances of their arrest, whence ye may judge how matters stand."

The judge put his fingertips together. "Master Eudoric," he said, "ye may plead innocent, or as incurring sole guilt, or as guilty in company with your servant. I do not think that you can escape some guilt, since Master Jillo, being your servant, acted under your orders. Ye be therefore responsible for his acts and at the very least a factor of dragocide."

"What happens if I plead innocent?" said Eudoric.

"Why, in that case, an' ye can find an attorney, ye shall be tried in due course. Bail can plainly not be allowed to foreign travelers, who can so easily slip through the law's fingers."

"In other words, I needs must stay in jail until my case comes up. How long will that take?"

"Since our calendar be crowded, 'twill be at least a year and a half. Whereas, an' ye plead guilty, all is settled in a trice."

"Then I plead sole guilt," said Eudoric.

"But, dear Master—" wailed Jillo.

"Hold thy tongue, Jillo. I know what I do."

The judge chuckled. "An old head on young shoulders, I perceive. Well, Master Eudoric. I find you guilty on all four counts and amerce you the wonted fine, which is one hundred marks on each count."

"Four hundred marks!" exclaimed Eudoric. "Our total combined wealth at this moment amounts to fourteen marks and thirty-seven pence, plus some items of property left with Master Kasmar in Liptai."

"So, ye'll have to serve out the corresponding prison term, which comes to one mark a day—unless ye can find someone to pay the balance of the fine for you. Take him away, jailer."

"But, Your Honor!" cried Jillo, "what shall I do without my noble master? When shall I see him again?"

"Ye may visit him any day during the regular visiting hours. It were well if ye brought him somewhat to eat, for our prison fare is not of the daintiest."

At the first visiting hour, when Jillo pleaded to be allowed to share Eudoric's sentence, Eudoric said, "Be not a bigger fool than thou canst help! I took sole blame so that ye should be free to run mine errands; whereas had I shared my guilt with you, we had both been mewed up here. Here, take this letter to Doctor Raspiudus; seek him out and acquaint him with our plight. If he be in sooth a true friend of our own Doctor Baldonius, belike he'll come to our rescue."

Doctor Raspiudus was short and fat, with a bushy white beard to his waist. "Ah, dear old Baldonius!" he cried in good Helladic. "I mind me of when we were lads together at the Arcane College of Saalingen University! Doth he still string verses together?"

"Aye, that he does," said Eudoric.

"Now, young man, I daresay that your chiefest desire is to get out of this foul hole, is't not?"

"That, *and* to recover our three remaining animals and other possessions left behind in Liptai, *and* to depart with the two square yards of dragon hide that I've promised to Doctor Baldonius, with enough money to see us home."

"Methinks all these matters were easily arranged, young sir. I need only your power of attorney to enable me to go to Liptai, recover the objects in question and return hither to pay your fine and release you. Your firearm is, I fear, lost to you, having been confiscated by the law."

" 'Twere of little use without a new supply of the magical powder," said Eudoric. "Your plan sounds splendid. But, sir, what do you get out of this?"

The enchanter rubbed his hands together. "Why, the pleasure of favoring an old friend—and also the chance to acquire a complete dragon hide for my own purposes. I know somewhat of Baldonius' experiments. As he can do thus and so with two yards of dragon, I can surely do more with a score."

"How will you obtain this dragon hide?"

"By now the foresters will have skinned the beast and salvaged the other parts of monetary worth, all of which will be put up at auction for the benefit of the kingdom. And I shall bid them in." Raspiudus chuckled. "When the other bidders know against whom they bid, I think not that they'll force the price up very far."

"Why can't you get me out of here now and then go to Liptai?"

Another chuckle. "My dear boy, first I must see that all is as ye say in Liptai. After all, I have only your word that ye be in sooth the Eudoric Dambertson of whom Baldonius writes. So bide ye in patience a few days more. I'll see that ye be sent better aliment than the slop they serve here. And now, pray, your authorization. Here are pen and ink."

To keep from starvation, Jillo got a job as a paver's helper and worked in hasty visits to the jail during his lunch hour. When a fortnight had passed without word from Doctor Raspiudus, Eudoric told Jillo to go to the wizard's home for an explanation.

"They turned me away at the door," reported Jillo. "They told me that the learned doctor had never heard of us."

As the import of this news sank in, Eudoric cursed and beat the wall in his rage. "That filthy, treacherous he-witch! He gets me to sign that power of attorney; then, when he has my property in his grubby paws, he conveniently forgets about us! By the God and Goddess, if ever I catch him—"

"Here, here, what's all this noise?" said the jailer. "Ye disturb the other prisoners."

When Jillo explained the cause of his master's outrage, the jailer laughed. "Why, everyone knows that Raspiudus is the worst skinflint and treacher in Velitchovo! Had ye asked me, I'd have warned you."

"Why has none of his victims slain him?" asked Eudoric.

"We are a law-abiding folk, sir. We do not permit private persons to indulge their feuds on their own, and we have some *most* ingenious penalties for homicide."

"Mean ye," said Jillo, "that amongst you Pathenians a gentleman may not avenge an insult by the gage of battle?"

"Of course not! We are not bloodthirsty barbarians."

"Ye mean there are no true gentlemen amongst you," sniffed Jillo.

"Then, Master Tiolkhof," said Eudoric, calming himself by force of will, "am I stuck here for a year or more?"

"Aye, but ye may get time off for good behavior at the end—three or four days, belike."

When the jailer had gone, Jillo said, "When ye get out, Master, ye must needs uphold your honor by challenging this runagate to the trial of battle, to the death."

Eudoric shook his head. "Heard you not what Tiolkhof said? They deem dueling barbarous and boil the duelists in oil, or something equally entertaining. Anyway, Raspiudus could beg off on grounds of age. We must, instead, use what wits the Holy Couple gave us. I wish now that I'd sent you back to Liptai to fetch our belongings and never meddled with his rolypoly sorcerer."

"True, but how could ye know, dear Master? I should probably have bungled the task in any case, what with my ignorance of the tongue and all."

After another fortnight, King Vladmor of Pathenia died.

229

When his son Yogor ascended the throne, he declared a general amnesty for all crimes less than murder. Thus Eudoric found himself out in the street again, but without horse, armor, weapons, or money beyond a few marks.

"Jillo," he said that night in their mean little cubicle, "we must needs get into Raspiudus' house somehow. As we saw this afternoon, 'tis a big place with a stout, high wall around it."

"An' ye could get a supply of that black powder, we could blast a breach in the wall."

"But we have no such stuff, nor means of getting it, unless we raid the royal armory, which I do not think we can do."

"Then how about climbing a tree near the wall and letting ourselves down by ropes inside the wall from a convenient branch?"

"A promising plan, *if* there were such an overhanging tree. But there isn't, as you saw as well as I when we scouted the place. Let me think. Raspiudus must have supplies borne into his stronghold from time to time. I misdoubt his wizardry is potent enough to conjure foodstuffs out of air."

"Mean ye that we should gain entrance as, say, a brace of chicken farmers with eggs to sell?"

"Just so. But nay, that won't do. Raspiudus is no fool. Knowing of this amnesty that enlarged me, he'll be on the watch for such a trick. At least, so should I be, in his room, and I credit him with no less wit than mine own. . . . I have it! What visitor would logically be likely to call upon him now, whom he will not have seen for many a year and whom he would hasten to welcome?"

"That I know not, sir."

"Who would wonder what had become of us and, detecting our troubles in his magical scryglass, would follow upon our track by uncanny means?"

"Oh, ye mean Doctor Baldonius!"

"Aye. My whiskers have grown nigh as long as his since last I shaved. And we're much of a size."

"But I never heard that your old tutor could fly about on an enchanted broomstick, as some of the mightiest magicians are said to do."

"Belike he can't, but Doctor Raspiudus wouldn't know that."

"Mean ye," said Jillo, "that ye've a mind to play Doctor Baldonius? Or to have me play him? The latter would never do."

"I know it wouldn't, good my Jillo. You know not the learned patter proper to wizards and other philosophers."

"Won't Raspiudus know you, sir? As ye say he's a shrewd old villain."

"He's seen me but once, in that dark, dank cell, and that for a mere quarter hour. You he's never seen at all. Methinks I can disguise myself well enough to befool him—unless you have a better notion."

"Alack, I have none! Then what part shall I play?"

"I had thought of going in alone."

"Nay, sir, dismiss the thought! Me let my master risk his mortal body and immortal soul in a witch's lair without my being there to help him!"

"If you help me the way you did by touching off that firearm whilst our dragon was out of range—"

"Ah, but who threw the torch and saved us in the end? What disguise shall I wear?"

"Since Raspiudus knows you not, there's no need for any. You shall be Baldonius' servant, as you are mine."

"Ye forget, sir, that if Raspiudus knows me not, his gate-

231

keepers might. Forsooth, they're likely to recall me because of the noisy protests I made when they barred me out."

"Hm. Well, you're too old for a page, too lank for a bodyguard, and too unlearned for a wizard's assistant. I have it! You shall go as my concubine!"

"Oh, Heaven above, sir, not that! I am a normal man! I should never live it down!"

To the massive gate before Raspiudus' house came Eudoric, with a patch over one eye, and his beard, uncut for a month, dyed white. A white wig cascaded down from under his hat. He presented a note, in a plausible imitation of Baldonius' hand, to the gatekeeper:

> Doctor Baldonius of Treveria presents his compliments to his old friend and colleague Doctor Raspiudus of Velitchovo, and begs the favor of an audience to discuss the apparent disappearance of two young protégés of his.

A pace behind, stooping to disguise his stature, slouched a rouged and powdered Jillo in woman's dress. If Jillo was a homely man, he made a hideous woman, least as far as his face could be seen under the headcloth. Nor was his beauty enhanced by the dress, which Eudoric had stitched together out of cheap cloth. The garment looked like what it was: the work of a rank amateur at dressmaking.

"My master begs you to enter," said the gatekeeper.

"Why, dear old Baldonius!" cried Raspiudus, rubbing his hands together. "Ye've not changed a mite since those glad, mad days at Saalingen! Do ye still string verses?"

"Ye've withstood the ravages of time well yourself, Raspiudus," said Eudoric, in an imitation of Baldonius' voice.

" 'As fly the years, the geese fly north in spring; Ah, would the years, like geese, return awing!' "

Raspiudus roared with laughter, patting his paunch. "The same old Baldonius! Made ye that one up?"

Eudoric made a deprecatory motion. "I am a mere poetaster; but had not the higher wisdom claimed my allegiance, I might have made my mark in poesy."

"What befell your poor eye?"

"My own carelessness in leaving a corner of a pentacle open. The demon got in a swipe of his claws ere I could banish him. But now, good Raspiudus, I have a matter to discuss whereof I told you in my note."

"Yea, yea, time enow for that. Be ye weary from the road? Need ye baths? Aliment? Drink?"

"Not yet, old friend. We have but now come from Velitchovo's best hostelry."

"Then let me show you my house and grounds. Your lady . . . ?"

"She'll stay with me. She speaks nought but Treverian and fears being separated from me among strangers. A mere swineherd's chick, but a faithful creature. At my age, that is of more moment than a pretty face."

Presently, Eudoric was looking at his and Jillo's palfreys and their sumpter mule in Raspiudus' stables. Eudoric made a few hesitant efforts, as if he were Baldonius seeking his young friends, to inquire after their disappearance. Each time Raspiudus smoothly turned the question aside, promising enlightenment later.

An hour later, Raspiudus was showing off his magical sanctum. With obvious interest, Eudoric examined a number of squares of dragon hide spread out on a workbench. He asked:

"Be this the integument of one of those Pathenian

233

dragons, whereof I have heard?"

"Certes, good Baldonius. Are they extinct in your part of the world?"

"Aye. 'Twas for that reason that I sent my young friend and former pupil, of whom I'm waiting to tell you, eastward to fetch me some of this hide for use in my work. How does one cure this hide?"

"With salt, and—*unh!*"

Raspiudus collapsed, Eudoric having just struck him on the head with a short bludgeon that he whisked out of his voluminous sleeves.

"Bind and gag him and roll him behind the bench!" said Eudoric.

"Were it not better to cut his throat, sir?" said Jillo.

"Nay. The jailer told us that they have ingenious ways of punishing homicide, and I have no wish to prove them by experiment."

While Jillo bound the unconscious Raspiudus, Eudoric chose two pieces of dragon hide, each about a yard square. He rolled them together into a bundle and lashed them with a length of rope from inside his robe. As an afterthought, he helped himself to the contents of Raspiudus' purse. Then he hoisted the roll of hide to his shoulder and issued from the laboratory. He called to the nearest stableboy.

"Doctor Raspiudus," he said, "asks that ye saddle up those two nags." He pointed. "Good saddles, mind you! Are the animals well shod?"

"Hasten, sir," muttered Jillo. "Every instant we hang about here—"

"Hold thy peace! The appearance of haste were the surest way to arouse suspicion." Eudoric raised his voice. "Another heave on that girth, fellow! I am not minded to have my aged bones shattered by a tumble into the roadway."

Jillo whispered, "Can't we recover the mule and your armor, to boot?"

Eudoric shook his head. "Too risky," he murmured. "Be glad if we get away with whole skins."

When the horses had been saddled to his satisfaction, he said, "Lend me some of your strength in mounting, youngster." He groaned as he swung awkwardly into the saddle. "A murrain on thy master, to send us off on this footling errand—me that hasn't sat a horse in years! Now hand me that accursed roll of hide. I thank thee, youth; here's a little for thy trouble. Run ahead and tell the gatekeeper to have his portal well opened. I fear that if this beast pulls up of a sudden, I shall go flying over its head!"

A few minutes later, when they had turned a corner and were out of sight of Raspiudus' house, Eudoric said, "Now, trot!"

"If I could but get out of this damned gown," muttered Jillo. "I can't ride decently in it."

"Wait till we're out of the city gate."

When Jillo had shed the offending garment, Eudoric said, "Now ride, man, as never before in your life!"

They pounded off on the Liptai road. Looking back, Jillo gave a screech. "There's a thing flying after us! It looks like a giant bat!"

"One of Raspiudus' sendings," said Eudoric. "I knew he'd get loose. Use your spurs! Can we but gain the bridge . . ."

They fled at a mad gallop. The sending came closer and closer, until Eudoric thought he could feel the wind of its wings.

Then their hooves thundered across the bridge over the Pshora.

"Those things will not cross running water," said

235

Eudoric, looking back. "Slow down, Jillo. These nags must bear us many leagues, and we must not founder them at the start."

". . . So here we are," Eudoric told Doctor Baldonius. "Ye've seen your family, lad?"

"Certes. They thrive, praise to the Divine Pair. Where's Lusina?"

"Well—ah—ahem—the fact is, she is not here."

"Oh? Then where?"

"Ye put me to shame, Eudoric. I promised you her hand in return for the two yards of dragon hide. Well, ye've fetched me the hide, at no small effort and risk, but I cannot fulfill my side of the bargain."

"Wherefore?"

"Alas! My undutiful daughter ran off with a strolling player last summer, whilst ye were chasing dragons—or perchance 'twas the other way round. I'm right truly sorry. . . ."

Eudoric frowned silently for an instant, then said, "Fret not, esteemed Doctor. I shall recover from the wound—provided, that is, that you salve it by making up my losses in more materialistic fashion."

Baldonius raised bushy gray brows. "So? Ye seem not so grief-stricken as I should have expected, to judge from the lover's sighs and tears wherewith ye parted from the jade last spring. Now ye'll accept money instead?"

"Aye, sir. I admit that my passion had somewhat cooled during our long separation. Was it likewise with her? What said she of me?"

"Aye, her sentiments did indeed change. She said you were too much an opportunist altogether to please her. I would not wound your feelings. . . ."

Eudoric waved a deprecatory hand. "Continue, pray. I have been somewhat toughened by my months in the rude, rough world, and I am interested."

"Well, I told her she was being foolish; that ye were a shrewd lad who, an' ye survived the dragon hunt, would go far. But her words were: 'That is just the trouble, Father. He is too shrewd to be very lovable.' "

"Hmph," grunted Eudoric. "As one might say: I am a man of enterprise, thou art an opportunist, he is a conniving scoundrel. 'Tis all in the point of view. Well, if she prefers the fools of this world, I wish her joy of them. As a man of honor, I would have wedded Lusina had she wished. As things stand, trouble is saved all around."

"To you, belike, though I misdoubt my headstrong lass'll find the life of an actor's wife a bed of violets:

Who'd wed on a whim is soon filled to the brim
Of worry and doubt, till he longs for an out.
So if ye would wive, beware of the gyve
Of an ill-chosen mate; 'tis a harrowing fate.

But enough of that. What sum had ye in mind?"

"Enough to cover the cost of my good destrier Morgrim and my panoply of plate, together with lance and sword, plus a few other chattels and incidental expenses of travel. Fifteen hundred marks should cover the lot."

"Fifteen hundred! Whew! I could ne'er afford—nor are these moldy patches of dragon hide worth a fraction of the sum."

Eudoric sighed and rose. "You know what you can afford, good my sage." He picked up the roll of dragon hide. "Your colleague Doctor Calporio, wizard to the Count of Treveria, expressed a keen interest in this material. In fact,

237

he offered me more than I have asked of you, but I thought it only honorable to give you the first chance."

"What!" cried Baldonius. "That mountebank, charlatan, that faker? Misusing the hide and not deriving a tenth of the magical benefits from it that I should? Sit down, Eudoric; we will discuss these things."

An hour's haggling got Eudoric his fifteen hundred marks. Baldonius said, "Well, praise the Divine Couple that's over. And now, beloved pupil, what are your plans?"

"Would ye believe it, Doctor Baldonius," said Jillo, "that my poor, deluded master is about to disgrace his lineage and betray his class by a base commercial enterprise?"

"Forsooth, Jillo? What's this?"

"He means my proposed coach line," said Eudoric.

"Good Heaven, what's that?"

"My plan to run a carriage on a weekly schedule from Zurgau to Kromnitch, taking all who can pay the fare, as they do in Pathenia. We can't let the heathen Easterlings get ahead of us."

"What an extraordinary idea! Need ye a partner?"

"Thanks, but nay. Baron Emmerhard has already thrown in with me. He's promised me my knighthood in exchange for the partnership."

"There is no nobility anymore," said Jillo.

Eudoric grinned. "Emmerhard said much the same sort of thing, but I convinced him that anything to do with horses is a proper pursuit for a gentleman. Jillo, you can spell me at driving the coach, which will make you a gentleman, too!"

Jillo sighed. "Alas! The true spirit of knighthood is dying in this degenerate age. Woe is me that I should live to see the end of chivalry! How much did ye think of paying me, sir?"

The employees of Five Star hope you have enjoyed this book. All our books are made to last. Other Five Star books are available at your library, through selected bookstores, or directly from us.

For information about titles, please call:

(800) 223-1244

or visit our Web site at:

www.gale.com/fivestar

To share your comments, please write:

Publisher
Five Star
295 Kennedy Memorial Drive
Waterville, ME   04901